A LIFE FULL OF HOLES

You know what we're going to do now? We're going to make a glass of tea and come back here and lie down a while. Then we'll get a good dinner.

Ouakha. When a man and a woman are lying in bed together, nothing matters. Not even hunger, she said.

While we were waiting for the water to boil I sat beside her and kissed her. Then I made the tea and we sat kissing while we drank it.

Let's pull back the blanket and get into bed. After that we'll make dinner.

Whatever you like, she said.

But she wanted to even more than I did.

Get up and sit in the chair while I make the bed, I told her.

I got the bed ready and took off my shirt and trousers. Then I got into bed.

Take your clothes off, I said.

No. It's shameful.

There's no shame. Just you and I are here.

She took off everything but her serouelles, and got into bed, and I was kissing her. . . .

Driss
ben Hamed Charhadi
(Larbi Layachi)

A Life
Full of Holes

A novel tape-recorded in
Moghrebi and translated into
English by
PAUL BOWLES

A Grove Press Outrider Book
Grove Press, Inc., New York

First Black Cat Edition 1966
This Printing 1982
ISBN: 0-394-17946-3
Library of Congress Catalog Card Number: 81-47638

LIBRARY OF CONGRESS CATALOGING IN PUBLICATION DATA

Charhadi, Driss ben Hamed.
  A life full of holes.
  I. Title.
PJ7818.H35L5   1982   892'.736   81-47638
ISBN 0-394-17946-3

Manufactured in the United States of America

GROVE PRESS, INC., 196 West Houston Street, New York, N.Y. 10014

CONTENTS

Even a life full of holes, a life
of nothing but waiting, is better
than no life at all

*Charhadi's commentary on
a Moghrebi saying*

THE man who invented this book, and along with it the name of Driss ben Hamed Charhadi, is a singularly quiet and ungregarious North African Moslem. His forebears are from a remote mountainous region where, however, Moghrebi Arabic rather than a Berber tongue is spoken. He is totally illiterate. His speech in Moghrebi is clear and correct. Like a peasant's, it is studded with rustic locutions and proverbs. The fact that translating and compiling the novel was a comparatively simple process is due mainly to the sureness with which he proceeds in telling a story. He knows beforehand just what he is going to say, and he says it succinctly and eloquently.

The book came to exist in a roundabout fashion. Charhadi used to call by to see me from time to time, usually in the evening on his way home from the cinema. On one of these occasions he had been to see an Egyptian "historical" film. People in this part of the world are prone to confuse the intent of feature films with that of newsreels. Was it possible, Charhadi wanted to know, that the entire city of Cairo had been destroyed without his having heard about it on the radio? When I told him how fictional films are made and what they are meant to be, he was particularly struck by the fact that it is not forbidden to "lie". I said that no one thought of film-making in those terms. "And books, like the books you write," he pursued. "They are all lies, too?"

"They're stories, like the *Thousand and One Nights*. You don't call them lies, do you?"

"No, because they're true. They happened long ago when the world was different from the way it is now, that's all."

I did not argue the point. Instead, I asked him: "And how about the stories the men from the country sometimes tell in the market place? Are they true, too?"

"Ah, but they're only stories. Everybody knows they're just for fun."

"That's like my books. And that's like the films. Everybody knows they're only stories."

"And it's not forbidden," he said half to himself. "But then anybody would have the right to make a book! I could, or my mother could. Anybody!"

"That's right. Anybody can, if he has a story to tell and knows how to tell it."

7

"And he doesn't have to send it to the government for permission?"

"Not in my country," I told him.

A few days later he telephoned me. "May I see you tonight? It's about something important."

We set the time, and he arrived. He did not come at once to the point of his visit. Presently he said: "I've been thinking. I want to make a book, with the help of Allah. You could put it into your language and give it to the book factory in your country. Would that be allowed?"

"I told you anything's allowed. But making a book is a lot of work. It would take a long time."

"I see. And you haven't enough time."

"I would have, if it were really good," I said. "The only way to know is to tell some of the story. Come tomorrow night and we'll try it."

The next night when he came, he said: "I thought about it last night before I went to sleep, and I know everything I want to say."

He sat down on the m'tarrba beside the fireplace. I put the microphone in front of him and started a tape-recorder. After a long time he began to speak.

Immediately I knew that whatever the story might turn out to be, his manner of telling it left nothing to be desired. It was as if he had memorized the entire text and rehearsed the speaking of it for weeks; there was no indication that it was being improvised. About an hour later I had "The Wire" complete on tape.

"That's not the beginning," he said. "I thought I'd tell that first, and see if you liked it."

"What do you think about it?" I countered.

"I think it's a good story, but maybe no one else will."

"It sounds very fine in Moghrebi," I said. "But I can't tell you anything until I've changed it into English."

When I had the first half-dozen pages translated, I told him that I thought we should do some more.

"Hamdoul'lah," he said. "Thank God."

Perhaps two months later I had finished putting "The Wire" into English. At the outset I had seen that the translation should be a literal one, in order to preserve as much as possible of the style. Nothing needed to be added, deleted, or altered.

During this period Charhadi came several times a week, while we went over the spoken text word by word. The apocryphal material disclosed by this examination had its own philological and ethnographical interest, and would have filled a book by itself. One day when we had nearly completed the translation of "The

8

Wire," he asked me to play the tape back to him from the beginning. Halfway through, he called out: "Please stop the machine! Here I want to tell something more, if it's all right." What he inserted was not a supplementary incident; it was a sequence which would give the piece a sense of the passage of time. With the intuitive certainty of the master storyteller, he placed it precisely where it made the desired effect. In the course of dictating the book he made only a half-dozen such additions to his original text.

One of these was the short episode in "The Shepherd," where the narrator insists on spending the night at the tomb of Sidi Bou Hajja in order to see if the "bull with horns" will appear. When he had appended this bit and listened to the playback, he decided that it was not interesting, and was for leaving it out. This was our only occasion for disagreement. I wanted to include it because, although it was incidental to the story, the passage was a clear illustration of the persistence of pre-Islamic belief: the appearance of the ancient god in a spot whose initial sanctity has been affirmed by the usurping faith. (During rural celebrations the bull is still decorated with flowers and ribbons and medals, and led through the streets to be sacrificed.) I explained to him the reason why I thought the passage ought to be included, knowing in advance that he would disapprove any suggestion to the effect that his ancestors had been something else before embracing Islam. We let the subject drop, he having agreed, if not wholeheartedly, to allow the episode to be incorporated into the text.

The good storyteller keeps the thread of his narrative almost equally taut at all points. This Charhadi accomplished, apparently without effort. He never hesitated; he never varied the intensity of his eloquence. When, now and then, I stubbornly insisted, for the sake of experimentation, that he give me his personal opinion of the behaviour of one of his protagonists, he held back. Probably because he had fashioned them with actual acquaintances in mind, he was loath to pass moral judgment upon his characters. From time to time he would recount a section before we taped it. On such occasions my reactions may have influenced him in his decision to include or excise certain details, but I made no suggestions one way or the other. Apart from the exceptions mentioned and the few passages whose intelligibility depended upon some elaboration, the procedure followed was that once the material was on tape, it was considered to be final and inalterable.

P.B.

CHAPTER ONE

THE ORPHAN

WHEN I was eight years old my mother married a soldier. We lived in Tettaouen. One day my mother's husband came home and told her: We've got to go to Tanja. They're moving the barracks there, so we have to move too.

All right, she said. If we have to go to Tanja, let's go.

Get everything ready. When the truck comes to the house, we'll put it all in and go.

Ouakha, she said. She packed everything, clothes and mattresses and cushions, and at noon a truck came. They put the things in. Then we got into the truck too, and they drove us away. We went to Tanja and took a house in Dradeb.

We had been living there three or four months. One day I went out of the house by myself. I did not know the houses or the people in the quarter. I went out and started to walk along, and I kept walking, walking, until I was far away, up on the Boulevard. And night came and I began to cry. A man said to me: What's the matter?

I don't know where my mother is and I don't know where my house is.

He said: Come with me. I'll take you home. He took me to the comisaría. A policeman was sitting in a chair in the doorway. He asked me: Where do you live?

I told him: In Tettaouen.

Poor boy, he said. Come on. He gave me a mat and told me: Sit down there. Are you hungry?

Yes, I said. Then he brought a little food and a piece of bread.

Have you finished? Give me the bowl. I gave it to him and he took it away. Then he said: Come here. Take off those old trousers. Take them off. Don't be afraid. So I took them off. Come here, he told me. Sit down on my lap. He was unfastening his trousers. Don't be afraid, he kept saying. Then I thought I saw a snake in his hand, and I jumped down and ran out of the room. He ran after me, but another man caught me.

What's the matter? Where are your clothes?

In the room, I said. The first policeman came running. Grab him! He's lost. Give him to me.

He put me in another room and brought me my trousers. Get

11

in here. Stop crying. I didn't do anything to you, did I?

No.

And don't say anything to anybody.

I won't.

He shut the door and left me there, and I slept. In the morning a Spanish man came. The policeman told him: Somebody brought the boy here last night. He's from Tettaouen. He's lost.

Where do you live? he asked me.

In Tettaouen, I told him.

Come on, he said. And he took me to Tettaouen.

The police looked everywhere in Tettaouen for my mother, and they could not find her. And they said: This boy has no family. We'll put him into the Fondaq en Nedjar.

They put me into the Fondaq en Nedjar, where they send children and women too, who have no families. In the fondaq they said to me: Boy, where do you live? I told them: Here in Tettaouen. And they too looked and looked for my house, and found nothing, nothing.

And I stayed there. They gave me clothes and shoes and everything I needed. We ate every day and had blankets to sleep under. And I was still small and not yet circumcised. They saw that and said: You'll have to be circumcised. I was afraid, and I said: No! When I find my mother I'll do it.

They called the pacha. He came and said: That boy must be circumcised now. Two men took hold of me and handed me to the women who lived there. They killed two rams and then they circumcised me. I stayed with the women there until I was well. Some of them gave me candy, and some gave me money, but I did not know what money was. When I was well I went back to live with the others. I was learning to read. From one day to the next I was beginning to know something.

One day the khalifa came to the Fondaq en Nedjar to see the pacha. You must give all the children and women new clothes, he told him, because now I am having my wedding feast. I'm going to take them all to my orchard, so they'll be happy. They have no one to do anything for them.

The pacha called us at noon. Listen, he told us. Go and eat now, and when you've finished come back here. I'm going to give you all new clothes.

Why? we asked him.

Because you're going to the khalifa's orchard. He's going to be married.

We went and ate, and we were talking among ourselves. Allah, my friend, the khalifa's getting married! Now, we're going out to his orchard and everything will be good. A big orchard. We can hide in it and everything. Yes, we told each other.

After lunch we went out to the storeroom and they gave each one of us a shirt, a pair of trousers, a jacket and a pair of sandals. All the children. Then the women came and they gave them clothes too. We went upstairs into the mosque and studied all afternoon. When twilight came they called us. Come down and eat, they told us. When you've finished, you're going in the soldiers' truck to the khalifa's orchard.

We went down and ate. When we all had finished eating they said: Now you will not go up and sleep. Just stay here.

We sat there. Then they said: Go on out. We went into the street and walked through the Medina to the Feddane. In the Feddane under the palm tree we saw the soldiers' truck. We climbed into it. And we went riding, riding, at night, until we got to the khalifa's orchard at the foot of the mountains. We went to sleep as soon as we got there.

The next day we saw that there were trees everywhere. And many of them had fruit in them. Apples, pears, peaches. And when we picked the fruit they let us keep it and eat it. And we stayed there playing all day. It was a day when we were all happy. And I said: Allah, let me live here forever! It's a good place for me.

The next day at noon they gave us a feast. Steamed rice with cinnamon and sugar on it. I had never had such a good meal. Eat, they said, and if you haven't had enough, we'll give you more.

I turned to the boy beside me and said: You see, my friend? It would be better if they'd leave us here always. This is the best place for us. Yes, he said. Al Allah!

So we ate all we wanted, and there was still food left. Everybody had enough. Then they took away the dishes and bowls. There were many musicians there, and they played Andaluz music for us. That way we lived for a week, and then they took us back to Tettaouen.

One day my mother's husband found out that I was in the Fondaq en Nedjar, and he came to see me. I was sick that day, lying on the floor.

So you are here. Do you want to go home? he asked me. I want to stay here. It's better here. It's a good place.

No. You should come home. Your mother wants to see you.

But I want to stay here.

Yes. Well. I'll tell her to come and see you.

My mother's husband went back to Tanja. He told my mother:

Your son is in Tettaouen at the Fondaq en Nedjar. And he's sick. I asked him if he didn't want to come home, and he said no. He wants to stay there. You'll have to go and get him and bring him back.

Yes, she said. I must. He should be with me.

He gave her some money and told her: Go and get your son. Bring him back here.

When my mother came to see me, I told her: No. I won't go. It's better here. I can study and everything, and on Fridays we go to the mosque with the khalifa and afterward we go to the beach at Rio Martin. I sleep well and I eat well and I like to study. It's the place I like best.

No, aoulidi, she said. You should come with me. I want you with me. You come to Tanja and you can study there.

No, Mother. Leave me here. It's better.

You know best, she said. And she went away by herself. When she got home she told her husband: That boy. We've got to make him come back. You must go to Tettaouen and see the pacha, and tell him the boy's mother wants him with her.

He said: Ouakha. I'll go. So he went back to Tettaouen and told the pacha: His mother can't live without him. He must go home as soon as possible and be with her.

The pacha said: We'll ask the boy. If he wants to leave, we won't stop him.

They came to see me. Which do you want, the pacha asked me. To stay here or to go and live with your mother?

I told him: I'd rather stay here. I know the other boys and everything. It would be better if I stayed here.

You hear? said the pacha. Listen to what he says.

I want him to come with me and that's that.

There he is, said the pacha. I have nothing more to say.

So I went with him in the bus to Tanja. And there nothing happened. They did not send me to school. Nothing.

And time went by. One day my mother said to her husband: The boy should go to school. He knows a little already and he can learn more. He's still young. He's not doing anything now.

All right, he said. I'll take him down to the school. He took me to the school and I was learning the Qor'an, perhaps for a year. Then my mother gave birth. It was a boy. When her husband saw the baby, he did not like me any more. He began to tell my mother: That boy of yours isn't learning anything. Everything he does is wrong.

After that he could not say anything good about me. I'm not going to give him any more of my food, he told my mother.

You know best, she said. But if you're willing, please let him stay in school. He's nothing but an orphan, I know. But it would be good if you would let him go to school. The boy has no one in the world.

No, he said. I can't let him study any more and I can't give him any more of my food. He can go out and work.

Even if he goes out and looks, said my mother, he's not going to know where to go to get work.

He said: It's not my business what he does. It's between you and him. I don't care what he does, but he can't stay here without working.

I went to work on the beach, helping the fishermen pull in their nets. And at home my mother and the man were always fighting about me.

I would go in the morning and pull on the nets until the end of the afternoon. They gave me two rials. If they caught a lot of fish, they gave me three, but that was not very often. I stayed like that today and tomorrow, today and tomorrow, for a long time. After two years I was earning four rials a day.

When I was about thirteen I was a man, and I began to think. I said to myself: If I had stayed in the Fondaq en Nedjar, I'd have known something when I came out. I thought about it for a long time. One day I decided to go to my mother and talk to her.

Mother.

Yes?

You know, Mother, tomorrow I'm going to Tettaouen.

What are you going to do there, aoulidi?

I want to look for the Fondaq en Nedjar. If I find it and they take me back, I want to stay there.

It's a long time since you were there. You're grown up now. I don't think they'll let you in. You don't know Tettaouen. You won't know where to go. You don't know anybody there, and yet you want to go! But if you do, I can't say no.

I said: Mother, I've got to go, and that's all. Your husband shouts at you all day, and it's about me. I'm going to go and take the life Allah gives me. I'm tired of looking for better work here. But if I can't find the Fondaq en Nedjar I'll come back.

She said: Yes, aoulidi. If you want to go, you must go.

But give me something to eat on the way, I told her.

Ouakha, she said. In the morning.

I went to bed. I got up at seven, and I told my mother: I should go now so I can get there early. Give me the food. She gave me a loaf of bread, and said: Take it, aoulidi, and go. I don't want you to go, but if you want to, I have nothing to say.

I went down the road, through Souani and Beni Makada, and into Mogoga. There I got onto the highway. Walking, walking, until I came to the border where the Spanish customhouse was. I tried to go by behind the buildings, but a soldier saw me and called to me.

Boy, come here! What have you got there?

Nothing.

He said: That blanket. Where did you get it?

I brought it from home. I said, and I'm going to Tettaouen to see my uncle. I said nothing about the Fondaq en Nedjar.

Have you got a passport?

No, I told him. I haven't got one.

How old are you?

Thirteen. But I have no passport.

Let me look in your bundle, he said.

Here. I opened it for him. It's a blanket with bread inside.

He said: Go on your way.

I went on, walking, walking, until I came to a river. The day was hot and the sun was shining, and I said to myself: This river has good clear water. I'm going to sit down here and rest a little and wash my shirt, and then I'll go on.

I sat down and rested and ate a little bread. Then I washed my shirt and spread it from the top of my head to dry, and started out again on the road. Walking, walking, until I came to a place called Fnidaq. By then I was tired and I could not go any farther. I saw a palm-fiber factory not far off, and I thought: I'll go and look at the factory. If there's any work there, I'll stay and work. I went up to the factory, and saw a man standing in the doorway. Mohammed, listen, I said. I want to talk to you. When he came over I said to him: Are you taking on any workers?

I don't know, he said, but ask that Nazarene. That Spaniard over there. Ask him.

I went to speak to the Spaniard. Please, I want to talk to you. If you need anyone to work for you, I'll stay here and work.

Do you know anything? Have you got a trade of some kind? he asked me. I told him: No.

You've never worked with iron?

No.

You see these pieces of iron here? You make a hundred pieces a day. We have to keep putting new teeth into the machine.

I said: All right. I'll try.

He took a hammer. Here, he said. He showed me how to use it on the piece of iron. Then he gave me the hammer. I worked

16

about an hour, and by then I had not made even one piece. The Spaniard said: You won't do. You don't know how to do this work here. The people from the mountains can make ten pieces in an hour. You can't even make one.

You know best, I told him.

No, you can't work with us, he said.

I went out. I walked up to the barracks on the hill where the soldiers live, and an army truck was coming along the highway. It stopped there and some soldiers got out. And I was very tired and could not walk any farther, so when the truck started out again for Tettaouen I caught onto the back of it and climbed up. I rode in the back of the truck until it had almost arrived in Tettaouen. Then some motorcycle police stopped it. One of them looked over the top into the back and saw me inside.

Where did you come from? he asked me.

I told him I had come from Tanja and got as far as Fnidaq, and couldn't walk any further and had got into the truck.

Come on. Get down, he said.

I was afraid. I thought: This one is going to do something.

Climb down from there and get out of here.

A good man after all, I thought. And I kept walking until I came to the city, and I went into Tettaouen. I went first into the Feddane where the khalifa's palace is, and kept walking around. The blanket was under my arm and I was hungry, but I did not know anyone in the city. Who can I talk to now? I thought. I can't ask anybody for a duro. Nobody's going to give me anything. I don't know anybody. I'm going to sleep here on these steps as Allah wants it and in the morning I'll look for the Fondaq en Nedjar. If I don't find it, I'll look for work. I took the blanket, folded it in the middle, and lay down to sleep with half of it under me and half of it over me. Very early in the morning the street sweepers came down, cleaning the steps. Come on, they said. Get up! Morning is here. And I got out from under the blanket, put it under my arm, and started to walk.

Walking, walking, looking for the Fondaq en Nedjar. And I could not find it. In the middle of the Medina there was a small restaurant that sold white bean pudding. I went in and said to the owner: Can I work with you?

Yes, he told me. Come in. He gave me some pudding and a little bread, and I ate. Then I washed dishes for him all day. Late in the afternoon many men came to eat, and then he gave me more bean pudding and bread. At dark the men stopped coming. The owner said to me: Put all the dishes together and wash them. I'm going to close up now.

I took the dishes and bowls and glasses and washed them. He was counting his money, and he took out a peseta and gave it to me.

Here. Take this, he told me. Go and sleep in the baths and come back in the morning.

Ouakha, I said. I took the peseta, and I thought: I'll go to the hammam and in the morning I'll come back.

I went to the hammam, took out my blanket, folded it in half, and slept in it. When I woke up in the morning, I began to think: Now I'm going to the restaurant and work again all day, and he'll give me food. And when night comes he'll give me a peseta and tell me to go to the baths again. And I'll never find the Fondaq en Nedjar. I ought to have stayed in Tanja. It would have been better for me.

I decided to go out onto the highway and go back to Tanja. I'll leave Tettaouen right now, I said to myself. I put my blanket under my arm and went out into the street and started to walk. And I walked out of the city. Walking, walking, walking.

And I thought: I'll make a short cut here, off the highway, along the mountain, and come back onto the road beyond. People are always talking about a short cut here. I wanted to get back onto the highway at Et Tnine. And I was not following any path, just walking along the side of the mountain. Soon I came to a patch of forest. I looked around and there was nobody, no sign that people had ever been there. I thought that if I went farther I would get lost, and so I turned back and went out of the forest. I looked down to the highway, and I saw some shepherds, and some men plowing. One of my sandals was loose, and while I was running down the mountain the strap broke. I took it off and carried it in my hand. Then the other one broke too, and I carried them both. I kept going. There were thorns everywhere so that it was hard for me to put my feet down. Then I came out into a plowed field.

Four shepherds saw me. They called to me: Yah, Si Mohammed!

What is it?

Come here! Come here! they called.

Yes. I went to where they were. Maybe they'll have a little bread, I thought. When I got to them, one of them said: What have you got there in that bundle? They were a little older than I was.

I've got nothing here, I said. A pair of broken sandals and a blanket.

What were you doing way up there on the mountain? Where are

you walking to? We're going to hand you over to the soldiers.

I said: You're going to hand me over to the soldiers, are you?

One of them turned to the others and said: Let's all grab him and do it to him! One after the other.

When I saw what they were going to do, I began to run. They all ran after me. I was running and yelling. There was a farmer plowing in front of us not very far away. I ran toward him.

You're not ashamed, you shepherds? he said. Is this what you do to strangers? Stop them and throw them down by force? I'm going to take you all to the soldiers now.

And I said to the farmer: They weren't ashamed.

The man said: Now go on your way, my son. Go quickly.

So I went to the highway and followed it, walking, walking, until I came to a souq in the country, called El Arba. When I got there I could not go on. I was hungry and tired, and my feet hurt from going barefoot, and the hot sun had been burning me all day. I fell down on the ground in the market and lay there.

After a while some people began to come out of a palm-fiber factory that was across the highway. One of them said: What's the matter with that boy lying there? I heard the words but I could not move. A man bent over and touched my head. This boy is either hungry or thirsty, he told them. I don't know which.

Wait, said a woman. If he's thirsty I'll bring him a bowl of buttermilk. And she brought it and I drank it and sat up. She said: Do you want to eat?

Yes, I told her.

She brought me country bread, made of corn and oats. And I ate. At first the bread tasted sweet, sweeter than any bread I had ever tasted. But by the time I had finished eating, it seemed like ordinary country bread. I said to myself: You see what hunger can do? When I was hungry the bread tasted like honey. Before I ate I couldn't even move my knee, and now that my belly is full I feel strong and I know the bread isn't sweet at all. But I gathered up all the pieces of bread that were left and wrapped them in the blanket and started out again. Thanks to Allah, I thought. Now I have life in me, and I'll be able to get to Tanja.

I went along, walking, walking, and the end of day came when I was in Ain Michlaoua. There is an old gasoline station there. I thought: Now it's getting dark. I'll go on as far as the garbage dump. There was a lot of paper there day before yesterday when I came through. I'll find some and spread the blanket on top and sleep there until morning. Then I'll go on into the city.

And I went on walking until I came to the garbage dump. I climbed up there in the dark and began to pick up papers. Then

I spread them out and slept.

In the morning I got up. I looked at the papers and thought: This can be sold. I'm going back into the town without a franc. I've got to do something to get hold of some money.

I picked up about fifty pounds of paper and twisted wires around it and carried the bales along with me. It was five kilometers to the beach, but I carried them there, to an old Frenchman who had always been in Tanja and had always bought old paper. And I sold them to him. When that was over I thought: Thanks to Allah! And I went to see my mother.

Well, my son, she said, did you find the Fondaq en Nedjar or not?

I said: No, I didn't find it. But for a long time I've had the idea in my head about going to Tettaouen and looking for it, on the chance that I'd find it. I wanted to see it again looking the way it did the first time. I went. It was hard, but I thank Allah that I went. In my head and heart I was always in the Fondaq en Nedjar. It's an orphanage, and I'm an orphan. And I've always said to your husband: Let me go! Let me go! And even you wouldn't let me stay there. You came to see me there and said to me yourself: Come. Come with me. I told you: No, Mother. Leave me here. It's better here.

And now see how much time has gone by, and I still say the same thing to you. For five years I've been telling you my place was in the Fondaq en Nedjar. If I'd stayed there, I'd have learned to read. I'd have learned some trade, or at least how to take care of myself in the world. Now there's nothing I can do. Allah will judge you, you and your husband.

No, my son. It's not my fault, she said. I can't do anything for you. That's just an idea you've put into your head.

I said: No. You did it. You sent your husband to get me. Now I can't read, and I have no trade. And I have no one to follow.

CHAPTER TWO

THE JOURNEY TO MENARBIYAA

WHEN I was about nine years old I was going to the French school down in Bou Khach Khach. I went there for six or seven months, and then vacation time came. One day my mother told me: I'm going to the country to see your grandfather. I haven't seen him in a long time. I don't know how long!

Now that you have three months of summer with no school, you can go with me.

She went to her husband and told him: I must go and see my father. It's a long time since I've seen him.

All right, he said. But wait until the end of the month so I can give you some money.

Good.

When the end of the month came he got paid. Then he said to my mother: I've got the money now. Come and I'll buy you some clothes to take to your family.

She went with him and they bought tchamiras, foqiyas and serraoual for the family, because country people wear those clothes. And they bought shoes for my mother. When they came home they had shoes and a shirt and a jacket for me. And we packed all the clothes together and got ready to leave the next day.

Early in the morning, before daylight, at the hour of the fjer, we went down to the beach. My mother's husband said good-bye to her. Then my mother and I got on a bus. We went to Tettaouen first. There we got out and went into the Medina to look for a fondouq to stay in. We found one and took a room with a mat on the floor. A man came and told us he knew where he could get us food, and my mother gave him money to bring us some dinner. He brought us rice full of red peppers. It was so hot that it burned my mouth and I could not eat it. I ate bread and olives. Then we slept. In the morning we got up and caught another bus for Bab Taza.

When we got to Bab Taza we got out and followed the other travelers and were examined by the soldiers. Then we sat down by the side of the trail to see if a truck might be coming past. There were two women and a man from the bus waiting with us. All day long nothing passed, and when it was night we all went a little way into the forest beside the trail and slept. In the morning a truck came by, and the two women and the man got in. My mother and I stayed behind because the truck was going to El Had, and we wanted to go to Beni Ahmed.

A soldier had been standing on guard on top of a hill. When he saw my mother and me alone in the trail he came running down.

Woman, he said. Where are you going?

I'm on my way to the Beni Mzguilda country.

Have you got a pass?

No, I haven't, she said.

I see. Come with me.

And he took us up to some barracks, where the mountain

21

patrol stayed. We went into a room. A Nazarene was sitting there. I found these two on the trail, the soldier told the Nazarene. This woman has no pass. She says she's been living in Tanja for eight years.

The Nazarene asked my mother: Where are you from?

Menarbiyaa.

And where are you coming from now?

From Tanja.

Are you married?

Yes.

Your father. Where is he?

My father's in Menarbiyaa and I'm on my way there now.

And why did you go from Menarbiyaa to Tanja?

She told him: People were going, and I went with them.

You'll have to wait here, he told her. In the afternoon the soldiers will come and take you to the Beni Mzguilda.

Later that day a soldier came and looked at us. They told us: This soldier will go with you.

Let's go, said the soldier. And we started out. It was the hour of the afternoon prayer. We walked along the trail for a while, and then the soldier took us onto a path that had many stones in it. There were albiota trees along the way, and we crossed streams and climbed around big rocks. Each time I saw an albiota tree I would go and climb up and pick some albiota nuts. I ate them as I walked along. I kept running and climbing up the trees until my mother said: Come here. That's enough. Walk in front of me. I had filled all my pockets with the nuts because each time I saw a tree I thought there would be no more of them. But the trees were everywhere. The nuts in my pockets were heavy. When I got tired of carrying so many of them, I began to throw them away. First I emptied one pocket and then another. We walked and walked, and a little after twilight we came to some barracks on top of a high hill.

We're going to stay here tonight, said the soldier. And in the morning you'll start out again. I'll go back to Bab Taza.

The next day before the sun came up, a different soldier woke us. Get up, he said. You've got to go now. I'm going with you.

He got on a horse, and we started out after him on foot. Walking, walking, through the country. Sometimes we saw a piece of plowed land, but it was small and then we would have to walk several hours before we would see another. And we never passed anyone on the path. We walked all day, and at the end of the day we came to some more barracks. We slept there, and they changed the soldier again. Each time the man who had come with us the day before stayed behind, and a new man went out with us. Walking, walking, walking, on the third day, through the mountains, and the soldier always on a horse.

Once we sat down by the path to rest for a few minutes. The soldier let the horse go and eat by itself. Then he sat down under a tree. He was from the Andjra country. Where are you from? he asked my mother.

Menarbiyaa, she told him. Where are you taking us?

To Beni Mzguilda to leave you with the caid.

A little later he said: We can't wait here. Let's go.

Yes, she said. We'll go on with you, but if we get tired we'll have to rest again.

We had not gone very far before I was tired. I told my mother: I can't walk any more. My mother called to the soldier: Ya, El Andjri!

What is it?

The boy is tired. We must rest. He can't go any further now.

That won't do, he told her. I can't stop again. I have to get to the barracks. The boy can rest when he gets there.

She said: Allah, ya sidi! We've walked for three days. Today we've been walking since early morning, and now it's past sehel time. The sun will soon be going down, and we're still walking. You soldiers change every day, but we never get a chance to rest.

He said: There's nothing I can do about it. I'm carrying out my orders, and you've got to keep walking until we get to the barracks. Then you can both sleep, and tomorrow you'll have a different soldier with you.

I tried to go on walking, but I could only sit down. This boy can't walk any farther, said my mother, so we can't go on.

Well, said the soldier, we'll rest a minute. So we sat down and rested a little. We were thirsty too, but there was no water. After a while, when the sun had set, the soldier stood up. Come on, he told us.

We started walking again, walking, walking, and we got to the barracks as night fell. When we went in, we saw some other people sitting there waiting. My mother looked at one of the women and remembered her. She had known her many years before in Menarbiyaa.

Why did they bring you here? she asked her.

We were carrying kif, said the woman. They're going to take us to the caid at Menarbiyaa. The caid will give us justice. He'll let us go.

The soldiers had taken the people because of all the kif they were carrying with them. They had a donkey and they had filled

23

the baskets at each side with many pounds of kif. Then they had cut wheat and spread it on top of the kif. But now the soldiers had taken everything. The woman was telling my mother all about it. And my mother was telling the woman of the things that had happened to her since she had seen her.

Allah! the woman said to my mother. If they take you to Menarbiyaa to see the caid, from there they'll send you to jail.

My mother said: When you leave here, go and see my father and tell him his daughter was on her way to see him, but now the soldiers have her. If we all stay together, that will be that, but if we separate, give my father that word from me.

In the morning they called us and got us together, and we all started out together with two soldiers. Walking, walking, the two soldiers too, until we came to a river. The rivers there have good water in them. Then the soldiers told us: Sit down, and we'll stay a little while here. Whoever wants to drink can drink.

We drank for a long time. Afterwards we sat there a while beside the river, and the water went by. And we rested a little and ate some bread and olives. When we felt better we got up and drank some more water out of the river, and we got back on the path and started to walk again. Walking, walking, walking, until I was very tired. So tired I couldn't walk any more. My mother called to one of the soldiers: Ya rajel! Ya rajel! My son can't go any farther. We've got to rest again now.

Keep him going as far as where those men are cutting wheat, he said. They'll give us some sort of animal and we'll put the boy on it and go on that way.

So we walked on until we came to the field where the men were cutting wheat. When we got there the soldiers called to them and said: May Allah bless your parents. Have you got an animal you can lend us? We have a child here who can't walk any more. We'll bring the animal back with us tomorrow. It will go only to the last barracks at Beni Ahmed, and come back.

One of the men said: Ouakha. I'll get my donkey and go with you. That way I can bring it back myself. So they got that donkey and set me on top of it. I went on, riding, riding, until we were at the last barracks of Beni Ahmed. The farmer got on his donkey and went back home. We stayed there a while waiting. A soldier came and told us: As soon as it's dark you'll be leaving for El Qachla.

When it got dark the truck came and we got in and went to El Qachla. There the soldiers began to ask all of us many questions. Where are you coming from? Where do you live? What address? And you? And you? And you? Ouakha. To my mother they said: We're going to call your chikh. He'll tell us who you are.

They sent a message to the chikh. The Frenchman there told my mother: We've called the chikh. Tomorrow he's coming to look at you.

We had to sit on a wooden bench all night. The other people went away, and my mother did not know whether the woman would remember to go and see her father or not.

The next morning the chikh came down to the office and told them my mother's name: Aicha bent Mohammed Chafaai. The chikh said to my mother: I know your father.

The Frenchman asked the chikh: How long is it since she was last here?

Six or seven years, the chikh said. He did not want to tell him it had been eleven or twelve years.

Did you have that boy when you were here before?

No, she said. He wasn't born here. Then she gave him my father's name. He was already in my belly when his father divorced me, she said.

So the Frenchman said to her: Well, woman, why did you run away from here?

She told him: I saw people going, and so I went with them.

And now the government is going to put you in prison, he said. You know it's forbidden to go from one place to another.

If the government wants to put me in jail, I'm ready, she said.

So they put us in. They put us in jail. And we stayed on the wooden bench again that night, and in the morning they brought a truck and took us to the jail in Tseroual. I had never seen a jail made of crooked shacks until I went to Tseroual. Before we went inside, we saw that they had the women in one part and the men in another. They let me go with my mother. There were three other women already in the shack. The women had no blankets or mattresses. There was just a piece of matting on the floor. They gave us no food. If a prisoner had a family, the family was allowed to bring food on Thursdays, but it had to last all week.

Each morning the three women went out of the shack and each evening they came back. My mother and I stayed behind because the government had not yet condemned us. We sat in that place three days, and no one spoke to us. We did not know anyone there. And no one knew us. No one brought us anything to eat. The third day one of the women began to talk to my mother.

Ya lalla, whose daughter are you? Your father, who is he?

And your mother? Is it true? You're Aicha? How old you've got!

Yes, said my mother.

And is that your child?

Yes.

Aicha, I don't know what they'll do to you.

I don't know either, said my mother. And why are you here?

I fought with my husband, she said. And so they brought me. What sort of work do you have to do here? My mother asked.

When it gets light, they send us out to gather wood, she said.

We slept, and in the morning the women went out the same as always. That day the government wrote our papers. They sentenced us to stay in the jail of Tseroual, because my mother had gone to Tanja twelve years before.

The next day when the three women went out to gather wood, my mother had to go with them.

You'll stay here, she told me.

No, I said. I don't want to stay. I want to go with you.

I walked with her to the door. As we were going out a soldier said to me: You won't go with the women.

I said: Yes. I have to go with my mother.

My mother said: That's right. If he doesn't go, I won't go.

The soldier went to speak to the sergeant. There's a woman here who has a child with her. She wants to take the child out to look for wood. A small boy like that can't get through the forest. Something will happen to him.

The sergeant said: Let him go along. It will be all right. She can take him, but she'll have to carry a load of wood on her back like the others.

The soldier came back and said: The child can go. The sergeant says you can take him.

Good, she said.

So we went to the forest. My mother gathered wood while I played. The wild strawberries were sweet. I sat eating strawberries and listening to explosions that came from far away. Every few minutes there was a roar.

I asked my mother: What is that noise?

That's the war, she said.

But when she said war, I thought it was nothing. It was like a game, or the wind. What is war? I thought. Not something in the world, not something that is part of life.

The women spent the whole day in the forest gathering wood. Each one kept adding to her pile. There were two soldiers on horseback to keep us from running away. Late in the afternoon the women piled the wood onto their backs and started to the jail. And we went along through the forest, walking, with the soldiers riding behind us. The people who were carrying heavy loads went on foot, and those who had nothing to carry went on horseback. Nobody but the one who is carrying a load knows how much it weighs. And I walked along with my mother. She was bent over double under her load, and I walked in front of her.

This is what our life was like there in the jail at Tseroual. I said to my mother one day: What a bad way to live this is!

And my mother said: Ah, you see how hard life is?

And I did not understand anything. I looked at her and that was all. There was nothing I could do for her.

We stayed that way, today and tomorrow, today and tomorrow. One day the news got to our family that we were there. My grandfather and his wife and my uncle came to see us at the jail, and then my grandfather went to see the caid and spoke to him.

The caid went to the pacha. He said to him: I know the woman Aicha bent Mohammed Chafaai. And he told him the story of how she had left the country many years before and gone to Tanja. When he had spoken with the pacha they let us go, and we went to stay at my grandfather's house in Menarbiyaa.

At first I thought people in the country had to buy plums and other fruit the same as people in the city. And I thought I would get a pail and fill it with plums and take it to the house, so my grandfather would say: Look, the boy has brought fruit for us all. And then I thought I would tell him I had bought them. I got a small pail and filled it with plums and carried them to the house. I went in and said to my grandfather: Do you want to eat some plums?

Yes, he said.

I bought them, I told him.

Aoulidi, he said. In the city where you live, you buy everything, don't you?

Yes, I said.

Here we buy nothing, he told me. Nothing is bought. When we want to eat, we go into the garden.

I said: You have a wonderful life here. I like it here.

Would you like to stay here with us all the time? he asked me. Yes!

Very good. You'll stay with us, he said. I was happy, because I thought I was going to live always with my grandfather.

The roof of the farmhouse was thatched with straw, but the inside was very fine. The house had a great orchard with fig trees full of big black figs. I spent three or four days picking figs and eating them. My grandfather's wife saw me eating them, and did not like it, but she said nothing.

One day I was sitting with my mother in the house, and I said to her: Wait. I'm going to go and get some figs. I went out into the orchard, and I was going to climb up into a tree, when I looked up and saw something big and black sitting there in the branches, with hair falling on all sides of it. It was bending over, and its eyes were looking down at me through the hair. I ran out of the orchard to the house.

What is it? What is it, Aoulidi? cried my mother.

Aicha Qandicha is in a tree in the orchard! I told her.

No, no, she said. It's not Aicha Qandicha. Don't be afraid.

It is. Come and look. Come! I made her go out and look. When we got there she was gone. There was only my grandfather's wife picking some figs.

She was here, I said. By Allah, I saw her here!

My mother said: Yes. Maybe. It could be. Now come on into the house. And we went in.

Behind the house there was an old tomb where a saint had been buried. Each year it had been falling to pieces more, and no one came to repair it. I liked that place, and I played in it every day. I picked ripe figs, the best ones, and I took them into the saint's tomb and ate them.

One day I was out in the orchard, in the top of a tree, picking figs. From there I looked out and saw another tree not far away. It had better figs than the tree I was in. I climbed down and went over to look at them. These figs! I thought. They're the best of all. But I can't eat any more now. I'll go into the saint's tomb and play a while, and when I come out I'll go up and get some.

I ran into the tomb. It was very old and falling to pieces, without a roof. There was an olive tree growing inside. When I went over to the tree, I saw a snake wrapped around a branch, crawling along. It saw me and disappeared. And I ran back outside and played there. After a while I went again to look at the figs. There was an old man sitting in the orchard under a tree there. Every day he came and sat in the shade. I climbed up into the fig tree and began to eat the figs. And I stepped onto a rotten bough, and it broke, and I fell. On the way down I hit a sharp branch. It went through the side of my face and tore my cheek all the way to my mouth. Then I fell onto the ground.

My mother came and got me and put me into bed, and I knew nothing about it. The next day I woke up and found my face torn. My mother gave me boiled oats and milk. There was no doctor. I went on eating only boiled oats and milk until I was well. Then I went out into the orchard and picked figs again the same as before.

We lived there another month, and then my mother said she could not stay away too long from Tanja. She had sent her husband a message saying she was going back, and she was afraid he would be angry if she did not go back now.

All right, said my grandfather. I'll go down as far as Beni Ahmed with you. You can stay in the house there and start out in the morning. You'll have to leave before daylight. There are soldiers along the river. If they don't catch you, you can go on to Bab Taza all right.

Yes, she said.

A few days later my mother came and told me: Get up and put on your shoes. We've got to leave.

I thought I was going to stay there in Menarbiyaa, but now I knew I had to go back to Tanja with my mother. I got ready to go.

So we went down to Beni Ahmed. There we had our dinner, and afterward we made some raif to take with us to eat on our journey. When we finished we ate some of the raif, and after that we slept until the hour of the fjer. Then my mother told my grandfather: I must go. She woke me up.

It's still night, Mother. Where are we going?

We went out, and my grandfather went with us. We started to walk along the trail. It was dark and I could not see anything.

We went on walking, walking, until we came to the river. It was not yet daylight, but I could already see trees along the river. When we got to the edge of the water my mother said good-bye to her father. Then I told him good-bye too, and we crossed the river. We kept going.

It was seven o'clock in the morning, and the sun was shining. We came to some farmers who were getting ready to cut a field of wheat.

My mother told me: Sit here, and I'm going to work with these people until evening. Then we'll go on.

We were still near the river. If we went along the trail the soldiers would see us. If she stayed and worked with the farmers they would think we were with them.

My mother went and spoke with the women. The men were cutting the wheat and the women were waiting for them to carry it away so they could walk behind and pick up what the men had dropped. The men gave them half of what they picked off the ground.

Lalla, I want to work here with you today, my mother told the

29

woman. I'm traveling, and I can't go on until night comes. I'll stay with you until the end of the afternoon and then I'll go.

That's a good idea. Better for you, the woman said. Stay with us and go later. If you go now, they'll catch you.

Good, said my mother. And all day long she worked, picking up wheat from the ground where the men had dropped it. She gave the other women her share. At midday the farmers brought out their lunch, and gave us some. They had bread and split-pea pudding and olives and buttermilk. We sat beside the river because there were high oleanders growing there. After lunch they cut wheat again until the middle of the afternoon. Then they put all the wheat together and threshed it on the ground. I sat watching. They piled the wheat onto the donkeys and started out for their village. My mother and I went with them. They let us go with them as far as their village, so the soldiers would not capture us. After we had walked along a while I got tired and they put me on a donkey. It was getting dark. We kept going. When we had got almost to their village, they stopped. You have to go over that mountain, they told us. Behind the mountain there is another village.

The farmers went away, and my mother and I kept going. It was night and there was no path, but we could see the trees and rocks because the moon was strong. We climbed up to the other village behind the mountain. There was nowhere to stay there but the mosque. They gave us food in the mosque and we slept there.

In the morning we started out for Bab Taza. The Djebala told us we could walk there in one day. We thought it was far because the soldiers had taken us back and forth from one barrack to another, all through the mountains.

That day we came to a country souq and it was market day. We sat down there and stayed until night. When the merchants picked up their things and started out for Bab Taza, we went with them. It was night when we got to Bab Taza. There we sat waiting in front of the barracks to see if other merchants would be going our way. It did not matter any longer whether the soldiers saw us or not. The bad part had been along the river the day before. We slept a little on the ground there, and the next morning we spoke with some men who were going to walk to the market at Chaouen. We went out with them. Each man was carrying something different to sell. One had charcoal with him, another had onions, another wheat. And we kept going along with them, until at twilight we came into Chaouen. My mother's husband had

30

been waiting there for us for several days. He put us onto a bus and took us home.

CHAPTER THREE

THE SHEPHERD

THE year we lived near the barracks of Beni Makada, the Spanish soldiers were still quartered there. Our house was in an orchard on a hill behind the barracks. I used to go every day to see the soldiers. I would go into the kitchen and help them with their work. They let me peel the potatoes, and afterward I would pour the peelings into a wheelbarrow and take them outdoors to throw them away. I would carry out all their garbage for them and toss it into the field. When they cooked their food they would give me some, and I would take it home. On Sundays and Thursdays they made paella with rice. That was the food I liked best.

We lived there for a while, and then the Nazarenes said that all the Spanish soldiers had to leave Tanja. They were going to be sent to the chemel. After a time the soldiers packed up all their things. They brought old clothes to our house for my mother's husband to buy. And they brought us pieces of metal. Sometimes late at night when we were asleep, three or four soldiers would come to the door with something to sell. Wood, blankets, or paper, or something else they had stolen from the government. Soldiers always need money.

And so the Nazarenes gathered up all their things. They took their horses and their trucks and their soldiers. Everything that had been in the barracks was taken away. And we stayed on, living in the orchard.

One day my mother's husband went into the city. On the road he met a man who had been a caid under the Spanish. Caid Abderrahman said to my mother's husband: Now, Si Mohammed, how long is it you've been living in that orchard? It must be sad up there, now that the soldiers have gone. Why don't you come and live in the hut that's on my land, with my cows and donkeys? It's in Souani. You could be the watchman at night and work in the orchard daytimes. You have a boy who could be a shepherd. And you'd stay there.

Ouakha, said my mother's husband. And so we moved to Souani, and I began to go out every morning with the caid's shepherd. My mother's husband would call me and say: Go!

31

Go with that man! Some day he won't be here and you'll have to do it by yourself.

I went with the shepherd every day, today and tomorrow, today and tomorrow. One day he quarreled with Caid Abderrahman. After they had argued a while the shepherd said: May your parents be blessed. Please pay me what you owe me, and I'll go and work somewhere else.

Later Caid Abderrahman was talking with my mother's husband. Your boy here. He knows how to watch over the animals. He knows all the paths. He can be our shepherd.

Yes, said my mother's husband.

That's that. Allah ihennik. Tomorrow, incha'Allah, the boy will take the cows out into the country and bring them in by himself. You'll go to meet him in the afternoon, to see that he gets them all back here.

That night my mother's husband said to me: Now you're going to be a shepherd. Get ready to be a good one. Just take the animals out for fifteen or twenty days, and then I'll buy you a pair of slippers.

And so the next morning the shepherd went away and I took the cows out by myself. I went down the road with them, walking, walking, until we came out onto El Adir, below Beni Makada. I drove the cows there and stayed with them all day.

A shepherd who had ewes on the hill came down to me. Are you Caid Abderrahman's new shepherd?

Yes, I said.

The man who has the hut in his orchard, is that your father?

Yes, I said, my father. I did not tell him he was only my mother's husband.

It's a good life, to be a shepherd.

Good or not good, I'm a shepherd now, I told him.

So the other one stayed with me that day. And in the afternoon I got the cattle together, the cows and bulls and a thin old mare that had to be taken out with them. They went ahead and I followed them holding the mare's rope. Every day I would take them down from El Adir to Souani, and my mother's husband would come to meet me. And sometimes he did not come. As soon as he saw that I knew how to do it alone, he did not come at all. I did it alone for two months or so, and then it was summer.

Caid Abderrahman had planted wheat there in El Adir. And he had the men cut down all the wheat, and went to look for women to gather up what the men had dropped. My mother went with the other women and worked in the field. I would take my animals to a pasture near the field and talk to her. Some days I stayed with her all day, and we ate our food together. And the women worked picking the wheat off the ground, and each one took her share. The caid had to have his share too, and it was my mother who carried it to him. Each day when we had finished working, she and I would take our share of the wheat home. And this went on, today and tomorrow.

Beside the land where the wheat had been cut there was a field of corn. It was still not ripe, so the cows could not eat it. I took them there every day to eat the straw that was left on the wheatfield. All day long I would stay there, and when the day finished I would bring the cows together and drive them home.

One day that work was all done. The men were picking up straw there in the field. They saved it to give to the cows when the rainy season came. There were many big piles of straw, all over the field. I walked over to one of them and lay down. It was very hot there, and I fell asleep. When I woke up I walked around, looking to see if all the cows and bulls were there, and to be sure they were not eating any corn. If they eat green corn they can swell and burst. They were there, and they were eating straw. Thanks to Allah!

It was late in the afternoon, not long before sunset. It's time to go, I thought. I got the animals together and drove them ahead of me, walking, walking, until we got back to the house. And there my mother and her husband tied them up. While my mother was milking the cows, her husband said: Aicha, there's a bull missing.

There is?

Yes.

He called me. Ahmed!

What?

There's a bull missing. Where have you left him?

I don't know, I said. These are the ones there were. I watched them all day and brought them home. That's all there are. Wait and I'll look at them, I know them all.

I looked, and it was true that a bull was missing. There should have been seven bulls and there were only six. Yes, I said. One's gone.

Did you fall asleep?

I said: Yes. I slept a little.

Why? I've told you never to sleep. Who told you to sleep?

I didn't know I was going to sleep until I woke up.

Come on, he said. Get your stick and we'll go and look for him. So we went out to El Adir to look. It was very dark on the road.

33

Walking, walking, in the night, and when the muezzin was calling the aacha, we were still up there in El Adir, looking. My mother's husband went to the cornfield, and I was standing near a high stack of straw. It was very dark. I pushed my head, and then my whole body, into the straw, so that I was all inside. The only thing I could hear was the wind hissing in the cornfield.

After a while my mother's husband began to call me. Ahmed! Ya, Ahmed! Ahmed! I knew he had found the bull in the corn, but I was afraid to come out from inside the straw. And I heard the frogs crying, and there was only the night everywhere. If I go out, something's going to happen to me, I thought. Someone will steal me or something. My mother's husband went on calling me for a long time, but I did not move.

He can call all he wants. I won't go with him. I'm going to sleep here until morning.

He called some more, and then he took the bull with him and went away. And I stayed there until the morning. When the sun came up into the sky I started home, and on the way I met my mother's husband driving the herd back out to El Adir.

Where have you been? he said.

I told him: Last night I was in a pile of straw, and when you called I was afraid to come out. It was very dark and I couldn't see anything, so I stayed inside there.

Go back, he said. Here are the cows. Take them.

I took them and drove them back to the country. And that day I had no food. A few days later my mother's husband bought me a pair of slippers, the kind the Djebala wear. Here are your belrha, he said. But look out. The leather is new and the soles are smooth.

I put them on. I was very happy to see shoes on my feet. It was the first time I had ever worn any.

Allah! I thought. These Djebala shoes are beautiful!

When the other shepherds came by, they said to me: Those shoes. Live in good health with them.

Allah's health to you, I told them.

The corn was all cut. Now the cows could go where they wanted. We shepherds sat all day talking. Some played cards, some played kchira with a piece of cork and sticks. My work stayed like this until the end of summer. Then one day when the summer was finished, Caid Abderrahman came to the hut where we lived, and told my mother's husband: I'm going to sell all this cattle.

When? said my mother's husband.

On Sunday the men will be coming to look at them.

I went on working another two days. Sunday afternoon I brought the animals home. We tied them up and milked the cows. Then the men came to look at them. Caid Abderrahman came with them. They looked for a long time at the animals, and then they went back to Emsallah with Caid Abderrahman and made the price. And he sold everything to them. Nothing was left. I went and looked at the empty stalls where the cows had lived at night. Caid Abderrahman told my mother's husband: I'm going to fix up these stalls and rent them to people to live in. You can take one of them and live in it until I bring cement and rebuild it. Then you can either pay me rent each month or look for another place to live.

And we stayed on there for a month or so, and the stall was better than the hut where we had been living. Then my mother's husband found another house lower down in a place called El Adaoui, and he rented it. It had a strip of orchard with it. Some days he worked there, and some days he went to market to sell sheep and buy goats. And he was always saying to my mother that he was not making enough money to feed us all, himself, my mother, and me. Then they would quarrel, and he would tell her: It's my work that keeps the boy with life in him. Send him out to work. Send him again to watch somebody's flocks, or whatever you want.

One day my mother said: Why don't you go yourself and look for some work for him, and take him to it?

I will, he told her.

He went to see a man named Ben Aicha and said to him: This boy of mine. If you want him to be a shepherd for you, he can.

Ouakha. Bring him. I can let him watch my sheep.

The next day he took me to Ben Aicha's house, and said to me: There is the man. Go out with him.

Ben Aicha told me he would give me thirty rials a month and all my food, and that when my slippers wore out he would buy me a new pair. I said: Good, and I began to work for him. Time went by. It was almost the Aïd el Kebir, and people were buying their sheep for the sacrifice. The men with a lot of money wanted to sell the sheep they bought, and so they bought many of them and put them out to graze. The sheep would be fat afterward, and they could sell them better. With so many sheep in one place, each day the flocks got mixed together, and at sunset the shepherds had to separate one flock from another before they could drive their own home.

There was a playing field near the meadow where we let our sheep graze. The French used to play rugby there. One day there was a game going on, and I went to watch. When it was over I went back to my sheep and got them together to take them home, and I found that one was missing. Someone had stolen it. I knew that Ben Aicha would know because each night when I took them in he counted them. This night he said: You've lost one.

We went out and looked everywhere over the country where I had been all day, but we did not find it.

Ben Aicha let me go on being his shepherd. He did not say I was no good or that I would have to pay for the sheep. He only said: The sheep is gone. Another time Allah will help you look after them better.

When my mother's husband heard about it, he came and said to me: You don't even know how to be a shepherd. You don't know how to take care of people's things for them. All you know how to do is play all day long.

Ben Aicha told him: Don't talk about it to him. Let him alone. Now it's happened, and Allah will help him another time.

And I stayed on working for Ben Aicha. I was his shepherd for six or seven months. Summer came again, the time when the schools are shut. When Ben Aicha's younger son got out of school Ben Aicha said to him: Now you're not going to school any more. You've got to go out sometimes with the sheep and watch them. And he said to me: And Ahmed, you're going to rake up straw. I'll give you a rial for each netful you bring me.

And the little boy went out with me, and took care of the sheep, and I would spend the whole day raking straw to give the sheep when the rainy season came. Some days I took back two or three nets full, and some days only one. Whatever I found. I would rake up the straw, and his son would carry the bales back to the house on the donkey.

Ben Aicha had an older son named Abdallah, who was plowing every day in a field near the meadow where we let our sheep graze. One day he took the flock out to the country for me. The Nazarenes were there playing rugby on the field. Abdallah left the sheep by themselves and went to watch the game. When it was over he went back to gather the sheep together. And he counted them, and found two missing.

When he saw they were not there, he took the others home. Then his father counted them and told him: Boy, you've lost two sheep.

36

I don't know anything about it, Abdallah said. I wasn't taking care of them. Ahmed was watching them today. I took them to him and told him to look out for them, and then I went to see the rugby game.

Then Ben Aicha came over to me and said: The words my son has been saying. Are they true?

No. I haven't seen the flock today. When I went out this morning I took the donkey and the nets to hold the straw. I haven't seen the sheep at all. Not until now.

Listen! said Ben Aicha to his son. Listen to what Ahmed is saying.

I swear it was Ahmed! He was watching them.

I said to Abdallah: You're not ashamed to lie?

I was trembling, and I said to myself: Now Abdallah is thinking that because I lost one sheep once he can say I've done it again.

You say I had the flock with me? I asked him.

Ben Aicha said: That's enough. We're not going to talk about it.

I went to my shelter and sat down. The girl brought me my supper. I ate and went to bed. In the morning I went to take the nets and the donkey, but Ben Aicha said to me: Leave them there. Don't take them. Leave them today. You're not bringing straw today. Abdallah's going to get it.

You know best, I said.

Look. The month is not over yet. But I'm going to pay you the whole month. You can't go on being my shepherd.

Ouakha. As you want.

He paid me the full month. Here, he said. Go home to your father. He thought my mother's husband was my father. I took the money home and gave it to my mother's husband.

Here's the money, I told him. Take it. I'm not a shepherd any more.

Why not?

The man doesn't want me.

Why doesn't he want you?

I don't know. The boy lost two sheep and said it was my fault. And in the morning Ben Aicha said I couldn't work for him any more, and he paid me.

Yes, I know you, he said. You always lose everything. You haven't got work in your head. One time you lose a bull. Another time you lose a sheep. And now you've lost two.

I didn't lose anything, I told him. I wasn't even with the flock. You're talking, and you didn't see anything.

37

Shut up! Don't say any more!

And I stayed there at home in his house. He would take me to the orchard outside and give me a hoe. Here, he would say. Take this. Work.

How could I work? What kind of work could I do for him? It was more than five years since anyone had dug in that ground. After so much time the earth is like a rock. There was nothing I could do with it. And it went on for a month or a month and a half. I was living in the house with my mother and her husband. Some days he made some money in the market, and some days he did not make any. And when he came home without money he quarreled with my mother. He would tell her: Your son. See how long I've been working for him this time. Now you do something about it. Do something with him. I married you. I didn't marry your son.

And my mother was always unhappy, always worried.

One day when he was in the market he met a man named El Fellah, who lived up in Beni Makada. He said to him: El Fellah, I have a boy at home doing nothing. Can you take him with you as a shepherd?

I don't need any shepherds now. All my cattle and sheep are in the hills. I have no animals at home. I keep them up in the hills for the whole winter. Until spring. Then they bring them down to the farm. But spring will be coming soon, he said. If you want to bring the boy to me, bring him. He can gather fodder until the animals get back. And he can run errands and work around the house. Then when the animals come back he can take them out.

That afternoon my mother's husband came home and said: Ahmed.

What?

I've found you a fine place to live, with very good people. They have a lot of land and cows and sheep.

As you say.

Eat your supper now, because I'm going to take you there. Where?

To Beni Makada.

It was a long way to Beni Makada in those days, because there were no houses anywhere. Only the road with fields of corn and wheat on each side.

Now? At night?

Yes, he said. Now, at night. You'll sleep there so in the morning early they can show you what to do.

Ouakha.

We ate our supper.

Put on your shoes, he told me.

I put them on, and took a jacket, and said to him: Let's go.

When I went out the door I said to my mother: Good-bye. Try and come some day to see me.

I'll come soon, aoulidi. Just go now.

And we went walking, walking along the road. After the barracks there was no more road. We got to Beni Makada when the muezzins were calling. And my mother's husband was asking everywhere for the house of El Fellah, and people began telling us we must climb up to the tomb of the saint, because his house was in front of it. We climbed up the hill to the tomb, and dogs started to bark at us. My mother's husband shouted: Ah, Si Mokhtar! Ah, Si Mokhtar! And a man answered: What is it?

Come. I want to speak to you.

The man came out and saw who it was.

Here's the boy I told you I was going to bring you.

Come inside the compound, aoulidi. Come in.

Ouakha.

Now you'll want to go, said El Fellah to my mother's husband. Go on home. The boy will be all right with us here.

Good-bye. You stay here, my mother's husband told me. And then he walked away.

Come on, said El Fellah. Your mother's husband is gone now. He led me through the compound to one of the huts behind the house. It was a good hut, built of stones inside, and mud and cow-dung outside, with a roof of fine straw. He opened the door. On one side there was a pile of straw, and on the other there was a high stack of corn cobs. A man was sitting in the empty space between. I went over and kissed his hand. Then I sat down. El Fellah went away.

Sit down over there on the corn cobs, said the man. That's your place, if you want it.

I'll just sit here in the middle on the straw, I told him. There was no mat or blanket in the hut.

Sit where you like, he said. Sit on the straw or on the corn cobs.

The straw is softer, I said.

Yes, yes. Sit down, aoulidi.

We sat there. He was looking at me and I was looking at him. I waited for him to say something, but he did not say any more. And I did not want to talk by myself. After a while someone knocked on the door. A girl cried: Eh, plowman in there!

What is it? said the man. He got up and opened the door.

Here's your supper, said the girl. And this plate is for the shepherd. And she gave him two half-loaves of bread, one for him and one for me.

Here. Take this. Eat, said the man.

Give it to me, I said. Bismil'lah. I took the food and set it on the ground in front of me. Then I looked at it and looked at it. There was not much food. Six or seven pieces of fried potato. The potato had been fried the day before. And the bread was made of corn instead of wheat, and it was as dry as a stone. I began to cry by myself.

What's the matter? Why are you crying?

No. Nothing. Then I said: Is this the food you always have here?

Tonight they've given us a lot, because this is your first night here. It won't always be this good.

Where do you sleep? I asked him. Not here on the ground? That little rag you have there can't even cover you. It's no good at all. Don't you have anything to spread out?

It's warm in here, he said. There's straw and corn cobs everywhere.

Yes? I rubbed my eyes with my fingers.

Well, eat, he said.

No. You take it if you want. Eat it. I ate at home before I came. Probably my mother's husband knew the food was going to be like this, and that's why he fed me before we came.

Then I asked him: Aren't they going to bring anything for us to sleep on?

Just sleep like that in your jacket and pants, he told me. With that jacket and pants and shirt. Sleep like that with them on you.

Then the girl came back. Eh, plowman! Give us the dishes.

Take them, he said. But this new shepherd here won't eat what you brought him. His food and his bread, here they are still.

Eat! Eat, ya raai! she cried.

No, I said. I don't want it. I ate at home before I came.

You know best, she said. But if you want it, there it is. Nobody's going to take it away from you.

I know, I said. But I don't want it. I just ate. I can't.

Ouakha. As you like.

Then I said to her: Haven't we got anything to sleep on?

It's almost summer now, she said. It's warm.

Where's the summer? I asked her. It's a long way off. Spring hasn't even started to come yet. The wind is still blowing.

She only looked at me.

You know best, I told her.

When the girl had gone, the plowman told me: If you want to get warm, climb up on top of that pile of corn cobs and sleep. It's warmer than straw, I swear.

Ouakha, I said. So I climbed up to the top of the pile of corn cobs and pushed myself into them and tried to sleep.

All night long I scratched. The corn cobs were full of fleas. And I spent the night scratching until morning came.

Very early in the morning they cooked soup with grease in it and brought it to us. We sat on the ground outside the hut. Take it, they told us. Eat. And they gave us bread made of corn instead of wheat. They baked the bread every three days. The plowman took it and ate very fast, until he had finished everything. I broke my bread into pieces and put a little into my mouth. Then I took a mouthful of soup. I did not like either the soup or the bread. The people stood around looking at me, and said: Eat your breakfast.

No, that's enough, I told them.

The plowman took two bulls with him and went out to plow. When he had gone, they told me I was going to clean out the stalls where the bulls lived, and that afterwards I would go to the spring below the mosque to get water. And a woman gave me a broom and a shovel. Sweep, she said. Here's the basket to put the dung in. Carry it all over there behind that fence.

I swept and swept until I had a big pile of dung. Then I put it into the basket and carried it to the place where she had told me to take it.

Don't lose any of it, she told me. Keep it all. We need it to make fires with next winter. Spread it on the wall there to dry.

I don't know how to do it, I said. I've never worked with dung. Why don't you do it now yourself and I can watch. Then the next time I'll know how to do it by myself. I don't know anything about dung.

Just take it, she said, and spread it and pat it like dough and leave it.

So I did that, and she told me: That's right! That's it, aoulidi! Now you know how.

Yes, I said. I kept working there until I had finished. Then the woman said: Now you can go to the spring for water.

I told her: I don't know where the spring is.

You'll see it below the mosque, she said.

Her granddaughter, the girl who had brought us our food, said: I'll go and show him where it is.

Yes. Go with him, Seudiya.

The girl came with me. She was eight or nine years old. Come on, shepherd, she said. She took me behind the mosque and told me: You see this place? This is our spring.

I saw the water. Beside it there was an empty clay pot. Why is this pot out here? I asked her.

Because there's a djinn living in the spring. The djinn beat a man of our village. And always every Thursday we bring food for him. But food without any salt in it. We bring it to the spring and leave it here.

And the food? Who eats it?

The djinn. My grandmother says he eats it.

Is that true?

I swear, she said.

That's something new. I never saw anybody leave a pot full of food by a spring before.

Every Thursday at sunset we bring it out, and the djinn eats all the food in the night.

Let's fill the pails and go, I said.

The next time you have to get water, come here, she told me.

I carried water until noon from the spring to the house. I filled a barrel that held two hundred litres. Is that enough? I asked the woman.

No. We need more. You have to fill another barrel so we can take it to the nouedder.

Yes, I said. But now I'm very tired. I want to rest a little.

Sit down a while. You can bring it later.

So I filled the other barrel. When I had finished, I had no legs to walk with any more. I was like a piece of rag. And I was hungry. I had not eaten any breakfast and I had filled two barrels with water.

When do you eat here? I asked Seudiya.

When we feel like it, she said. Sometimes at the hour of the dhor, sometimes at the hour of the sehel. Any time.

That day they made white bean pudding with turnips in it. When the time came to eat, they gave me my food by myself, and I ate it outside in the compound. Even if they had served me stones then, I was so hungry that I would have tried to eat them. When I had finished eating, they brought the plowman's food and put it on the ground inside the hut so I could take it to him where he was working.

Where is the plowman? I asked them.

You see that hut down there on the plain? they said. There's a man working near it there. That's our plowman. There.

How do I get down there? I don't even know the way out of the village.

Go with him, Seudiya, they said, and show him the way.

The girl went with me through the village, until we came to the last shop on the road. From here you can see the whole path, she said. Go down there until you come to the hut.

That's the man, beside the hut?

Yes.

I walked all the way down until I came to where he was. I said to him: Friend!

What?

Here. Take the food the woman has sent you.

Good.

I told him good-bye and climbed back up. When I got to the house, the woman said: Now take the sickle and the basket and go and cut food for the bulls to eat tonight.

Where am I going to cut it?

Go, Seudiya, and show him.

So the girl went with me again. Behind the house there was a big orchard. Barley grew there under the trees, and that was what they fed the bulls. I did not know how to use a sickle, and so I pulled up the barley with my hands.

Seudiya said: No. Not like that. Look!

You know how? I asked her. And you're so young?

Yes. This is the way people do it.

I took the sickle and began to use it the way she had. Little by little I filled the basket, and then I took it to the house. They sent me back three tines for more. Then they told me: The cold water in the spring is good. Go and get some for us.

Ouakha. I got two pails and went to the spring. I took them back full.

Now sit down, said the woman. Rest a little. I sat down for a few minutes. The sun was setting. At twilight the plowman came back.

Get up, shepherd! he said. You've got to tie the bulls.

I took the bulls into their stalls and tied them.

The plowman had work to do there at the house, but when he saw I could do it for him, he made me do it all. Do this. Bring that. Give them some barley. Each evening when he came back, he sat down and called to me, to tell me what to do. Every morning I would get up, sweep, bring water, eat, and then take the plowman's food down to him, until he had planted all the corn.

The plowman finished planting the corn at the beginning of

43

spring. El Fellah came and said to me: Now the animals are coming down from the hills. Two shepherds are bringing them down. One of them will be going with the plowman to take care of the cows. And you, Ahmed, you'll go out with the other and watch over the sheep.

Two days later the animals got to the house. And the next day I went out with the shepherd whose name was Bouchta. He had more in his head than anyone else in the village, and I was his friend. He showed me all the lands that belonged to El Fellah. This valley is his, he would say, and all that hill is his.

Tbarak Allah! They have a lot of land!

When did you come to work here? he asked me.

I've been here a long time, I told him. About two months now.

What sort of work have you been doing?

Sweeping, carrying water, cutting barley, taking the plowman's food down to him.

I see.

And you? I said. How long have you been working for them?

I've been with them four years.

How is it to be a shepherd with them?

It's all right.

And you stay six months in the hills every year?

Yes.

And the rain and the cold and the wind? Do you have a place to stay?

We make a shack out of canes and stay in it. Every week on market day El Fellah comes on his mare and brings us food.

I stayed and helped Bouchta all that first day. In the afternoon we drove the flock ahead of us and went walking, walking to the house. When I got back there I found the corral full of dung. No one had swept it up all day. I got all the sheep in, and the woman came. Ahmed, we have to have two pails of water, she told me.

Ouakha. I went to the spring below the mosque and got them. When I came back I swept up the dung and carried it behind the fence and spread it on the wall. Then we all sat down together, three shepherds and one plowman. We were talking with one another, and the plowman told the other shepherds: The day Ahmed came here, he wouldn't eat his supper or his breakfast. He thought he was still in the city, in Tanja, where they eat white bread half a metre long. Nothing like that here, aoulidi. Only corn bread, and Allah's white bean pudding and buttermilk. Now you can drink all the buttermilk you can hold.

In a while El Fellah called me. Look, he said. Only one shep-

44

herd will go out with the sheep every day. You've got to stay here at the house. My wife is tired. She can't sweep or do anything.

Ouakha. So I stayed at the house and did the work there the same as before, except that I took the food for the shepherds out to them. Bouchta worked alone, and the other shepherd worked with the plowman.

Then summer began, and the plowman and his shepherd went to help cut the wheat and barley. One day El Fellah came again and spoke to me: Now, Ahmed, we have a lot of work in the fields. You'll have to go down and help the plowman and the shepherd with their work.

And I began to work with them in the field. They would cut the wheat and I would pick it up. When I had made a big pile, every two or three days, we would carry the wheat up to the nouedder. I would fill a net, and they would pile the bale onto the horse and take it up to the house. We finished cutting everything and carried the last wheat up to the nouedder. Every morning we took out four horses and tied them in a row together, each horse's head beside the next one's head. The last horse had a long rope tied around its nose and ears. We would take the rope in one hand and a stick in the other, and beat the last horse. He would walk around the outside of the circle and the other three would turn beside him. They were used to this, because they did it every year. The nouedder was covered with a powder made of dung and fine straw, and the wheat was spread out on top. The four horses kept walking over the wheat this way for many days. At that time of year the wind blows every day. There has to be wind so that the chaff can fall to one side. When a pile of wheat was finished we would take it away and spread more down. All the time we were there I was learning how to work with wheat, because I had never done it before. At the end I knew almost as much about it as they did.

And every day the sun was very hot. The plowman would drive the horses only a minute, and then he would give the rope to me, because the sun was burning him, and I was young. And we stayed working like that until we had finished the wheat.

One day I said to myself: Here I am, working for these people, and they haven't given me any clothes or shoes. And the slippers I have are broken on the bottom. I'm going around almost barefoot. If I want to wash my shirt or trousers I have to borrow somebody's djellaba for a day while they dry.

I went up from the nouedder to the house, and called to El Fellah.

What is it, shepherd?

45

Allah! I said. I'm almost barefoot now. Here it is five months that I've been working with you. Aren't you going to buy me anything? No shoes or sandals or slippers? And the shirt I have is so dirty it's sticking to my back.

Good, he said. When we get the wheat out of the nouedder I'll buy you some shoes or a djellaba or something. You know your money has been going every month to your mother's husband.

Is that true? I said.

By Allah, it is.

And haven't you told him I need some clothes?

No. All I told him was that I'd pay your wages to him each month.

It's very good this way, isn't it? I said. I do the work and he takes the money.

I'll talk with him, he told me, and we'll see what he says.

So we went on working until we finished the wheat. Then we carried the last of it from the nouedder to the house. El Fellah bought me a new pair of belrha and a long woolen tunic and a djellaba.

Here, aoulidi. I bought these things for you out of my own money. I'm giving your full wages anyway to your mother's husband.

May Allah bless your parents, I told him. And I took the tunic and the slippers and the djellaba, and I was very happy.

I said to myself: Allah! Now I'm going to be a real shepherd like the ones they used to have long ago! I put on the new clothes. That's it, I said. I'm even better than the Djebala now!

The shepherds talked a lot about the tomb of a saint named Sidi Bou Hajja. No one could sleep there, they said, because there was something the matter with the place. They said there was no one who would dare to stay the night near the tomb. A shepherd who worked for the moqqaddem told me that I would never dare to sleep there.

I don't know, I said. They all had talked so much about it that I thought perhaps it was true. These people have been here a long time, I thought, and they must know whether the tomb has something wrong with it or not.

That tomb, I said. What's the matter with it, if nobody can sleep there?

A bull with big horns comes out at night, he said.

A bull with horns comes from inside the tomb, you mean? Have you ever seen it?

Yes. Some of the people in the village have seen it, too.

I wonder, I said. Even I was afraid of the tomb. If the old people had seen it, what could I say?

It was summer, and one day there was a wedding in the village. We shepherds went to the wedding and sat in a hut apart from the rest. The guests ate wheat couscous with lamb in it, and they gave us couscous made of corn, because we were only shepherds. It got very late, and we went on talking, sitting in the hut. Then I said to the others: Good night. I'm going to sleep.

One of the boys said to me: Wait a while. We can go together later, you and I.

No, I said. I'm tired. I want to sleep. I'm going now.

I got up and put my djellaba over my shoulder. Then I went out. I had to go along the road that went by the grave of Sidi Bou Hajja. When I was almost up there, I felt my hair getting stiff.

Ah, I thought. See what is happening to me because of all the things they've told me about this place. I'd better curse Satan and bless Allah now, because I'm going to spend the night here and see what happens. And I went across the stones that were painted white, and walked up to the tomb, to the spot where they light candles on Friday. I spread out my djellaba on the ground and lay down on top of it.

I went to sleep. Sometimes I opened my eyes. Then I sat up and looked all around. There was nothing but the owls calling. When morning came I went back to El Fellah's house and carried the water up from the spring. Then the woman gave me my food. When you finish, take the plowman's food down to him, she told me.

I was going through the village with the food, and on the way I met the shepherd who had wanted me to wait and go home with him the night before.

Is it true that a bull comes out of the tomb? I asked him.

I swear it is. With my own eyes I saw it.

I don't know, I told him. Think a little. Perhaps you're lying.

That's enough! That's enough! I've been a shepherd all these years here in Beni Makada, and now you tell me maybe I'm lying!

I told him: I didn't see anything. Last night when I left you I went up there and slept beside the tomb until morning. And there were only owls talking to each other.

You're lying, I swear. I know you could never sleep there in that place.

I told him: All right. Let's go together tonight, both of us, and sleep there.

47

No, no! If you want to go, go by yourself. I'm not going near that tomb.

I went back and spent three nights there, and never saw anything at all.

One day El Fellah said: We're going to plant melon vines today.

The two shepherds and the plowman began to dig the holes. The flocks and the herd could go where they liked now. There was room for them everywhere, and the men were free to do the planting. They put the melon seeds in the holes and covered them up with earth. I began to go down in the afternoons to help them water the field.

When the melon vines grew up out of the ground, it was time for the corn to be cut. Then when the corn was cut the melons were ready to be taken and sold in the market.

Today and tomorrow, today and tomorrow, El Fellah was selling the melons and making a lot of money. But he never gave us any of it. Only melons. Eat all the melons you want, he told us.

I've been with these melons since they were seeds, I said to myself. Now they've grown, and people are buying them, and what am I getting out of it? He hasn't given me ten rials or five rials or two rials or one. Allah yaouddi!

One day I spoke to Bouchta because he was my friend. Listen! Has El Fellah given you any of the money from the melons?

Yes, he said. He gave us a rial for every four vines we planted. Is that right?

Yes, he said. Hasn't he given you anything?

No, he hasn't.

Do you know what we'll do?

What?

El Fellah has pink-eye, you know. He can't see very well. In the middle of the day, when the sun is strong, he can't go out at all. When he's asleep inside, we'll take the donkey and load her with melons and go and sell them, and we'll divide the money between us.

Ouakha. I haven't had a franc from those melons, I said. I haven't been paid for my sweat. I've worked for nothing!

You'll have to do what you can. If you want some money, we'll try it this way. But don't say a word to El Fellah.

I'm going to talk to him? You and I together are going to take the melons, and I'm going to tell him?

Let's go, he said. At noon you bring the donkey and the saddle and the panniers.

Ouakha. And at noon the sun was very bright and El Fellah went into the hut to sleep. I saddled the donkey and took her to Bouchta.

Here she is.

Sit down here, he told me. I'll go and cut the melons and leave them piled on the ground. Then you carry them and put them into the panniers.

Where am I going to sell them?

Just take them to the market and sell them to anybody who wants to buy them.

He went to cut the melons and I stayed with his sheep. Then he came back and said: Now you can go. They're all ready.

I took the donkey and went to the field. I put a stick across the donkey's back so the panniers would not reach the ground. Then I filled both panniers with melons. Bouchta was waving to me, calling: Go now!

I started out, walking beside the donkey, and we went along the road on our way to the city, until we came to the barracks of Beni Makada. Once I turned my head around to look back, and I saw that Bouchta and El Fellah were running along behind me. Bouchta called to me: Ahmed! Ya Ahmed! Wait!

I said to myself: That's El Fellah with him! What's the matter with that shepherd? You can't trust anybody.

Wait! Wait! he called.

I stopped the donkey and waited there for them to catch up with me. When El Fellah got to me he began to shout at me. No shame! You dog! You thief! Is this the way people behave?

What's the matter?

You went and saddled the donkey. You cut the melons. And now you're on your way to sell them.

No, I said. I didn't saddle the donkey or anything.

Shut up! Bouchta says you did

And did I go and cut the melons? I asked Bouchta.

Yes! Yes! You did! And to El Fellah he said: You can see with your own eyes it's not a lie, what I told you.

El Fellah did not answer, but I told Bouchta: I understand. Then I said to El Fellah: It wasn't like that. I asked Bouchta if he had earned any money from the melons. He told me you'd paid the others a rial for every four vines we planted. Then I said I hadn't got anything from it. Think how many melons have been sold, and I haven't had anything at all. And Bouchta told me: If you want money for your work, you'll have to take the donkey and fill up the panniers with melons and take them to market. He said: I'll go and cut them for you, and when I come back you load them onto the donkey and go and sell them. The money will be half for you and half for me. That's what Bouchta told me.

You're both sons of whores, said El Fellah. Neither one of you is any good at all.

We've never done anything before, I told him. But you hadn't paid me anything, and you'd paid everybody else. We were only going to sell this one load, and then my work would have been paid for.

El Fellah said: Why didn't you speak to me about it?

It's your fault, I told him. You're a man. You're forty years old and you have land and money. You know what Allah does to men who don't pay people for the work they do. When I finished watering the field, that was the time to call me and say: Here. Take this money for your work.

He did not want to listen. Come on. Come on, he said. Turn the donkey around. We're going back. Nobody can trust either one of you.

It's not my fault, I said. See how long Bouchta has been with you. And he was my friend.

I know, said El Fellah. Yes, Bouchta. You're not ashamed?

So we went back with the donkey, and El Fellah unloaded the melons and piled them on the ground. Then he sat down beside them. When some woman walked by he would give her one. All that afternoon he sat there. He gave them all as gifts to the country women. Some of the melons were ripe and some were still green, but he gave them all away.

Late in the afternoon El Fellah came to me and said: Come on. Put the saddle on the donkey.

It was nearly sunset time. I saddled the donkey and El Fellah got on her, and we went up to the house. When we got there he began to talk to his wife in front of me: Do you know what the shepherds did this afternoon? They tried to steal all the melons out of the field while I was asleep. I found Ahmed with the donkey and the melons in front of the barracks in Beni Makada.

Allah, ya aoulidi! she cried. Is that the way to act, Ahmed?

I didn't do anything. Bouchta said we'd do it that way, and I said all right.

There's no harm done, she said. Allah forgives everything. It's over.

But, lalla, I worked a long time with those melons, and he's never given me five or even two rials or anything.

And we left it that way. They never paid me anything for the melons. I stayed with them until winter came. One day I went to El Fellah and said: I've been with you a long time. Almost a year

50

I've been your shepherd. And for all that work I have only a pair of slippers and a tunic and a djellaba. I'm the shepherd and I should be the one to get the money, not my mother's husband.

He said: Wait until market day, and I'll meet your mother's husband there and talk with him. We'll see what he says.

Yes, I said. I'm the one who does the work, and I'm the one who ought to get the money.

The words I just said to you are the way it will be, he told me. On Thursday I'll meet him and speak with him.

Thursday El Fellah went to market. When he came back he said: Do you want to know what your mother's husband told me? You work for me and I pay him. If you need anything he'll buy it for you.

I knew he would never buy me anything. Ouakha, I said. We'll see what he buys me at the end of the month.

At the end of that month El Fellah paid my mother's husband and he bought me nothing. This is no good, I said to myself. I'll never earn any money here. I'm working for nothing. It's no use.

There was nothing I could do. I went on being El Fellah's shepherd.

CHAPTER FOUR

THE OVEN

Two years later I was still a shepherd, but I was working for my mother's husband, and sleeping in his house.

There was a boy named Rhanrha who worked with me, watching the cows and sheep and goats. One day Rhanrha told me: My friend, I'm going into the city and look for work. This is no work.

Where are you going to work? I asked him.

I'm going to try and find some man with an oven who'll let me carry the bread for him.

I said to Rhanrha: Good. Do what you can. If you want to go and be a terrah, go.

Tomorrow I won't be here with you watching the animals.

You know what you're doing, I told him. I did not believe he meant what he said.

All that day we stayed in the valley watching the animals. Evening came, and we drove them ahead of us and took them back home. He went with his goats and I went with my cows and sheep. The next day I took them out again. I went to the valley, and there I met another shepherd.

Hasn't Rhanrha come yet? I asked him.

No, he said. I haven't seen him. I wonder where he's taken his goats.

I don't know.

Six or seven days went by, and I did not see Rhanrha. I had not seen him since the day he had told me he was going to look for an oven. One day I went into the city, and I met him.

Ahilan, Rhanrha! Is everything all right? Where are you these days?

I'm working, he said.

Where?

At an oven near here. That oven by the steps of Ibn Batuta.

Near the cinema?

Yes, that one, he said.

Is it good? Look and see if you can't get work for me there too, with you, or at some other oven.

Yes, he said. There's a maallem who's looking for a terrah now. If you want to work I'll take you to him.

Where is the maallem?

His oven is in Djenane el Kaptan.

Ouakha, I said. I'll go home and talk with my mother, and tomorrow I'll come and find you at the oven.

I went home. Mother, I said.

Yes?

I'm not going to be a shepherd any more. I'm going to work in the city at an oven.

Do as you like, she said. Go if you want.

Tomorrow morning I'm going to go and see Rhanrha, I told her. He's the one who's going to take me to the maallem.

The next day I got up, put a basket on my arm, and went to the oven at the foot of the steps. Let's go, I told Rhanrha.

We went into the Medina. I did not know any of the streets. We climbed up to Djenane el Kaptan, and Rhanrha took me to a man named Maallem Mohammed.

Maallem Mohammed, here's the terrah I told you I was going to bring you.

Come in, my son, come in, he said. Hang your basket up on that nail.

There was already a terrah named Abdeslam working there, but the maallem needed an extra one because so many people brought him bread to bake for them.

I hung up my basket. The maallem told Rhanrha: Go now. If

Ahmed doesn't know the way, you can come by for him this evening after work.

Rhanrha went back to his work, and I stayed sitting in the oven. Soon a woman came by and stuck her head inside. My bread is ready to be baked, she said. I need a boy to come and get it.

Go with her, the maallem told me. I went with the woman to her house, got the bread, and carried it to the oven on my head. When it was baked, I took it back to her, and she gave me a quarter of a loaf. Each woman gives something when the terrah takes her back the bread. Some give a quarter of a loaf and some give a half. The first day I did not get very much. Three pieces of bread, no more. I put them into my basket, and at sunset Rhanrha came to get me. We went home.

Ah, aoulidi! So this is the work you're doing! said my mother. No money. Only a few little pieces of bread.

Just let me learn, I told her. When I'm bigger I'll know all about how to bake bread, and I'll have my own oven. I'll be a maallem and everything.

Whatever you like, said my mother.

I went to sleep. In the morning I got up and went to Rhanrha's house, and we walked together to the Medina. I went up to my oven in Djenane el Kaptan, and he went to his oven by the steps of Ibn Batuta. And a woman who made bread to sell in the street came to the oven and said to the maallem: I need a boy to bring my bread from the house. When it's baked he must carry it down to the bread market in the Saqqaya.

I thought the maallem would tell Abdeslam to go. But he asked me: Can you do it?

Yes, I told him. I thought it would be like carrying any other bread.

Good, he said. Take these three boards and go with her.

I took the boards and put them on my head. Each one was as big as a door, and could hold thirty-five loaves of bread before it was baked. And I went to the woman's house. I put the boards down outside the door and stood there. She came and got them one by one, and put the loaves of bread on them. I went in and carried out the first board covered with loaves of bread, and took it to the oven. Then I went and got the second, and then the third. When the bread was baked, I piled it all on a different board, still bigger, and started down the steps to go to the Saqqaya. The woman was walking behind me. There were a hundred loaves of bread, and they were very heavy for me. My legs would not stand up under them. I tried to put the board down on the steps, and it slipped. All the loaves of bread were rolling down the steps, and many people were picking them up. And the woman was screaming: Allah! Allah! The terrah has ruined all my bread! A man who was coming up the steps said to her: A small boy like that can't carry so much bread all at once. The woman went back up to the oven and got Abdeslam. He wiped the bread off and carried it to the Saqqaya for her. When Abdeslam came back I asked him why the maallem had not told him to carry the woman's bread for her in the first place.

He knows I don't like to work for her. She's stingy, he said. She sells bread, and so she wants to keep all she can.

The next day I went by the oven where Rhanrha worked. I said to him: Look. This work I'm doing up there is hard. I had to carry a hundred loaves down the steps from Djenane el Kaptan to the Saqqaya. Can't you look around for some other work for me?

I'll see, he said.

I went on working at the same oven for a month or so, and one day Rhanrha came to see me there. Do you want to come and work at my oven? he asked me. The maallem says if you want to you can.

Ouakha, I said. I spent that day working for the Maallem Mohammed, and the next day I went with Rhanrha to his oven.

Rhanrha said to the owner of the oven: Si Larbi, here's the terrah I said I'd bring you.

Well, my son. Do you want to work?

Yes, I said. I came to work.

You've been working in Djenane el Kaptan with the Maallem Mohammed? Sit down.

And I sat down. There were several terrahs working there, and they knew all the houses in the quarter. I did not know any. I went with them to learn, but I did not carry any bread that day, and I went home with nothing in the basket.

Not even one piece of bread today, aoulidi? my mother said. Yesterday you brought bread.

I'm working now at a different oven, I told her. This one is better than the other. I'll get bread later.

For a few days I went with the other terrahs to learn about the houses in the quarter. When one of them went to a house I went with him. I got to know the houses, and when somebody came to the oven asking for a terrah I would start to run, and try to get to the house before any of the others. The first one who got to the door took the bread and carried it up to the oven. I needed the bread for my mother, and more than that, I did not want to be beaten by the maallem. Each terrah had to have at least ten pieces of bread by the time the maallem went home at night. If he had fewer the maallem would beat him. Every maallem knows each loaf of bread he bakes, so we could not buy pieces of some other bread and say it was his.

Today and tomorrow I worked at the oven by the steps of Ibn Batuta, and two years went by that way. And I was earning money. I got money from the Jews. On Fridays I would carry their pots of skhina, with meat and eggs and vegetables in it, to the oven, and take them back when they were ready, and they would give me money. Sometimes I slept at the oven for two or three nights at a time, until I had enough money or bread to take home. Friday night nobody could sleep at the oven, because the Jews sent their hazzan to lock it up. That night all the ovens are full of pots of skhina. The Jews think that if a Moslem sleeps in the oven he may open one of the pots and eat some of the skhina. If he does that, all the pots will have to be thrown away, and they will have no skhina to eat on Saturday.

One day a Jewish woman came to the oven and asked the maallem: Do you want to buy some firewood?

The maallem said he would look at it. There was a Riffian boy named Gordo working there with me. He was about five years older than I was. The maallem said to him: Go with her, Gordo. And he told me: You go too. Both of you go with her. Look at the wood, Gordo, and come and tell me if it's good. You can bring it back in the handcart.

We went through the streets with that Jewish woman. When we got to her house we climbed up with her to the roof, and Gordo began to talk with her about how much the wood was worth. After a while they made a price, and we went back to the oven and told the maallem. He gave Gordo the money, and we pushed the cart to the Jewish woman's house. After Gordo paid her, we began to carry the wood down from the roof to the street. We filled the cart and took it to the oven, and we went back for the second load.

The wood on top of the pile was very old, and at the bottom it was still older. When Gordo lifted up one of the logs, there was a bundle there, covered with a rag.

What's that? I asked him.

Shut up, he said. It's an old bundle.

Open it up. Let's see what's in it, I told him.

He undid the knot in the rag. It was full of Spanish banknotes. The rats had bitten pieces out of them.

It's money, he said.

Half of it's mine, I told him.

Shut up! Do you want me to kick you off the roof? He says I've got to give him half! The maallem sends me to buy wood from the Yehoudía, and I'm supposed to give you half! And now keep your mouth shut and I'll give you five rials. But keep quiet.

He was much bigger than I was. All right, I said.

And we carried all the wood to the oven on the second trip. When it was piled next to where the maallem sat, Gordo took me out and gave me five rials from the inside of the bundle where the notes had no holes in them. Then he said: This money. Where am I going to change it?

I don't know, I said. They might take it at some bacal.

And if the maallem finds out about it?

Don't worry about the maallem, I told him. He won't do anything. He's not going to see you.

I left him standing in the doorway of the oven and began to walk down the street. I was thinking. Then I went back to the door. Give me one of the hundred peseta notes, I told him. I'll see if I can change it for you. He took out a bill and gave it to me. Here, he said. It was one of the old banknotes that the rats had been chewing.

I went into a bacal in the Calle de Italia and asked for a pack of cigarettes. The man looked at the bill. This bill has no numbers on it, he said. You'll have to take it to the bank.

I went back to Gordo and told him: It's no use. They won't take it. How much will you give me if I change it all for you?

Where?

Don't worry about that. I can change it. Tomorrow, incha'-Allah, I'll give it to somebody I know. He'll change it for me.

You will? Is that the truth?

I swear!

So he said: Ouakha. Here it is. He took the bundle out of his pocket.

How much is there? I asked him.

Count it, he said. There's five hundred rials in there.

I don't know, I told him. There may be five hundred or three hundred.

I did not know how to count the money. I said: I'll get it changed for you. You give me another five rials and it's finished. Take it, he said.

I took the bundle. That night I slept at the oven. In the morning about ten o'clock I climbed up to the Boulevard. There I asked a man where the Banco de España was. Over there, he said. The one with two doors. Go in there.

I went across to the bank and walked in. There were people

56

waiting in line. One of the Moslem guards saw me. He kept looking. Then he came over and said to me: What do you want here, boy?

Nothing, I said. I have some money, and I want to change it.

Go over there, he said.

And I went up to a Nazarene who stood behind a counter, and gave him the money. He began to count it, and he counted and counted. Then he gave me new bills. I looked at what he had handed me. It was only a little, and I had given him a big handful.

I gave you a lot, I told him. Look how little you gave me back.

That's the right amount, he said. Count it. Don't you know how to count?

Yes, I said. I put the money in my pocket and went out. That day I did not go back to the oven. I stayed in the street drinking gaseosas and playing ruleta in front of the cinema. I bought a pair of sandals, because I was barefoot. And I walked through the second-hand stalls in Bou Araqía and bought a shirt and a jacket. I slept at home that night. The next morning at half past ten I went back to the oven.

When I went in the maallem said: Where have you been?

Maallem, I said, yesterday they took me to the police station. And I stayed there all night.

What for?

Nothing. I was fighting with somebody, that's all.

You always go into things that aren't your business, he told me. You see what happens? You sleep in the comisaría. Why do you get into fights?

It's all over now, I said.

I went out and called Gordo. You know what happened? Because of you I had to sleep last night in the comisaría. And this afternoon at three o'clock I've got to go back there. All because of your money. And the money's at the comisaría too. What they're going to do to me at three o'clock I don't know. But I've got to go, and if they ask me about the money I'll have to tell them it's yours.

No, no! he said. By your mother, don't tell them that! The money's not mine. We just happened to find it together. If they want to keep it, let them keep it. But don't tell them it's mine! If the maallem hears we found it with his wood and didn't give it to him, he'll say we're thieves. We'll have no work.

I told him: If you want me to say that to the police you'll have to give me ten rials.

All right, he said. I'll give you the money. We went to the street where the oven was, and he said to me: Wait here for me.

57

Don't come to the oven with me.

He went into the oven. Each terrah had his own money-box inside. In a minute he came out with the money.

I took the ten rials and put them into my pocket. Allah ihennik, I told him. If I come back tonight, you'll see me. If I don't, you'll know they kept me there again.

That afternoon I walked all around the city. After a while I got tired, and I said to myself: This is the time to look for a woman. Everybody says it's good. Now I've got the money I can try it. I can take one and see what it's like. I was in the Derb el Oued. There were houses in that quarter, with Spanish women. I went into the alleys and began to look. In front of some of the houses there were girls standing. I saw one Spanish girl and I thought: That one is good. I'm going up with her. I said to her: Shall we go up?

All right, she said.

How much? I asked her.

Five rials.

Ouakha, I told her.

When I came down from the room and went out into the street, I was thinking: It's true! Women are good! I'll come back and do it again.

It was almost dark. I went by the oven. The maallem had gone home but the oven was open. At night the owner, Si Larbi, always stood in the doorway selling pastries. If one of the terrahs wanted to go in and sleep, he could. Gordo was sitting inside in the dark.

What happened, Ahmed?

Thanks to Allah! I said. We're out of it. The police kept the money. They beat me again. All on account of you. Anyway, it's finished. This isn't the time to complain.

You're right, he said. Let the money go. We can't do anything about it.

You see? I told him. I asked you to give me half, and you wouldn't do it. That's what happens. Neither one of us got anything out of it.

The money's gone, he said. It's all the same.

Every day I went to the Spanish girl until all the money was spent. And I went on working at the oven. One house would give me skhina, another sweets, and that was the way I lived. Two or three rials a day and the basket full of bread. And my mother was much happier.

One day Si Larbi, the owner, came by the oven. He began to talk with the maallem. I'm going to rebuild my house, he told him. The next day he took workmen and materials to his house. Then he came again to the oven and started to talk to me.

Ahmed, you've been working a long time here. Why don't you come and help the workmen at my house?

I said: Si Larbi, if I go and work on your house I won't be getting any money or any bread either. And who'll keep me alive?

Work here at the oven in the morning, and come to my house in the afternoon. When the Aïd el Kebir comes, I'll buy you some new clothes.

Ouakha, I said.

And I began to work that way. We tore down two rooms, and we built up walls and put in two doors, one on each floor. Every afternoon for two months or so I worked there for him. We had to finish the house in time for the Aïd el Kebir.

Two or three days before the festival, Si Larbi came to the oven. The other terrahs were there. I said: Si Larbi, now the day is almost here. It's time to buy what you promised me. We've finished the house, and now I need the clothes. If you will.

Have you got any money? he asked me.

No, I told him. But you said you were going to buy them.

If you have the money, he said, I'll buy you the clothes. If you haven't, I won't. I'm not going to pay for your clothes.

I see, I said. You know best. And I was thinking of what my mother had always told me: If you see a Moslem who has been lucky, you'll know he didn't have another Moslem with him.

I went outside. There's a rich man who has everything he wants, with houses and an oven and everything, and he does that to me! Let him have his money. Allah will arrange it when the day comes.

I heard Gordo behind me. You know, he said, I've been giving Si Ahmed a few pesetas each day because he told me he'd buy me a pair of trousers for the Aïd el Kebir. And now he's got twenty rials of mine, and he says I never gave him any money.

Then Hamadi, another terrah, came out of the oven. He had been working six or seven years there. Do you see this broken tooth? he asked me. I said: Yes.

I had a fight, he said. And when Si Larbi saw the tooth he told me: Give me a little money every day. I'll save it up for you, and when there's enough, I'll have a gold tooth made for you. You have to have a hundred rials. A hundred Spanish rials to get a gold tooth! So when I'd given him a hundred rials, I said to him: Si Larbi, will you have the tooth made now? And he said: I've got no money to spend on teeth for you.

Yes, I said. A man who has his own and wants everybody else's too. But that's all right. Let him have it. He cheated me,

59

but I'll get it back.

So I kept on working there. After that, everytime I had the chance, I stole from Si Larbi. If he sent me to buy something, I would buy half and keep the rest of the money, and when he said: Is that all? I would say: That's all, Si Larbi.

Today and tomorrow, today and tomorrow, I went on working. One day a boy who sold pastries at the door of the oven said to me: Ahmed, the Nazarenes' big holiday will be here soon. The festival when they get drunk in the street and put trees inside their houses. My father knows a Spaniard who'll buy an arar tree from you. Why don't you and Pitchi go and get one and sell it to him?

How much will he pay? I asked him.

Maybe a hundred or a hundred and fifty pesetas.

I called Pitchi. Tomorrow is Sunday. Let's go to Boubana and cut down an arar tree and see if we can get something for it.

Yes? said Pitchi. You believe that? A dead tree?

I turned to the boy who was selling pastries. Is it true, Mohammed? That Nazarene your father knows will buy a tree if we bring it down to him?

I swear he will, he said. I know he will. Just get it and bring it.

So we went. We slept that night at the oven, and the next morning we walked out into the country to Boubana. There is a forest of arar trees on the mountain above the place where the Nazarenes play golf. We were standing there, and in a little while a Nazarene came by in his car. He stopped and got out, and began to cut down a young tree. He went on cutting trees until he had six or seven small ones.

We said to the Nazarene: Can we have one of your trees?

Cut one, he said. You can cut all you want.

Are they yours? I asked him.

Yes, they're mine. Don't you see how many I'm taking with me? He got into his car and went away. I began to cut one of the young arar trees with a saw. When I had four trees I told Pitchi: That's enough. We'll sell one to the friend of Mohammed's father, and the others we'll take to the market.

Let's go, he said.

You take two and I'll take two.

They were heavy. We carried them, one over each shoulder, until we got to the Souq el Bqar. We rested a while. Then we carried them on down to the market, and I waited there with three of them while Pitchi took one up to the oven. He came back and sat down with me. In a little while a Moslem walked up and said: Do you want to sell those trees?

Yes, we told him. Do you want to buy them?

I'll give you ten rials for the three.

More. They're worth more than that, we told him. One of them costs twenty rials, and you want three for ten?

Ten rials, if you want to sell them.

No, we said.

We were sitting there, and a policeman came up. Those trees, he said. Where did you get them?

They're ours, we told him.

Who gave them to you?

We were in a forest near Boubana and a Nazarene came and was cutting trees, and he said we could cut some too. We asked him for a tree, and he said to cut them ourselves. We asked him if they were his, and he said yes.

Pick up those trees. Come with me.

We picked up the trees and went with the policeman down to the comisaría in the Souq Ndakhel.

Ahah! they said to us. So you steal trees! Sit down.

They took the belts out of our trousers, and the laces out of our shoes, and they took away our cigarettes, and then they said: All right. Go on in, you two. And we stayed in there in the dark until the next day.

In the morning they came and said: Where are the ones who stole the trees?

Here we are, I said. They took us out into the corridor. The three trees were there. Pick up those trees, they told us. We picked them up and carried them outside, and went on carrying them through the street. Two policemen were walking with us. At the bottom of the steps by the Cinema Americano there was a police jeep waiting. We got into it and they drove us to the comisaría at Oued el Ihud.

Inside there was a very fat Belgian. I used to watch him get into a jeep. It leaned to one side when he got in. He looked at us and began to shout: Ha! So you're the thieves we've been looking for! You're the ones who've been cutting down all the trees!

Then he looked at me and yelled: Say something!

I told him how we did it.

What's that Christian's name?

He had a green station-wagon, I told him.

Lies! Sit down! There!

And we sat down and waited while they sent a jeep to the forest at Boubana. They came back with a shepherd. The Belgian asked the shepherd: Did you see these boys cutting the trees?

Yes, said the shepherd. There was a Nazarene there cutting trees too.

I said to the Belgian: You see? I wasn't lying. He said they were his.

So you stole them! The Belgian began to slap my head back and forth with his hand.

You aren't supposed to hit me, I said. You make out the papers here and send us to the Mendoubía.

Shut up, you son of a whore! Lie down there!

I lay on the floor and he stepped on my belly. You're going to kill me! I cried. Then he sat down on top of me. I couldn't move or shout or do anything, he was so heavy. He was like a truck on top of me.

When he got up he hit me some more, and then he put us into the cellar. The next day they wrote out the papers and took us to the Mendoubía to Monsieur Bompain's office. He said to us: Now where did you take those trees from? We told him the story.

Nothing but lies. I'm going to send you to jail.

So they put us in jail. That was the first time I had ever been sentenced to jail. They walked with us through Djenane el Kaptan and Pitchi was handcuffed to me. We went by the oven, but the maallem was not there. Mohammed was standing in the doorway selling pastries.

And there was hunger there in the Casbah jail. At meal-time they gave out the bread first. By the time they served the soup everybody had finished eating the bread. The bread had worms in it. They were dead. The oven had killed them.

When I did not go home for several nights, my mother went to the oven. The maallem told her I was in the Casbah jail. Then every day she brought me food.

I was talking to Pitchi. You know, I said, my mother's bringing me food now. If you want to eat it with me, you'll have to pay me a rial a day.

But I haven't got any money here, he said.

When we get out you can give it to me.

Ouakha. And we began to eat the food together.

We stayed on there. And each day my mother was running up and down, talking to the khalifa, trying to help me get out, but it did no good. One day Si Larbi went to the Mendoubía. Those two boys work for me, he said, and I'll be responsible for them.

They let us out. We worked four or five days there at the oven. Then they called us to the Mendoubía. There they said: You stole those trees?

We started to tell them about it, but they only told us: Get out of here! Don't do it again. You should have ten days in jail. But this time you can go.

So we went back to the oven. Now that I had been in prison, the maallem did not like me. He shouted at me and blamed me for everything. And each time I could, I would steal two or three pesetas from him. One day he took a broom and began to beat me with it.

I said to him: Look! If you don't want me to work for you, say so, and I'll go and work somewhere else.

No! You'll stay and work here whether you like it or not, he said. You're not going to work anywhere else. You think I want to teach a new terrah how to work?

If I stay with you, keep away from me.

I stayed working for him, but he went on beating me every day and shouting at me, until it was very bad. One day he took the bread shovel out of the oven and tried to hit me with it. I pulled it out of his hand and threw it on the floor.

That's enough of you and your oven! I said.

The terrah says that to the maallem? He picked up the shovel and pushed it hard into my belly. I grabbed it away from him. I let it come down on his shoulder. Then I ran out of the oven.

I was walking around in the Calle de Italia in front of the cinema, and one of the terrahs came by. Allah, Ahmed! he said. What's the matter?

The maallem's gone to get Si Larbi. You'd better not go back to the oven again.

Why shouldn't I go back? I said. I'm going back now. I want my things.

I went up to the oven. Si Larbi was there. So the terrah wants to be the master? Have you gone crazy? Don't you know what you're doing any longer?

The maallem took the bread shovel and tried to break my belly with it, I said.

Pack up your things, he told me.

I took everything and went home. My mother was there.

What's the matter? Why don't you want to work there any more? What's the matter with you?

They're no good! Si Larbi cheated me. Every day the maallem hits me. And I'm going to carry their bread?

CHAPTER FIVE

THE WHORES

I HAD no work, and I used to walk around the streets all
day watching the people. One night about ten o'clock I was
standing with the crowd outside the cinemas in the Calle de Italia.
Mustapha was there with a friend of his. He called to me. Ahmed,
he said. Let's go down to the Haouma dl Bnider. I'll find you a
girl.

Al Allah! I hope you can, I said. I've never even been down
there. This will be the first time.

The three of us, Mustapha, Mohammed, and I walked down
to the Haouma dl Bnider and began to look into the doorways
of the different whorehouses. Then we went into one of the houses
and sat down in the courtyard. Mustapha called to the padrona:
Bring me a bottle of lemon soda. A girl brought it to him. What
are you going to drink, Ahmed? he asked me.

I'll have a lemon soda, I told him. And Mohammed asked for a
lemon soda, too. And while we were drinking a girl came over to
the table. Mustapha, she said. You're drinking lemon soda? And
I'm not drinking anything? You're drinking alone? Shame on
you!

If you want to drink something, drink, he told her.

Then she called out: Bring me a lemon soda. Mustapha's
paying for it. The padrona brought another lemon soda for her.
I was just looking at the girls. They were sitting in two rows, all
dressed in fine caftans. This is something new, I thought.

In a little while Mustapha turned to me. Which one do you
like? he asked me.

That one there in the middle. The light-haired one, I told him.

That one? Yes?

Yes.

And how much are you going to pay her?

I've got ten rials on me. I can pay her.

I'll talk to her for you.

Good. That's the one I want.

And you've never been here before?

That's right. Tonight with you is the first time.

Don't you ever go with women at all?

I had a Spanish girl in the Haouma dl Oued, I told him. But
that's all I've had up until now.

All right. Don't talk about it here. I'm going to speak with her.

And Mustapha and Mohammed got up and began to walk around the room and joke with the girls. Finally Mustapha went over to the light-haired girl and said: Get up! Go and talk to that boy over there. You're sitting alone.

She got up and came over to me.

Brother, she said. Aren't we going to have a drink inside or anything? Look at your friends. Each one has a girl to talk to. And you're all alone.

How much does it cost to have a drink in the other room? Six rials.

I have ten, I said. I'll give them to you. We'll have a drink in the other room and then go to bed, and that will be it.

Wait, she said. I'm going to talk to Mustapha.

Mustapha, she said. This boy here has only ten rials. He needs more money for a drink.

Mustapha said: That's all right. I'll pay for him, whatever he needs.

We went into the other room, the three of us, and sat down at a table, and the three girls sat on the other side of it. Each one had his friend sitting across from him. They were all drinking wine, and the girl with me drank it too. Mustapha wanted to give me some, but I said: No. I have enough with the soda. We sat there for a half hour, and then the padrona came to take away the glasses. That's enough, she said. We all got up and each one went to a different room with his girl, and got into bed with her.

Afterwards we went out to Mustapha's café and sat down with him.

Was Khemou good? he said. Did you like her?

Yes, very good, I told him. She was wonderful.

Well, it's up to you. Be careful. Look out for her. She was broken in by a dog. She's the blonde who used to work for a woman who lived on the Boulevard. The woman's husband had a big dog. And when the woman and her husband went away they left the dog for her to take care of, and she took down her clothes and made the dog come and do it to her. And she was a virgin, too. That dog was her first lover. You'd better be careful of her.

I don't know, I said. That's her business. If she likes to do that, I don't care. With me she only wanted a lot of money. When I have money I'll go and see her.

I did not say any more then. And when I was walking around the town, I always had to go by and see Khemou. I began to stay all night with her. When she saw that I was bringing her a lot of money she said: Now you're not living any more at your mother's

65

house. Why don't you just move into the whorehouse? You can live here in this room with me. I'll talk to the padrona. It will be all right.

One day I have money and another day I don't, I told her. And afterward the padrona is going to make trouble for me.

You don't understand, she said. When you have money, you give it to me, and when you don't, you come and sleep and eat and drink with me.

All right, I said. I'll do it.

And then I was always looking for money to take to her. Wherever I could find it, working or borrowing or stealing. Anything to have money in my pocket to give her. When I had enough I would go and stay with her three or four days at a time, and never go out of the room at all. Then I would go out again and look for more money, and stay looking for it as many days as it took me to find it. Sometimes I found no work. And when I would go back without any money she would have an angry face and would not talk to me. Ah, I said to myself. What a race of creatures women are! See how they act when a man has money, and how different they are when he has none. They think only about what they want and how they're going to get it. It's hard to believe anybody could be like that. The first day we arranged everything, and now see how it is! This isn't the way we planned it. I'm going to get out. I'm going to pack up and go, and not come back.

I put my things together and went out of the whorehouse, to Mustapha's café.

What's the matter? he asked me. Have you fought with her or what?

I told him how it was, and how much money I had to take her each time. No matter how much you take a whore, she'll never say it's enough, I told him.

Money is all they think about. But be careful of Khemou. You're not going back to her?

That's right.

Be sure you don't, then, even once. If you do, anything can happen to you.

I'll go to the Haouma dl Bnider, I said, but not to that house.

It's your business, he said. But if you leave her at all, don't ever go back.

A long time went by, and I did not go back. One day I met a boy named Tsetsa who worked at the sawmill in Bou Khach Khach, where they made crates.

Brother, I said to him. Is there any work there at the sawmill?

66

I'm not doing anything now.

Yes, there's work there, he said. But it's piecework. They pay you by the crate.

It doesn't matter. Any kind of work at all.

Come by tomorrow, he told me. But bring your own hammer with you. The workmen have stolen all the hammers that belonged to the owner, and there aren't any left.

Ouakha.

That afternoon I went to the café and borrowed Mustapha's hammer. I slept there in the café that night, and the next morning I went to the sawmill. Tsetsa took me into an office to see a Nazarene. Here's the man who wants to make crates by the piece, he told him.

The Nazarene said: The wood and everything he needs is there. All he has to do is work like the others. Take him inside and show him around, and leave him by himself. If he wants to work, he will.

Tsetsa took me inside. There are the nails and there's the wood.

And I began to do that work. A month or so I had been working there. I was earning money and wearing good clothes. And I began to go down now and then to the Haouma dl Bnider, just walking from one house to the next, talking to the girls. Nothing more. Then I found one girl I liked more than the others. One day Mustapha came into the whorehouse where I was sitting talking to Mekraiya. That was her name.

What are you doing here? he asked me.

Nothing. Just sitting.

I thought you weren't coming back here.

Why not? I said. This isn't the same house. And I haven't done anything with any of them. I'm not stealing now, or doing anything bad.

Do as you like. You said you weren't going to come back. If you have any brains you won't keep coming here. This isn't the right place for you now. You're too young. I don't know. Do as you please. I'm telling you this, but you do what you want.

I'm not a boy any more, I told him. If I feel like coming I'll come. It doesn't do any harm. I don't get into fights or anything. This is a whorehouse, and it's open for anybody who wants to come in.

As you like, he said. It's up to you.

He went out. I stayed there. After a while I said to Mekraiya: Now I have to go.

You've got to go? Will you come tomorrow?

Yes. I don't know. Maybe I'll come. Maybe I won't.

If you want to come, she said, tomorrow's Sunday. Come early in the morning and we'll go to the beach and stay all day and come back late in the afternoon.

Yes, but I'm broke. I haven't got a franc.

Just come, she said. Don't think about money.

All right, I said. Thank you.

Come in the morning, she told me.

Ouakha. I said good-bye and went home to my mother's house. I slept and got up early. Look, I said to my mother. If you have two fresh loaves of bread, give them to me so I can take them with me.

Where?

I have to go to the beach with a friend.

She gave me two fine loaves of bread, and I took them and went to the whorehouse. There were four girls who wanted to go to the beach, and they all had food to take with them. We went down the stairs to the tannery where the taxi-stand is, and got into a taxi. Then we drove out along the beach, all the way to the Villa Harris. We took everything out of the taxi and walked across to the beach. Near the water we stuck canes into the sand and hung the girls' haiks across them and made a tent. We set all the food inside the tent, and the girls began to undress. They had put on their bathing suits at the whorehouse. When they had taken their clothes off they went into the water.

Aren't you going to swim? they asked me.

No, I said. I'm not going to. I sat with their clothes and they swam for a long time. Then they ran up and down the beach and played. Later they came back to the tent. We're hungry. Good, I said. Let's eat. We took out the food. One had brought fish, one had brought potatoes. Another had some meat with her. What did you bring? they asked me.

I just brought bread. That's all I had.

All right. Let's eat now, they said. So we ate, and we sat there all afternoon. Then we picked up our things and walked to the bus stop on the road. The bus came, we got in, and we rode back to the town. When we got to the Souq el Berra I said good-bye to them and went home.

I went on working at the sawmill. Working, working, until one day one of the men there cut his hand on the circular saw. The Nazarene came to me. Ahmed, he said. You work at the saw now with the maallem until the other one comes back from the hospital.

Ouakha. And I began to work at the saw with the maallem. The saw was in the middle between us. The maallem was on one side of it pushing planks toward me. After they were cut through I pulled them out and stacked them. The first week went by, and I did not go to the Haouma dl Bnider. And the second week I did not go, either. The third week I went back.

When I went into the whorehouse they all began to talk. Ah, how are you? How's everything? You haven't been here for a month.

I haven't been feeling well, I told them.

We're going to have supper now. Don't you want to eat with us?

No. Not now. You eat and I'll watch. They brought the table and uncovered the dishes. Come on, they said. Eat with us.

No, I can't. I've already eaten at home. Eat with good health.

Do as you like, they said. The food is here in front of you. If you want to eat, eat. If you don't, you know best.

That's right.

And so they ate, and I watched them. You know me, I said. If I'm hungry I eat.

They went on eating. When they were nearly finished, a girl walked into the courtyard from the street. It was Khemou, the light-haired one I had lived with before. She looked at me when she came in. I turned my head the other way. She came over and sat down on the mattress with the others, and began to talk, She did not look at me again.

Aren't you going to the cinema tonight? she said to one of the girls.

Yes, I'm going.

And you? Are you going, Mekraiya? she said.

If my friend Ahmed will take me, she told her.

Yes, I said. The cinema. All right. If you want to go, I'll pay for you. It's nine o'clock. I'll go out and get the tickets now, and at ten we'll go. I got up.

Good.

I went to the theater and bought two tickets, and took them back to the whorehouse. When I got there Khemou had gone out, and so I asked Mekraiya: Khemou's not going with us, is she?

Yes, she is.

If she goes, I'm not going.

What difference does it make if she goes? You don't have to talk to her. That's all. You're with us, not with her.

If you like, I said.

We sat talking in the courtyard until ten. Then I got up. Let's go now. Khemou was at the door with the others.

When the film was over, we were standing in front of the

theater. I've got to go home, I said. And I go up that way. You'll be going down there. That's your street.

But come by and see us some day, said Mekraiya.

Incha'Allah. Some day I'll come.

And a few days went by, until Saturday came again. I got my pay at the sawmill. I went home and changed my clothes, and walked down to the Haouma dl Bnider, to the house where Mekraiya lived.

Salaam aleikoum, I said to the girls.

Ah, Ahmed! How are you? Why haven't we seen you? You come by once a month, about like the moon. It had not been even a week, but whores always talk like that.

Life isn't made that way, I said. There isn't enough time to come here every day. Are you getting supper ready?

Ah! Tonight you feel like having some supper, do you?

That's right. Tonight I'm hungry.

I forgot that I was not going to eat their food.

We're getting it ready, said Mekraiya.

Good. I went out to a store in the street and bought half a kilo of bananas. When I went back into the whorehouse I said: Is supper ready?

Yes, they said. Almost. And it was not ready. We sat there talking for a long time. Then the padrona came in and said: If you want to eat, get up. The food is on the table. We went into the other room and sat down on the mattresses and began to eat. We were talking and laughing. I had put food into my mouth and swallowed it maybe five or six times when I began to feel something inside my belly moving and pushing. Then it felt as if my guts were cutting each other in pieces.

What's the matter with me? I thought. No food has ever done this in my belly before.

Eat, Ahmed, said one of the girls.

No, I said. That's enough. Then I turned to Mekraiya. Can you look and see if you have some bicarbonate?

Yes, they said. Get him some bicarbonate, Mekraiya. Have you got any?

Wait, she said. I'll go out and buy some at the bacal.

Those were the last words I heard. When I came back into myself and opened my eyes I was looking at a floor of black and white tiles and it was going around and around. There was a bottle in front of my nose with a smell like fire coming out of it. I was hanging upside down and my feet were strapped together. And I was vomiting all the time. While I vomited my mind was coming back, and I began to know what was happening. When they saw I was awake, they took me down and let me sit in a chair.

The doctor said: What did you eat?

Nothing, I said. I had my supper, that's all.

Where?

In a house somewhere.

Where?

Haouma dl Bnider. Where am I now?

This is the emergency hospital. The Cruz Verde.

Who brought me here?

There was a lot of trouble up there. They told us on the telephone that a man had died. We sent the ambulance for you.

I said to him: That's all the food I ate. Nothing more.

When you feel all right, you'd better go up to the comisaría, he said. Then he telephoned the police and told them about it, and he gave me a paper to give them when I went. A little later I went out to the comisaría. I spoke to an inspector there, a Nazarene. He asked me which house I had been in, and I told him. Then he sent some policemen to the whorehouse, and they came back with all the girls and the padrona too. He called me into the room where they all were.

Who was eating with you? he asked me.

That one, and that one, and that one, and that one, I said. Four of them.

The padrona. Was she eating with you?

No.

And this one? And these?

No. Only the four. And I was the fifth.

The inspector went over to one of the girls who had eaten with me. He drew back his hand and hit her hard. She fell against the wall.

What did you eat for supper? he said.

We just ate kifta with eggs and fried fish, said the girl.

Is that what you ate? he asked me.

Yes.

Then he hit her again. Why don't you tell me the truth? I'll send you all out into the mountains if you don't. I'll shut down every whorehouse. You wanted to kill this boy, didn't you?

He was just talking. He would never have shut the whorehouses because he made money out of them. Every day there are whores at the police station, and they pay the police to let them go.

The girl was crying and saying: No! No! I didn't do anything. I don't even know the boy. I don't know anything!

71

Nothing, said the inspector. Put them all in the cellar.

They took them downstairs and locked them in. The inspector told me: Go home and come back at nine in the morning.

I went home and slept. The next morning I went back to the comisaría. When I got there a different Nazarene was in command. He had his men bring the girls upstairs. What were you doing with these whores? he said to me.

Nothing at all, I told him. I work at the sawmill in Bou Khach Khach, and now and then I go down to the Haouma dl Bnider to that house and sit there and talk. A whorehouse is a place where anybody can go in and sit. And so I was sitting there.

That's all?

That's all. I'm not sleeping with any one of them, and I've had no fights with them either. There's been no trouble.

Listen! the girls cried. Listen to what he's saying. He says he didn't eat at our house or anything. We didn't even see him. Nothing. Who is he?

The inspector asked them: Where did the police find him?

In the street outside the door. He had a cramp or something, and fell against the door.

I told him: No! They're lying. I was eating with them. I fell over. I came back into my head in the hospital, hanging by my feet with my face on the floor.

I'm going to have you put in prison, the inspector said to me. Look at you! You're only a boy. And here you are mixed up like this with whores and savages!

The Nazarene went on scolding me. He said everything. Then he shouted: Get out of here! But tomorrow I'm going to tell the police in the Haouma dl Bnider. If they find you there again, they'll bring you to me. And I'll send you to jail.

Ouakha, I said. I'm going.

Wait a minute, he said. Do you forgive these whores?

They say they didn't do anything. I forgive them. What else can I do? I don't want to do anything to them.

I went out. I was thinking how the one who had made the poison for me had not even been in the comisaría. But the other girls and the padrona had helped her. Whores always protect each other. Now I see what the Haouma dl Bnider is like, I thought, and what happens in it. Why do I go there?

I decided not to go back. I thought: I'll look for a girl in the street, or some woman, and then I thought about how I would get married or live with her or take her to a room or somewhere. And I went around with this idea in my head for four or five months, and all that time I did not go back to the whores. I was busy working at the sawmill.

One day the saw cut my hand. I waited for the next three days to get permission to go to the doctor. My hand swelled up. Then I went myself to the Spaniard who ran the sawmill, and said: Look! Three days ago I hurt my hand, and now it's swollen, and you won't give me a paper to go to the doctor. And I can't work or anything.

No, he said. I hired you as a pieceworker and they're not insured like the others.

But the man who was working at the saw before me was insured, I said. I wasn't doing piecework when I got hurt. I was working at the saw!

There's nothing more to say. That's the way it is.

He went back into his office and shut the door.

I said to myself: I can never get anywhere talking with this Nazarene. There was a big bar of wood standing against the wall by the door. I'll get him with that, I thought. I'll take it and wait outside his door. If he doesn't give me the paper for the hospital I'll take care of him. And later I went and stood by the door with the piece of wood in my hand. When he opened the door he saw me and he called inside to a boy named Aziz.

Give him a paper, Aziz, he said, so he can go to the doctor. That hand of his is bad. It's all puffed up. Then he called to me: Come in. Entra.

Aquí estoy, I said. He handed me a paper, and I went to see the doctor. The doctor bandaged my hand. For three weeks I was going to his office. Then he gave me another piece of paper, and told me: You're all right now. Take this paper to where you work.

I went back to the sawmill and told the Spaniard: Now I'm cured. I've come back to work.

There's nothing for you to do now, he said. We've got somebody else doing your work.

So I had no work. Today and tomorrow, without work, today and tomorrow, looking everywhere for something to do. My mother's husband would say to me: Here you are again, lying around, not working.

Lying around! I said. That's right. Do you want me to go and steal something so I can go to jail? Would you like that?

He did not care where I was, so long as I was not in his house.

I thought to myself: I'm going to get out of here. I'm going down to Mustapha's café and live there. So I went and began to stay there in the café. I had no food and no money, and the poison was still in my stomach, so that I did not feel like eating.

Once in a while Mustapha would give me ten rials, or sometimes twenty.

My mother's husband had a son who was always going to school. One day I met him in the street. We were talking, and he told me that there was a new sawmill behind the Charf, where the railroad crosses the river on a bridge. I kept thinking about the new sawmill. I wanted to see it, and one morning I walked out there. I was happy when I got back because they had told me I could work for them.

I did not want to sleep any longer on the floor at Mustapha's café. But I lived another few months there. Then I had enough money to take a room for myself. I moved out of the café and rented a mahal in the Djenane el Kaptan.

CHAPTER SIX

MALABATA

I WAS working at the sawmill on the Charf. One Thursday I said to myself: Tomorrow's Friday and I won't be working. I'm going out to Tanja el Balia to see Hamadi in his orchard.

In the afternoon they paid us. I went to the market to buy food. Then I walked back to my mahal and cooked my supper. At the same time I fried some fish to take with me the next day.

I'll leave the fish until tomorrow, and I'll buy some tomatoes, and take it all to Hamadi's, and we'll have lunch.

I got everything ready, ate my supper, and went to sleep. In the morning I put the food into my kouffa and carried it out to the Souq el Berra. There I took a bus and went on my way. I got off at Tanja el Balia and walked until I came to the powerhouse. Behind it was Hamadi's orchard. I went up along the path to the orchard gate.

I began to call. Hamadi! Hamadi! Ya Hamadi! Three times. What do you want? Who is it?

Me! Ahmed!

Ah, Ahmed! He came down to the gate. It's a long time since you've been here to see me.

There hasn't been enough time to come. But today here I am.

Come in. He opened the gate and I went in. We walked under the trees. How is the city? he said.

You know the city. I don't have to tell you anything about it.

Yes. What have you got to eat in your kouffa?

Nothing but bread and fried fish and green tomatoes.

Good. Let me have it. We'll cook the tomatoes and put them in with the fish.

We sat down there. He took out his mottoui and his sebsi, and we began to smoke. Pipe after pipe of kif. The tomatoes were cooked, and we put them in with the fish. Come on and eat, said Hamadi. We sat down and ate. When we were almost finished, we heard a man's voice calling, down at the gate. He was calling: Mohammed! Mohammed! because he did not know Hamadi's real name.

What is it?

Come down. I want to talk to you.

Hamadi got up and went down to the gate. The man who was there said: If you want to buy some kif, I've got some with me.

I never buy kif, Hamadi told him. I grow my own here. But wait a minute. I've got a friend here who's from the city. And he's going back there. I'll see if he wants any.

Hamadi came up. Ahmed, he said. There's a man here selling kif. If you want to buy some, he'll sell it cheap.

Will he?

I swear. I can get it cheap.

Call him, I said. Tell him to come up.

He cried: Come on up! And the man walked up through the orchard.

Salaamou aleikoum.

Aleikoum salaam. Here's the boy who's going to buy from you, said Hamadi. Where's the kif?

The man took the sack he had over his shoulder and put it on the ground. Here it is, he said. Here's the kif.

I told Hamadi: Talk with him about the price.

How much do you want for it?

There are three kilos here. Give me two hundred rials for it.

Two hundred rials is a lot, Hamadi told him. I'll give you a hundred.

No, I can't sell three kilos for a hundred rials.

If you want to sell it, good, said Hamadi. If you don't, it doesn't matter.

No. Not at that price.

He went down toward the gate. Then he turned and came back. All right. Give me the money.

I took out a hundred rials and gave them to him. But you don't know me, I told him. And I don't know you either.

We're men, he said. Not boys.

That's right.

He went away, and we stayed there. We made a pot of tea, and Hamadi took three or four bunches of kif and chopped them. We smoked, and it was good kif.

Allah! Allah! I said. This is really good.

Yes, it's good. But only if I chop it, said Hamadi.

We'll smoke this, I told him. And I'll leave you some so you can cut it. And next Friday, incha'Allah, I'll come back here and see you.

Ouakha.

We drank the tea and smoked the kif. Then I said: Now, Hamadi, I'm going. It's getting late.

Right.

Allah ihennik. I put the sack over my shoulder and walked down the hill. I had my kouffa in my hand and I kept going. Walking, walking, until I got to the bus stop. I waited there. The bus came and I got in and sat down. When the conductor came around, he said: What have you got there in that sack? If it weighs more than ten kilos, you'll have to pay.

I lifted it up and swung it in front of him. No. It's just a little straw, I told him.

All right.

I paid for my seat and gave him nothing for the sack. We drove into the Souq el Berra and I got out.

Here I am in the middle of the souq with a sack of kif, I thought. I'll be lucky if nothing happens. I'll go into the Café Rhali and see if there's anybody I know in there. If there is, I'll talk to him about it.

I went into the café and sat down. I ordered a glass of tea, and then I saw a man I knew called Cherif sitting in the corner. He worked in the port. Whenever he spoke to me he did not call me by my name, but only: Friend.

Cherif! I called. Sit a little nearer.

He came over. Ah, friend! How are you?

I have some kif here, I told him. If you can sell it to somebody here I'll give you a good commission.

Ouakha, he said. You stay here, and I'll go and see if I can find somebody.

Yes, go. I'll be here. You'll see me.

He went out. I sat there thinking: I don't know. That Cherif. That one could play me a trick. I don't know. Allah yahfudd!

I left the sack under the table and went outside to watch him go. He walked up the hill. I crossed over to the door of the joteya and stood there.

After a while I saw Cherif coming back down the street from

the boulevard toward the café. He was walking alone.

No! Cherif is all right, I said to myself. He's a good man.

I went back over to the café and sat down. Cherif came in. He sat down beside me and said: I've found somebody who'll buy it from you.

Yes?

That's right.

How much?

He'll give you forty rials a kilo.

Ouakha, I said. Where's the man?

He'll be here in a minute. He's gone to get the money. Order a glass of tea if you want, I told him.

Make me a glass of tea, he said to the qahouaji.

The qahaouaji made the tea. At the moment when he was setting it on the table, I saw two men standing in the doorway. One was named El Maati, and the other was called the French-woman's Son. They both worked for the secret police. They came into the café. El Maati came over to our table and said: Ah, Cherif, what are you doing here? And to me he said: And you? What are you doing here?

Nothing, I said. Just having a glass of tea.

And that sack there. Whose is it?

I don't know, I said.

Cherif, is that sack yours? he asked him.

No, sidi. It's not mine, the sack. It belongs to my friend here.

Allah yaouddi! Mine?

When I came over to the table it was on the floor beside you, he told me.

Naal alik Cheitan, Cherif! That sack isn't mine!

The two men turned to Cherif. So, you're lying. It's yours. Come on, both of you.

They handcuffed us together, Cherif and me, and Cherif took the sack and carried it. We went up the steps with the two men to the comisaría. They put me into one room and him into another. In a little while I heard them calling him, and I looked through the door and saw them take him out of his room. I did not know where they went with him or what they said to him. Then a little later they came and called me. Come on, they said. They took me into another room where an inspector was sitting at a desk. The sack was there, and so was Cherif, and the two policemen too.

Is this kif yours?

Sidi, it's not mine, that kif. I went into the café and saw the sack there, and ordered a glass of tea. Then I saw Cherif in a corner and I asked him if he wanted a glass too.

No, said Cherif. It wasn't that way. The kif is yours. You brought it in and called me over and asked me to go and find somebody to buy it from you.

Allah yaouddi, Cherif! I asked you that?

Yes, he told me.

Then El Maati hit me in the face. You son of a whore! he said. You don't want to tell the truth? In a little while you will.

The inspector said to Cherif: You can go. And they put me back into the room where I had been before. I stayed there for two days and two nights, and no one said anything to me. The third day in the afternoon they came and got the prisoners out of the other rooms and took them away with them, but they left me there alone.

Allah! This is it! I thought. They've left me here. Tonight they're going to kill me, these police. But whatever they do, I won't say anything different. That kif isn't mine, and I didn't buy it from anybody. I went into the café and found it there. And those are the words I'm going to tell them.

And they left me there until night. When it was late they opened the door. Come out, they said. And my heart was beating fast. I was afraid, and I said to myself: Allah! Allah!

I went out of the room into the courtyard. Stand there, they told me. They brought a pail of water with two pieces of rope in it.

Come on, they said. Take off your clothes.

I took off my jacket, my shirt, and my undershirt.

Sit on that table.

I sat down.

Take off your sandals.

They tied my feet together and fastened a piece of wooden pole across my ankles. Then they lifted my feet into the air and began to beat the bottoms of them with the wet rope.

The kif is yours!

No! It's not mine!

After a while I could not talk any more. My feet were swollen and the blood was dripping from them. One man said: That's enough. Leave him now until another day.

They stopped beating me and untied my feet. Then they said: Now stand up and walk.

I tried, but I fell onto the floor. Then I pushed myself on my hands back to the room. They came and threw my clothes in on top of me. Here, they said. And I stayed in there like that. The floor was wet and covered with mold, and I was lying on it, and my feet were aching. This is real trouble, I thought. In the morning my feet hurt much more. They brought me a tin can of tea and half a loaf of bread. I did not drink the tea and I did not eat the bread. I stayed on there until ten o'clock. They came then and called me.

Come out!

I could not walk, but they pulled me along and took me back to the same inspector.

The kif is yours!

No!

And I said what I had said before.

They pushed me into a chair and the inspector began to write. At noon the police went out to eat, and in the afternoon they took me to the tribunal along with some other prisoners. We went into an office. A man was sitting at a desk.

The kif is yours?

It's not mine. And then I told them the same story again.

There's a witness who says you asked him to go out and look for a buyer, he told me.

No, sidi. It's a lie, I said. I showed him my feet. See what the police did to me.

There's a doctor in the prison, he said. That's all today.

When each prisoner had passed in front of the official, they put us all into the police van and took us to the jail at Malabata. When we got there we went inside, and a man said to us: Whoever has money, or a watch or a ring, he can leave it with me. And whoever has kif must give it to me now. Nobody can take kif into the jail.

Not one of us had any kif on him. We knew we could get kif inside the jail. When a man smokes he forgets he is in jail. He forgets everything. A packet of kif costs a pack of cigarettes. They put us all inside, took away our belts, and gave every man two blankets.

Go on in, they said. There were about thirty men in the room where they put us. We had gone all day without eating anything, and now we found that dinner was already over. I asked a prisoner about the food there. They give us bread and soup at noon and again at night, he said. You missed the meal because you stayed so long at the tribunal.

The jail at Malabata had been built for Europeans, so the cells still had beds and mattresses. I spread one blanket out on the mattress, lay down, and covered myself with the other blanket. That night I did not know anyone there. I lay on my bed watching the others. They were sitting in groups of three or four or five, smoking cigarettes and kif, and talking about the government. I felt like smoking, but I had no cigarettes. I was alone on my bed. A guard came by and switched the lights off and on three times. Go to sleep! he shouted. Ten minutes later all the lights went out. After it was dark and some of the prisoners were going to sleep, I heard a man singing somewhere in the jail. I said to the boy who had the bed next to me: Who's that?

That's El Mernissi.

Ah! The one who killed all the Jews and Nazarenes?

Yes.

How long has he been here?

It's about seven or eight months since they brought him.

He's alone?

Yes. They've put him in by himself.

Doesn't anybody talk to him?

All of us talk to him. But he won't take cigarettes or anything from the guards.

Why not?

I don't know, he said. He hates everybody except the prisoners.

Does he sing like this every night? I asked him.

He sings three or four songs and then he stops and goes to sleep.

No more?

That's all.

And his room? What's he got in it?

You'd be surprised if you saw his room, he told me. He's drawn all kinds of pictures on the walls. Tanks, airplanes, pistols, machine guns, submarines, everything.

He knows how to draw? I said.

Yes.

Listen. He's singing a song of Om Kaltoum's.

He knows some fine songs. But only the ones of Om Kaltoum and Abd el Wahab. Tomorrow when you go out into the courtyard you'll see him. He always sticks his head out of the window and talks to us.

Everybody knew the story of El Mernissi. He used to go around the Souq Ndakhel from one café to another, with a tray of pastries to sell. When we were making war against the French many people said he was an informer for them. When he heard anyone say that, he would get very angry. One day he bought two long knives, the kind butchers use to cut meat with, and he went to the mosque. When he had prayed he came out. His friends saw the knives and laughed. So even El Mernissi is going to make a sacrifice for the Aïd? they said. You'll see my sacrifice, he told them, and he ran down the street. In the Haouma dl Bnider he began to cut Jews and Nazarenes with the knives, one in each hand. Everybody was running. He even killed an English tourist who had just come from the ship. Eight of the people died in five minutes. The others went to the hospital. He thought people would stop saying he was an informer if he did this. But the police put him in jail.

I was thinking about El Mernissi, and I was very hungry. But I went to sleep. In the morning they called us new prisoners into the office. Each one had to take off his clothes and put on overalls sent by the government, and sandals and a straw hat. The prisoners' own clothes they tied up and put away. Then they sent us into the courtyard and we walked around. I looked for the boy who had the bed next to mine, the one who had been telling me about El Mernissi.

Where's El Mernissi's room? I asked him.

Over there, he said. That door over there, the one that's shut. That's his room.

Don't they ever let him come out and walk around the courtyard?

Not now, he said. They keep him inside until we go in. Then they let him out and he walks around alone.

Don't they even open his window?

Yes, when the guards call the prisoners outside to work. After that they open it.

A few minutes later the guards came to call the prisoners who were going out to work in the gardens. About thirty men went out and about sixty stayed behind.

Look! he said. That Spanish guard is going to open the window now. Wait. You can look in and see the pictures on the wall.

The Spaniard opened the window and went away. We went over and walked on that side of the courtyard. When we got to the window El Mernissi stuck his head out the window. He had a long beard. He was talking to a prisoner. Good morning, Chaib, he said. A cigarette for me, Chaib?

I'll go and get you one, said the prisoner.

El Mernissi saw I was new, and he called to me. When did they bring you, brother? he said.

Yesterday.

What did you do?

Nothing. They caught me with some kif, that's all.

Wait. Wait, he told me. Allah will take care of everything for you. Have you got a piece of pencil with you?

What are you going to do with a piece of pencil?

Just make some pictures, he said.

81

Where are you going to make pictures?

Here. He put his head back inside the window and said: Look. Look at the room. Put your head in and look, if you want.

I was going to put my head in, but the boy standing beside me touched me and shook his head. I knew he was saying: Don't put your head inside.

Look in, said El Mernissi.

I can see them from here, I said. There's a ship, there's a rifle. I can see them. They're very good pictures. But the one I like best is the one of the airplane carrier.

Do you know what ship that is? he said. It's an English ship, the one called Franklin Roosevelt. It came here once, and planes flew off it and wrote words in the sky. That's what I've put on the wall of my room.

Ouakha, I said. I'll find you a pencil somewhere.

We went back to our cell. The guard came and said: Everybody to his own place. So we had to stay inside, and I could not take El Mernissi the pencil. Then they brought the food from the city in a station wagon and put it in the courtyard. There was no kitchen at Malabata. A little later the workmen came in from the gardens and went to their rooms. The guards brought bread and passed it out to the prisoners. Then they brought soup. And we ate. Some men slept afterwards. I called to the boy who had the bed next to me. He was sitting somewhere else, and I asked him to come over. Why did you make signs to me and tell me not to put my head inside El Mernissi's window?

Once one of the guards put his head in and was talking to him, and El Mernissi took hold of his head and was choking him and beating him, trying to kill him. If the other guards hadn't come fast he would have done it. You have to be careful of him. If you put your head in his window, someday he'll grab it. You have to be careful what you say to him too. If he thinks you're making fun of him he gets angry. Be careful.

At three o'clock the guard came and opened the door. Into the courtyard, he said. We went out and walked some more. I was thinking: If El Mernissi calls me I'll go over, but if he doesn't, I won't.

I was walking around. A little later a guard came and opened El Mernissi's window. He put his head out and began to sing. He was singing and we were walking around. At five o'clock they told us: Come on. Everybody back into his own cell. And we passed each day this way, today and tomorrow, for ten days or more. One afternoon they came to get the prisoners who had to go to the city to the tribunal.

82

They took us in pairs, each one handcuffed to another one, in the police van, and we went inside and sat down. They called our names one by one, until they came to me.

Ahmed ben Said!

Here, I said.

Come up, they told me. Sit down.

Then they called Cherif's name and told him to leave the hall. He went out, and then the judge said to me: The kif was yours?

I told him the same story I had told each time. When I had finished he said: That's the way it was?

I said: That's the way it was.

Good. Sit down. He sent for Cherif, and they brought him downstairs. The judge said to him: Raise your right hand and swear you will tell the truth. Cherif raised his hand and said he would tell the truth. Whose kif was it? said the judge.

Cherif pointed at me. Sidi, the kif belonged to that man. He came in out of the street with it. Then he sat at a table and put it on the floor. He saw me and invited me to have a glass of tea. When I sat down with him he asked me to try and find somebody to buy the kif. I said yes. Then I went to the police and told them.

The judge looked at him and saw that he was badly dressed and had no jacket, and he said to him: Why do you tell the police what people are doing?

Sidi, that's my work.

He wanted the judge to think he was a real police informer, but I knew he had been arrested many times and put in jail like anybody else.

I see, said the judge. Then he had him taken out, and he called the lawyer for the government tobacco monopoly. The lawyer began to talk. This man had kif, he said. That is bad. People should smoke tobacco instead. We have to finish with kif in this country. He meant that the government makes no money from kif, but it does from tobacco.

When he had spoken, the judge thanked him. Then he called the head of the government monopoly and asked him how large a fine he would put on the kif I had bought. The man talked with the lawyer.

We ask half a million francs for three kilos, he said.

The judge asked me: Have you got half a million francs?

Sidi, I haven't even got enough money to buy my supper. Where am I going to get half a million francs?

Good. Sit down.

Then they all stood close to each other and talked. In a little while they separated, and the judge told me: Stand up.

I stood up, and he said: The government condemns you to ten months in jail. Or if you want, you can pay a half-million francs and go free.

Sidi, I said, I haven't got half a million francs. But ten months pass by themselves, as Allah wills it.

And I went back to Malabata, and they opened the door and let me in. They put me into the same cell where I had been before. The prisoners began to ask me: How much did they give you? What happened?

Ha! I said. We have a government of the wind! There's no justice anywhere in this country. Ten months for some kif. Ten months of jail. And the kif wasn't even mine.

You're lucky to get only ten months, they said. You see that Rhmari there? They gave him a year for carrying it on him. And they found only a kilo on him.

That one sells it, I said. I don't sell it.

Well, you're lucky. Ten months will go by like nothing at all.

If they want to go by, they'll go by. If they don't, what can I do about it? Whatever Allah has decided, that's all there is, and nothing more. I was working, and I went to visit my friend, and see what happened! And somebody brought some kif, and now, ten months in jail. Now I've got no work, no kif, and no money. Nothing.

Wait, they said.

I'm waiting.

That evening they brought the soup and gave it to us, and we ate. Then the prisoners began to play parchesi and checkers and dominoes and cards. Each one had some way of making the time go by. I went and sat near some boys who were playing dominoes. And I was thinking by myself. One of them said: You're crazy, sitting there worrying about ten months of jail. It's nothing. Some of us have two years, some have three, some have five. You have ten months and you worry.

Each man is different, I told him. One worries, another doesn't care. Each one does what he feels like doing.

Just sit and wait, he said. It's happened to you now. Worrying about it isn't going to change anything, except that you'll be sick. What Allah has given is given.

Ten months in jail is what's been given, I said. They'll pass.

The guard turned the light on and off three times. Sleep! he shouted. Each man spread his blanket and got into bed. They turned the lights out, and we went on talking. The guard came by. Shut up! he said. Don't talk so loud. This is the time to sleep, not to talk.

Ah, Mrrakchi, somebody said. You've got to tell us a story now.

Ouakha. I'll tell one if you want. But you've all got to be quiet. Nobody else can talk.

We all stopped talking. The Mrrakchi began to tell a story about Sidi Ali of long ago, when there was war. We all listened. Then each one of us began to go to sleep while he was still talking. When the Mrrakchi saw that almost everybody was asleep, he went to sleep himself.

And in the morning the guard came and said: Come on. Outside. We went out. Some of us took baths with pails of water, others washed their clothes, some talked. At ten o'clock they sent us out to work. Some worked in the vegetable gardens and some helped build a new wall. While we worked we talked. If a man has a long time to spend in jail they send him to Dar el Beida. There it is bad because the work is very hard and there is a lot of it. I was saying: I have only ten months. For ten months they won't send me there, will they?

One man said to me: They send you there if you have only six months. And you think with ten months they're not going to send you?

Allah! Allah! I thought. I've never been to Dar el Beida and now I've got to go like this. If they take me there, I don't know what will happen.

And that was our life there. Every morning at ten we went out to work and every afternoon at three again. And it was almost time for Ramadan to begin. On Thursdays and Saturdays people could come to see the prisoners and bring them food. There was a girl who used to come and see me every week. Sometimes she came with Aicha, her mother, and sometimes she came alone.

One Thursday she came to see me. I said to her: Now Ramadan is coming. See if you can bring me a little butter and some olives and some oil, so I'll have something to eat at midnight when they beat the drums.

Ouakha, she said. I'll bring it soon. Next Thursday I'll bring it all to you.

We talked that day a while, and she went away. The next Thursday she brought me everything I had asked her for.

Ramadan came. We would go into the cell in the afternoon, wait for the cannon to be fired, eat our supper, and go to bed. The guards would wake us up at three o'clock and bring us our dinner, and we would eat it. After that we would sleep again until morning, and then get up and work all morning. Then we would go in and sleep again until three in the afternoon.

One day I heard a man named Chaib talking to another in the

85

courtyard. He was saying: Now, you've got two years and that one there has three. Each one of us has a lot of time to stay in jail. And now Ramadan's here and we're going to spend the festival in jail. And the Sultan is coming to town for the feast, and we won't see him or anything.

The other one said: And what are we going to do about it, here in prison?

We can do one thing, said Chaib.

What's that?

Escape.

Escape? How are we going to do that?

We can grab the guards and tie them up. There aren't many guards here. Only five. That's nothing. Look how many of us there are. If everybody agrees on it, we can all escape.

The other one said: Yes. But we'd have to ask everybody here about it.

And they began to talk about it. Every time we walked in the courtyard those two men would talk to the prisoners who had long sentences to serve. Chaib would say to them: Do you want to get out? And they would say: Yes, if I find somebody to help me. And Chaib would tell them: You've got this one and that one and the others. He would give them the names of all the men he had already talked to and who had agreed on it.

This is what we're going to do and this is how we're going to do it, he would tell them. Ouakha, they would say. And Chaib went on talking to the prisoners and they all said: Yes, yes. Then he told them: There are two Nazarenes here who have a long time to stay in prison. I'm going to ask them, too. If they want to get out with us, good.

Chaib could get into the courtyard where the Nazarene prisoners were, because the chief trusted him and let him go everywhere inside the jail. The rest of us saw the Nazarenes only when they came to take a bath.

The others said that was good, if the two Nazarenes wanted to go with them. Chaib went to the courtyard where they were, and he talked to the two men. One was a Galician who had eight years, and one was a German who had twenty.

One night we were all talking together in the cell. Chaib, I said, that tall Nazarene, who is he?

That's the German. He's the one who killed his woman at El Aaqaba el Hamra.

Yes, I said. And who was the woman?

She came with him from Germany to work with him here in politics.

And why did he kill her?

Because she fell in love with somebody else. She wouldn't go with him any more. She didn't even like to talk with him.

How could anybody kill a woman for nothing? I said. That's nothing, what she did.

That's the way Nazarenes are, he said. If a woman doesn't like a man or something, he can kill her just for that.

How did he kill her? I asked him.

Just with rocks. He took her in his car out there to the mountains. They got out and were talking. He picked up a rock and said to her: Do you know how much this stone weighs? She said: How much? Six or seven kilos, he told her. Take it in your hand and see. She took the rock in her hand. It's heavy, she told him. Then she handed it back to him. He took it and banged it against her head. She fell down. Then he took other rocks and threw them at her. He kept throwing them until she was all covered up. When none of her showed under the pile of rocks, he got into the car and drove back to the Hotel Rif. And they caught him, and brought him here. And he's got twenty years.

He deserves them, I said. Because that woman did nothing bad to him. He had no right to kill her like that.

And so Chaib went to the courtyard of the Nazarenes and talked to the German. We're going to escape, he told him, and if you want to go with us, good. We're going to get everything ready first and all leave together. Do you want to come?

Yes, said the German. I'll go with you, beat anybody you say, do anything you want.

Good, said Chaib. But we've got to tell Miguel the Gallego.

It's better not to say anything to that one, the German told him. He's not going to be able to escape anyway.

Ouakha, said Chaib.

When are you going to do all this? asked the German.

Wait. In another two days or so I'll tell you.

That day went by. The next day Chaib was talking to everybody. You know, he said, tomorrow's Thursday, visitors' day. Each one of you who has visitors tomorrow must ask them to bring him some clothes on Saturday.

And so each one of us asked his friends and family to bring him street clothes so that no one would be wearing jail clothes after we escaped. Aicha came with her daughter, and I asked her to bring me some sandals and a pair of trousers. She said she would. But you must bring them Saturday, I told her.

Why do you want them Saturday? You've got sandals on.

Yes, but they're broken. Anyway, please bring them Saturday.

And she brought everything and gave it to the guard. He called me. Ahmed! Here. Take this package. It's for you.

That night when we were all in our cells we were talking together about the hour we were going to escape the next day. We had to be sure that every prisoner understood the exact time when it was going to happen. Tomorrow is Sunday, they were saying, and the guards on duty will be Cherif el Abbar, he's an old man, and Bba Miloud the Algerian, and two Nazarenes. And one more outside makes five. They're all old and married, with families, so they'll be afraid when we grab them.

But how are we going to do it? they were asking.

Hapot and Amar Riffi will begin to fight in the courtyard, the guard there will yell at them and try to separate them, and we'll grab him then.

Ouakha, ouakha, they said.

Now we won't save any more food, said Chaib. We'll eat everything tonight. Everyone brought out the butter and the oil he had been saving, and we rolled pieces of rags and dipped them in the oil and butter. Then we set the rags on fire and cooked our food over them. Whoever had tea or sugar or milk brought it out. And if a man had nothing, the others gave what they had to him. We did not want to leave anything there. All night we cooked and ate and smoked kif in the dark, until the cannon went off an hour before dawn. Then we all went to bed before it got light. A little later the guards came and knocked on the door. Get up! Get up!

And we got up. Each man put his street clothes on under his overalls. At nine o'clock we went out into the courtyard and began to walk around, the same as every day. In a little while Hapot and Amar Riffi started to fight with each other. The old guard Cherif el Abbar went to stop them, but when he got near them all the prisoners grabbed him. One of them hit him on the head with a rock. If he had hit him a little harder he would have killed him. They dragged him into a cell and threw him on the floor and shut the door. Then they ran to the office and saw Bba Miloud there. Some of the men got frightened then and began to run back, but the others cried: Go on! Go on, you Jews! Are you afraid? Then everybody went ahead.

Bba Miloud ran out to the other courtyard. One of the Spanish guards was standing there. When the Spaniard saw him with all the prisoners running behind him, he went into the nearest cell and locked the door. I was in the office, and I saw the German come running and take the telephone in his hands. He pulled the wire out of the wall and threw the telephone on the floor. Another prisoner broke off the head of a bottle and ran to cut Bba Miloud with it. I grabbed his arm and stopped him. No! No! he's the best guard in the jail, I told him. Be careful. If you kill him it'll be bad for you. Leave him and let's go. Then Bba Miloud took a big bunch of keys out of his pocket and threw them over the wall into the garden outside.

The German found a ladder and climbed to the top of the wall and jumped over. Then a lot of men took a plank and began to ram it against the door. The third time they hit it, it broke open. Half the prisoners ran out. The others were still in the office looking for money and other things to steal.

Between the men's and the women's courtyards there was a wall with a grill in it. One of the women guards began to shout: Don't break things! Don't break anything! Just go out! Just run! Run!

And they were breaking all the windows and tables, and throwing bottles of medicine and books and typewriters on the floor. And they tore up all the papers and threw them up into the air. Everything. It looked like the war.

There was a guard outside by the electric generator. When he saw what was happening he tried to take his pistol out of his pocket, but before he could get it out the prisoners threw rocks at him and he fell down. Everybody threw more rocks on top of him, and then they smashed the generator. Chaib was shouting: Come on! The door's open! Go on out! He went to El Mernissi's window and said: Wait. I'll get the key and let you out. But El Mernissi told him: No! No! I don't want to go out. You just go.

The woman was still yelling: No! Don't hit anybody! Run! Run! Then the prisoners broke the other door, the one that is on the highway, and they began to run out that way.

The guard who was outside was holding his head where they had hit him, and he was crying: Ay, yimma el habiba! Everybody was running, and I ran out the door with the others. It was raining hard then, and the mud was deep everywhere. I decided to go on the highway. I forgot to take off my overalls, and I began to run with them on. A little later I saw the truck coming from the city to bring water to the jail. Allah! I thought. Now they're going to catch us all! The truck's going to get to the jail and they're going to see what's happened and go back to tell the police. I'm going to take the river and cut through to Tanja el Balia. That will bring me out into Beni Makadi. That was where Aicha and her daughter lived.

I was going along the edge of the river. I turned around and saw the German running behind me. I made signs with my hand: Come on! He had one bad foot. He would run a little, and then he would stop and wait. He was carrying a leather case in his hand. I waited for him. Here, he said. Take this bag, please, and carry it for me.

Ouakha, I said. Give it to me. I began to run again. My feet were going deep into the mud and water, and I was getting tired. I left the river and ran across the fields, and he was following me. Then I came to another stream, and I thought it was shallow so I could get across it, but there was a deep part there, and I went down into it. The water was up to my neck.

Ya latif! I thought. This is trouble! If I'd known it was going to be like this, I'd have stayed in jail. The German gave me his hand and pulled me out of the water, and we began to run again. Then I shouted to him: I'm sick of this. Here's your bag! Take care of it yourself.

I threw the bag into a pile of brambles and ran ahead by myself. I kept running, running, until I came out onto the road. There I saw another prisoner named Hamouda who had escaped too. He was yelling: Run! Run! The soldiers are coming!

I was very tired from running. We got to the ruins of the Portuguese Fort by the road that goes to Tanja el Balia. We hid inside the ruins while the soldiers went by. It was raining hard, but from where we were we could see the road all the way back to the jail. There are no trees or houses out there. The trucks stopped in front of the jail and the soldiers began to go in all directions through the fields and over the hills behind, looking for the prisoners. And they found a lot of them and were taking them back into the jail.

We went into the village of Tanja el Balia and came out behind the power plant. Then we cut across to the abbatoir, climbed around the side of the hill, and came out by the bull-ring. It was not raining any more. From there Hamouda and I went to Beni Makada, to the house where Aicha lived. I knocked on the door, and she cried: Who is it?

Me! I said.

She came to the door. What's happened? They let you go?

No. We escaped. Come in! Come inside, quick!

I went in and told Hamouda to come in.

Are you hungry? she said.

No. It's Ramadan.

It doesn't matter, she told me. You ought to eat, both of you. And she cooked us some eggs, and we ate them. Then Hamouda got up and said to me: Now, my friend, I've got to go to my wife. It's very important for me to go.

Where do you live? I asked him.

Et Tnine Sidi Yamani, he said. It's a long way off.

But you can't go out now, I told him. Sit down. We smoked, and it was Ramadan. Then I said to Aicha: Go out and walk around the quarter. See what's happening, and if you hear any news come back and tell us.

Ouakha, she said, and she went out and began to walk around, listening to what people were saying. She heard the radios playing, and telling everyone how sixty prisoners had escaped from Malabata. Then she came back and told us what she had heard.

You see? I said to Hamouda. You mustn't go anywhere now. Wait here until the afternoon. I have a djellaba I'll give you, and you put it on. Then you can go.

He said: Ouakha. And he stayed with me there until evening. Then I said: Now's the time for you to go. Here. Take the djellaba. How much does it cost in the bus, to get to Et Tnine Sidi Yamani?

You can go for four rials, he said.

Aicha took out the money and gave it to him. Now you have enough to ride in the bus, she told him. Go.

So I said: Good-bye. And he said: Good-bye. And he went away and I stayed there in the house. After the cannon had been fired off and we had had our harira, Aicha went to my mother's house and told her: Your son has come. My mother put a big towel over her head and came quickly to Aicha's house in Beni Makada.

Aoulidi! she said. You're out!

No, I'm not out, I said. I escaped.

So you ran out with the rest of them? Even you? This morning the radio was telling the news.

Yes, I went with them.

Now I'm going back home and get you a djellaba, she told me. Perhaps you'll want to go out and take a walk in the quarter, and you won't have any way of hiding. I'll bring your brother's djellaba.

Good, I said.

So the poor woman went out in the night and walked to Souani and got me the djellaba and brought it to Beni Makada. When she gave it to me she said: Now be very careful. It would be better not to go out at all. But be very careful.

Then Aicha told us: That's enough talk. Come and eat your supper. And we sat down and ate. Afterward my mother said: Now I must go. May Allah be with you, aoulidi. Be careful.

Allah ihennik, I told her. Don't be afraid. Nothing will happen. She went home. I stayed sitting still for a little while. Then I said to Aicha: I'm going out. I want to go to a café and sit a while.

You know best, she said. Do as you like. She took out twenty rials and said: Here. I put on the djellaba and went out.

I went down the road to the bus stop. I stood there for a while. Then the bus came. Allah! I thought. I'm going down to the city and see what's going on there. I got on the bus and went down to the town. When I was in the street I put the hood of my djellaba up over my head and began to walk around, back and forth. Then I thought: I'll go down to the Cine Vox. If there's a good picture there I'll go in. So I went down to the Souq Ndakhel. I saw a lot of secret police sitting in the cafés, and two of them stood in the doorway of the Spanish telegraph office. Ah, I said to myself. See how the whole town is here tonight! I've got to go into the cinema no matter what happens. I bought a ticket and went into the theater. When the picture was over and I was on my way out, I saw that there was a secret police agent in each corner by the front door, looking at each man's face as he came out. When I saw that I thought: Now they're going to look under the hood of the djellaba and catch me. Wait. I'll take the hood off. So I put the hood down around my shoulders. Then I pulled my handkerchief out of my pocket and held it up in front of my face as if I wanted to keep out the dust. Many people do that when they go out of a building into the street. When I got outside I put my handkerchief away and raised the hood again because it was cold. Then I went home.

Where have you been all this time? said Aicha.

I was in the theater.

What!

That's right.

You must like living in jail, she said. It seems to me you're planning to go back right away.

I'm still here, I said.

I kept on going out whenever I wanted to. The police saw me, but they did not know who I was, and no one said anything to me. This is strange, I thought. I don't understand. Now there's El Maati, the very man who arrested me for having the kif. Why doesn't he see me? Why doesn't he arrest me again? Perhaps they've pardoned us all or something.

And nothing happened. It was almost the time of the Aïd es Seghir, and I was walking everywhere in the street and no one was paying any attention to me.

The feast went by. One day I was sitting in a café, and I saw a police van stop in front of it. The police came to the door, and one of them said: Get up! Get up, all of you! They made everyone go out and get into the truck, and they took us to the comisaría in the Souq Ndakhel. They took everyone's belt and money away, and they locked us inside. I asked one of the prisoners: Why are they picking up everybody like this?

It's just a raid, he said. They'll let us go afterward. It's nothing.

Hamdoul'lah, I thought. If that's all it is, tomorrow they'll take us to the Souq ez Zra and then let us go.

We slept there that night on the floor, and the next day they called us. Come out, they said, and they gave us back all our things and made us walk out through the street to where the truck was waiting. They drove us up to the Souq ez Zra. We went inside, and they called us one by one and asked us: Why were you arrested? Where were you arrested? What were you doing?

They had brought people in from all over the city. One would answer: I was sitting in a café. Another would say: I was walking in the street. Another would tell them: I was watching the cinema. When they called me, they said: Why did they bring you here? And I said: They found me in a café with a lot of others, and they brought us all.

You can go, they told me.

Allah! I thought. Now they'll never put me back in jail. They've pardoned me. I started to walk to the door. El Maati was standing there. Aha! he cried. You got out fast!

Yes, I said. They're through with me.

Come here, he told me. Come here. You're one of them, the ones who broke out of Malabata.

Allah yaouddi! The inspector just told me I could go!

El Maati went over and spoke to the inspector. This one escaped from jail.

Is that right?

I swear!

The inspector hit me in the face. Go back inside, you dog!

I went back in and sat down. That's it, I said to myself. Now I'm going back to Malabata. I got out and now I've got to go back again.

The inspector went away and came back with the book that had all the names of the prisoners who had escaped. He read through the names until he came to mine, and then he said: Your name is Ahmed ben Saïd Haddari?

Yes.

Good. Now you've got to tell me what happened at the jail. He wanted to know who had hit the guards, who had broken this and who had stolen that.

Sidi, I didn't see anything. I was playing in the courtyard.

93

When I heard the yelling in the Nazarenes' section I went and saw the doors open, and I said to myself: Everybody's running out. I'm going out too. I ran to the door. I didn't break anything or hit anybody. If you know somebody who says I did, bring him here so I can see him.

Ouakha, he said. I'll show you somebody. He put me into a jeep and drove me out to Málabáta. He took me inside. The guards were there and they were looking at me. I was afraid, and I thought: Allah! Now one of them is going to say I did something.

Bba Miloud said to the policeman: This one didn't break anything or hit anybody. One of the others was going to cut me with a bottle and he stopped him. He told him: No, no! Don't hit him!

Hamdoullah! I thought. He's being a good witness for me. Now nothing bad is going to happen.

Then the fiscal of the Tribunal told me: You didn't do anything. You're a good man. You must tell us the truth. How did it all happen?

I didn't see anything. How can I tell you? I was playing in the courtyard. I heard the noise. And when I saw the door open, I ran out.

Ouakha, he said. So they gave me the overalls, the sandals, the straw hat and the two blankets the same as before, and I went back to the same cell I had had the other time. And I saw a lot of the men who had been there with me. But the ones who had hit the guards had no blankets, and no food either. Only if their families brought them something. They just stayed in the cell sitting on the floor all day and all night. Eight days later the government called us all. They took us to the city and left us at the Tribunal. Then they called all our names, one after the other. The first name was Chaib's, and they told him: You did this and this and this. Chaib said: I didn't do anything. If anybody says I did, make him step up here and face me.

Then Cherif el Abbar the guard spoke. That man and another one, he said, grabbed me and threw me into a cell and locked me in.

Hear what the guard says, said the judge. Then he called another man and said to him: You stole money and a ring out of the jail's office. The man said: I didn't steal money or a ring or anything.

Sit down, all of you, the judge told them.

I was the last one he called.

You hit the guards, you broke the machine, you stole a lot of government property, he told me.

I didn't do anything, I said. Then I told him the same story I had told each time.

Sit down. The judges got together and began to talk. In a little while they started to call our names again, one after the other.

Chaib, they said. You had a year? Two years now.

Abdeslam ben Taieb. A year? Two years.

Mokhtar ben Mohammed. Eighteen months? Three years.

Mustafa ben el Hachmi. A year? Two years.

Eight men got double sentences, but when they came to the German, they gave him an extra six months. I was the last one. They said to me: The government pardons you this time. If you make any trouble another time, you'll be punished.

Ouakha, I said. Then we went downstairs. Thanks to Allah! I thought. The men who made the trouble are carrying all the punishment. They made a lot of noise, but they didn't even manage to stay out of jail.

So I lived on there in the prison. Three months had already gone by, and I had seven months left. After a while they had confidence in me, and let me go outside into the garden, and afterward to the highway. Sometimes they let me go alone to the beach to swim for a few minutes. Ah, I thought. This isn't jail at all! It's more like the Fondaq en Nedjar where the poor people live.

One night we were all sitting in the cell talking about the German. I asked one of the men: Did he ever get his bag?

When they caught him he wouldn't come back here until they let him go back to the river and get it.

I thought he wouldn't want to carry it with him, I said. It was very heavy.

It was full of papers, he told me. Every night when he went into his room he wrote more papers. He was telling how he killed his woman and everything. They let him take a typewriter from the office to his room. He said his papers were worth a million and a half francs. A newspaper was going to buy them. He didn't want to sell them until he'd finished writing the story.

I went on living there, today and tomorrow, today and tomorrow, until the seven months were finished. One day they called me. Ahmed, they said.

Yes?

Have you got anything here in the office?

I have a belt and a watch, I said.

And money?

No money.

Here's your belt. Here's your watch. And here are your clothes. Then they gave me a paper. Take this, they said, so when you get to the gate the guard will let you out.

I took the paper, went to the gate, and gave it to the guard. Sign here, he said. I wrote my name in Arabic, because I had learned how to do that in school. Good, he said. Allah ihennik. He opened the door and I went out.

When a man goes out of jail it is the happiest day of his life. His heart is open and he is not afraid of anything. That was the way I felt. And best of all, it was summer.

I'm going to the beach and swim, I thought. It's warm. I went down to the shore and swam in the sea for as long as I wanted. Then I said to myself: I'm going home and see my mother.

When I got there she said: How are you, aoulidi? Have you really finished this time? Not just escaped?

Hamdoul'lah, I said. This time I've finished it.

Another time you won't try to sell kif?

Never again in my life! I told her.

CHAPTER SEVEN

AT MUSTAPHA'S CAFÉ

My mother's husband would not let me live at home, and so I went to stay at Mustapha's café again. And one day we heard that the Sultan was coming back to us. Have you heard the news? they were saying. No, I haven't heard anything. The Sultan's coming back, and the French are going to give us our freedom. And the day after he comes to Tanja will be the Festival of the Throne. Ah, what a day that's going to be! The biggest day of the year!

Who knows? I said.

I was not working then. My clothes were ripped and ragged, and very dirty. One afternoon I went home to Souani to see my mother. When I got there I was hungry, and she gave me some food. If her husband had been there she could not have given me anything. But he was not at home. When I finished eating, I said to her: Look. If my brother has an extra pair of pants and a shirt, I'd like to have them for a few days. Until the festival is over. Then I can give them back.

She brought them to me. Here are the trousers and the shirt. But when the feast is finished give them back to me.

I'm afraid your husband's going to make trouble, I told her. They're his son's clothes.

96

No. Just take them. Don't worry about that. It'll be all right. If he says anything, I'll tell him I took them.

Oukha, I said. I put on the shirt and the trousers, and she gave me half a loaf of bread. Go now.

I went out. Everybody in the city was happy, everywhere in the streets. They were going to get their freedom. One man was saying: The Nazarenes are leaving! I'm going to have a big house on the Boulevard, and it will be all mine. Mine! Another was saying: I'm going to be a commissaire! And they were all telling each other they were going to be rich, and no one would ever have to ask for alms in the street again. They were all talking. But not one of them knew how to read or write.

The men of all the quarters in town were out collecting money to pay for the festival. In each quarter they would look for a big house where they could have the music and dancing. They filled the houses with mattresses and rugs, and decorated them with palm branches and flowers. Flowers everywhere. In Souani a man was building a big new house, but it was still not finished, and no one was living in it. The people in that part of the town asked him if they could use his house for the festival. Yes, good! he said. They could have it. Each family in the quarter gave something for the feast. One gave a rug, another a mattress, another cushions or haitis to hang along the wall, or just money to buy food and tea.

The festival lasted three days. The first day the men were all sitting on one side of the big room and the boys were on the other side. The women were in the street outside the doorway, because they were not allowed in. But there were five or six chairs in the street by the door, and when the women came by, they would say to the men: What is this? Here we are in the Festival of the Throne, and you're all inside eating. Aren't you going to give us anything? The men would say: Of course. Here you are. Sit down. The chairs were always full. When one woman got up, another sat down. Spanish women came by, too, and sat and had a glass of tea.

I was inside with the other boys, eating and laughing and drinking tea. We kept eating. It was all free. In the afternoon my mother's husband came by, looking for me. Have you seen Ahmed, my wife's son? Someone said: He's sitting inside, I think.

Go and get him, said my mother's husband. If he's in there, tell him I'm looking for him.

The boy came in and said: Ahmed. Your mother's husband wants to see you.

I went outside.

As soon as I saw him, I said to myself: Ah! He's going to say something about these clothes. I went over to him, and he said: Why did you put on your brother's pants and shirt?

Because today and tomorrow and the next day we have the festival. When it's over I'll take them back to the house. I'm not going to hurt them.

You'll do it now. Go and put on your own dirty pants.

Ouakha, I said. I could not say that my mother had given me the clothes. She had to tell him that. And I went home and took off the shirt and the trousers, and put on my own clothes that were torn and stiff with mud. My mother never had time to wash and mend them. When I had dressed I went back to the big house where the festival was going on. I sat down again. The boys around me began to whisper: Look at Laraïchi's son. Look at the clothes he has on. A little while ago he was wearing good pants and a new shirt. What's happened to him? And one boy said to me: Why did you change your clothes? Did you think the festival was over?

No, I said. I changed because I'm going to stay here all night. Until tomorrow morning. And I didn't want to get the other pants dirty.

Another boy said: Look at these clothes I'm wearing. They're all new. Everything. Look.

Yes, I said. Wear them in good health.

The three days of festival went by, and I went on wearing my old clothes. And the people began to empty the big house, taking away all the things they had brought for the feast. The wall-coverings, the rugs, the teapots, the stoves, everything. After it was all gone, I said to myself: Now the holiday is over. I've eaten and slept for three days here in the big house. I'm going down to Mustapha's café and see if there's any news. Maybe some work for me. Perhaps in the Calle de Italia I can find somebody who needs a porter to pull a cart.

I was living again in the café. Some days I found a man who needed a cart, and I worked. And some days I found nothing. But Mustapha always gave me two or three rials each afternoon. To help him I would get up early in the morning and build the fire for the qahouaji. I would take the chairs outside and put them in the alley while I swept the floor. Then I sprinkled water around on the floor inside and outside the door.

I stayed there six or seven months, working like that, and I got to know all the men who came to the café. There were thieves, pickpockets, all kinds of men. I used to listen to them when they talked. One day I said to one of them: Why don't you let me go with you some time?

No. You wouldn't know anything. You don't know anything about stealing.

Why don't you let me try? I said. But they would not listen.

One day I was hungry. I went home and knocked on the door. My brother opened it. When I went in I found only him and my mother in the house. I said hello to my mother.

Are you hungry? she asked me.

Yes.

She gave me a little food and some bread. Here you are. Eat. When I had finished she said: Look, son. There's a Nazarene who keeps pigs, and he needs somebody to work for him. You're there living in the town. Sometimes you eat, and sometimes you don't. Wouldn't you be better off working for him and always eating there at his house? You'd sleep there too, and it would be better than where you are now.

Yes, I said. Where is he, this Nazarene?

He lives in Oued Bahrein.

Do you know him?

Yes. Your stepfather met him and told him you were working in the city. And he said you could work there with his pigs.

Ouakha. Who's going to take me to see him?

Wait until your stepfather comes home. He'll take you.

We sat there talking, the three of us, and after a while my mother's husband came back.

Labess, he said. How have you been?

My mother told him: He's come so you can take him to see the Spaniard.

I had gone home because I was hungry, but she did not tell him that.

That one's going to work? said my mother's husband. He never works.

I told him: You're not the one who's going to do the work. I am. Just take me there. Don't worry about whether I ever work or don't ever work.

All right. Tomorrow morning. I'll take you to see him.

So I slept there at home that night. And in the morning I got up and had breakfast. Then he and I started out, walking to the Nazarene's farm. When we got to the orchard, my mother's husband began to call out: Pépe! Pépe! Then a man answered: Na'am? The Nazarene knew how to speak Moghrebi.

Here's the boy I told you about, said my mother's husband.

The Nazarene was young and short and fat. Have you ever

worked with garbage? he asked me.

Yes. Once I worked with it at the Monopolio on the beach.

Good. I'll give you two rials a day and your food, and you can sleep here.

Ouakha, I said.

You have to go into the city every morning with the donkey and fill the panniers with garbage and bring it back.

My mother's husband said: All right. I'm going now. Goodbye. You stay here.

Ouakha. And so he went away. And I stayed there with the Spaniard. He lived in the house with his father, his mother, his brother and his sister. Five of them lived there together.

I slept in the stall where they kept the straw. The next morning the Nazarene knocked on my door. Ya, Ahmed! he said. Buenos días.

Buenos días, I said.

Go to the kitchen. The coffee's ready for you. I'll get the donkey harnessed while you have your breakfast.

Ouakha. I went and washed my face. Then I went to the kitchen. Buenos días, Maria, I said.

Buenos días, hijo.

I sat down in a chair. She gave me a cup of coffee with milk, and some bread and butter. Then I went out. I cut a branch from a tree and shook it at the donkey. Let's go! I shouted. I was going to walk beside the donkey.

Pépe said: Nó, hombre! Ride him now. But when he's carrying the garbage, walk beside him.

So I started out to the town riding the donkey. Riding, riding, until I got to the Boulevard. Then I tied him to a tree on a back street, took the basket down, and started to look for garbage.

I was looking too for policemen because I knew it was forbidden to pick up garbage in the street. The police said the garbage belonged to the city. If they caught someone stealing it to carry away with him, they fined him and sent his donkey to the slaughter-house. But I knew about this before I went to take it. I made friends with the garbage-collectors, and sometimes I would help them carry the garbage to their carts. I had no trouble.

When I would find a pile of garbage in front of a door, I would empty it into the basket. Then I would look all through it and pull out the papers and cans and things that the pigs could not eat, and put them back on the sidewalk. What stayed in the basket was all food: potato peelings, banana skins, old bread, lettuce and things like that. When the basket was full of food I took it back to the donkey and emptied it into one of the panniers. Then I went and picked up more garbage, and I kept doing this until both of the panniers were full. I filled the basket too, and put it on top of the saddle. Then I unhitched the donkey and started out for the farm. When I got back, I set the panniers on the floor. I took the harness off the donkey and hung it up. Then I led him out into the orchard and left him under a tree where he could eat flowers. It was the largest and finest orchard anywhere around. There were many big trees, and there were flowers everywhere on the ground underneath the trees.

The first day, when I had tied the donkey to a tree in the orchard, I went into the pigpen. I was going to give the pigs the garbage then, but the Nazarene called to me. No! First you must sweep out the pen. I swept all the dung into a corner, and poured the garbage onto the clean side. While the pigs were eating I carried the dung out to the manure-heap in a wheelbarrow.

Each morning Pépe's mother went out to sell milk, and his sister went into the city to work. Some days I started out with them. They would put the milk cans into the panniers on each side of the donkey. The two brothers and the father stayed at home, feeding the cattle and cleaning out the stalls. In the morning they fed the pigs wheat chaff, and in the afternoon they fed them the garbage I brought back with me.

I stayed on there for a month and a half or two months, and then I went down to the town and bought some new clothes. I began to enjoy my work on the farm. I thought: This is better than living in the city the way I've been doing. In the café, I slept on the floor one night, in a chair the next night, and I never slept well. Now I sleep and eat well, too, and I feel better.

Today and tomorrow, today and tomorrow. One day the Nazarene said to me: I've got to sell the pigs. The government says I can't keep pigs here any more. People don't like the smell. We're going to move out of here and go to live at El Azib. We'll plant another orchard there.

If you want me to go with you, I'll go, I said.

No. We're selling the pigs. It's too near the road. The garbage smells. We won't have pigs in the new place.

Ouakha. You know best.

But we're not selling them for another month, he said.

And I stayed working with them until the end of the month. Then they brought a truck and put all the pigs into it. Before he drove away, Pépe said: Ahmed, sweep out the pen so we can gather up all the posts and planks in there when we come back. We don't want to leave any wood behind. Then he took the pigs to the slaughter-house by the river. When he had gone I went into

101

the pigpen and swept it clean. I went and sat under a tree in the orchard, and in a little while Pépe came back.

Ahmed, come here, he said.

I went over to him. What is it?

Look. We owe you a month. Here's the money for the month we owe you. And here's another month we're giving you as a present.

Thank you.

I had lunch there with them. After we had eaten I said to Pépe: Allah ihennik! If you ever need anybody to work for you, now you know me. And you know where to find me.

And his mother said: Adiós, mi hijo! Buena suerte!

I walked to my mother's house. Inside I found my mother's husband and my mother.

What's the matter? said my mother's husband.

Nothing, I said. The Nazarene has sold his pigs. He's got no more work for me.

Did he pay you?

Yes. He paid me. A month's wages and another month as a gift. A hundred and twenty rials.

Give me the money, he said.

I gave him a hundred rials. These twenty rials I'll keep, I told him. I've got to go down to the town and walk around a little.

Give me all of it. You've got no need for any money. What are you going to do with money?

No. I gave you a hundred rials. That's enough for you. I need twenty for myself.

You're not going to be working, he said. You're going to be living here at home, eating and sleeping here, and lying around here all day. What do you want with money?

So I gave him the other twenty rials and went down to the town without any money at all. I walked around, but I could not do anything or buy anything.

Now I had no money and no work, and when I would go into the town all I could do was look at what was in the street. And at home my mother's husband was always shouting at my mother and telling her I was no good. I thought: I'm going into the town and stay there. I'm not coming home any more. I'll manage to live somehow. If I can get hold of twenty-five francs now and then, and sit and drink a glass of tea, life will be a whole lot better. I'll get out of here and not come back. I can't listen to him yelling all day at my mother.

One day I said to her: Look. I'm going into the town and find some sort of work and stay there. Once in a while I'll come back and see you.

But why, aoulidi?

You and your husband fight every day because of me. It will be better when you're by yourself with him. If Allah wills it, wherever I go I'll be all right.

You know best, she said. But try and meet your brother in the street sometimes. In the morning when he's on his way to school. He'll have a little extra bread with him, and he'll give it to you.

Ouakha. And I went down to the town and stayed at Mustapha's café again. I began to go to the railway station every day. Sometimes I carried people's valises for them. Sometimes I pushed a cart through the town with trunks and packing cases in it. And I earned a little money that way. Late every afternoon I went back to the café, ordered a glass of tea, and sat for a long time drinking it. I would sit all evening talking, until twelve o'clock, and then I would shut the café. The men around there called me The Café Cat, because I ate so much tuna fish. There was a platform in the corner with a reed mat on it, and I slept there. Two other boys were staying there, and they slept in chairs or on the floor. I had the best place. Sometimes we did not shut the café until two or three in the morning, because the customers stayed so long smoking kif and playing cards.

There was a boy named Bouhoum who used to come to the café and stay all afternoon and evening. One night he asked if he could sleep there with me and the two other boys, and Mustapha said he could. But after he had looked at Bouhoum a while he came to me and said: Now there are four of you living here. You've got to watch out that one of them doesn't steal something. It's your job to keep watching everything. You're in charge.

Don't worry, I said.

And if you don't want anybody else here but you, you can put the others out, you know, he said.

All right.

Now all four of us spent the whole day in the street, looking for work. We always met back at the café at the end of the afternoon and had tea while we talked together.

One night Bouhoum had some money in his pocket. He did not say how he got it. He went into the Café Yasmina and began to play cards, and the others won all his money. When he had lost everything he came back to Mustapha's café. It was late. The café was shut and we were asleep. He began to knock on the door. Who is it? I said.

Bouhoum.

I opened the door. He did not look at me. Are you going to

103

sleep? I asked him. I wanted to go back to sleep.

Yes.

I shut the door and went over to my corner and put the key under the part of the mat where my head would be lying. Then I went to sleep.

In the morning Mustapha came and began to knock on the door. Taf! Taf! Taf!

Open up!

Who is it?

I got up and looked under the mat for the key. It was not there. Then I saw that it was in the door. I looked around for the radio, and saw that it was gone. That's it, I thought. Bouhoum's done it. Now Mustapha's going to say it's my fault. Maybe he'll put us all out and call the police. And the police will say we did it.

Mustapha went on pounding on the door. He thought it was locked, the same as always. I went and opened it.

Good morning, he said.

Good morning.

Put the chairs out and sweep now, before the qahouaji comes. Ouakha.

I was carrying the chairs out when I heard Mustapha say: Where's the radio?

I don't know, I said. Is it gone?

And where are my jacket and my djellaba? They were here.

I haven't seen them.

You were sleeping here, and you don't know what's happened to anything?

I said: Everything was here. Bouhoum came in late. I opened the door and let him in and he went to sleep. When you woke me up he'd already gone out.

Where do you think he might be now?

I don't know, I said.

He began to shout at me. Why do you let these boys in here in the middle of the night? I told you you could stay here alone if you wanted, and put them out. Nobody can make you open the door. It's your fault. I'm the owner of this café, and I've told you you're in charge.

Listen, Mustapha. There's no use yelling at me. The radio's gone, and the clothes are gone too. Wait a while. I'm working, and I'll give you a little every few days and pay you back.

I don't want anything from you, said Mustapha. Get out of here and don't come back! The day I see you in my café again, I'll break your head.

I did not say anything.

104

Then Mustapha's brother came in and began to say: Let the poor boy stay. He's done nothing. If he'd known the other one was going to steal he wouldn't have opened the door for him. He has no place to sleep. Let him stay here.

No, said Mustapha.

What he did wasn't very bad, his brother said. He's in the street all day and he only comes here at night to sleep.

No, said Mustapha. I don't want him in my café any longer. And the one who robbed me, I'll find him! No matter where he is!

That radio and those clothes, said Mustapha's brother. Forget about them. It's all the same. Allah takes care of everything in the end. Leave the poor boy here. He's got nowhere to go but his stepfather's house, and you know what his stepfather is like.

Mustapha said: All right. All right. He went out of the café angry, and his brother told me: Don't pay any attention. He's lost his things and he's angry. Every man is in a bad humor when he loses something. Go on out and work the same as always. And in the evening come back and sleep here. I'll talk with him about you.

I went out, but that day I had bad luck. I did not earn a franc. I thought: I'm going to Souani and see if I can find my brother somewhere in the street where he plays, and send him to the house to get me some bread.

I went to Souani and found him playing there in the street with the others. Mohammed, I said. Go home and get me a piece of bread.

He went to the house and said to my mother: Ahmed is out in the street. He wants some bread. If you have any, give it to me and I'll take it to him.

My mother found half a loaf of bread, cut it and spread a little butter inside, and handed him a rial. Give him this, she told him.

He came back and gave it to me. I found a piece of newspaper and wrapped the bread in it, and went back to Mustapha's café. I said to the qahouaji: Make me a glass of tea. And I paid him the rial, and he gave me back half of it. While I was eating, Mustapha came in. He kept looking over at me, but he did not speak to me. The café was full of men.

When it was time to close I went over to Mustapha and said: Brother, let me sleep here. I have nowhere else to go.

I leave it up to the qahouaji, he said. Amar is the head here now. If he wants you to stay, you can.

I said: You're the owner of the café. You have to give your permission. If you don't give it, Amar will never let me stay.

What's happened has happened. It won't help to keep thinking about it.

You people are no good for anything, he said. You don't even know how to take care of people's things for them.

He let me stay there, and I went on living that way, today and tomorrow. I would find what I could in the daytime and go back and sleep at the café at night. And the season of hindiyats came. The people in the country were picking them off the cactuses and beginning to bring them into town to sell in the street. Amar the qahouaji came to me and said: Look, Ahmed. Why don't you buy some hindiyats and sell them? Buy six or seven rials' worth and sell them. You'll make more money than at the station. And you'll be sitting down all day on the sidewalk, instead of walking up and down.

But I haven't got six rials, I said.

Ask Mustapha to lend them to you. He'll do it if you ask him.

Wait until he comes this afternoon, I said. I'll ask him and see if he will.

Late in the afternoon Mustapha came to the café. Brother, I said, I wonder if you could lend me six or seven rials to buy hindiyats. It would be a big favor you'd be doing me.

Where are you going to sell them?

Outside the café here in the street.

What is this, a café or a market?

I'll put them up the street away from the café, if you like, and I'll sell them to the Jews who live here in the quarter. I know all the Jews here.

But you'll have to give me six hindiyats every day, he said.

You can eat all you want of them, I told him.

He gave me six rials. There was another café up the street that belonged to an old man named Si Abdeslam. I went to see him. There is a crate in your garden, I said to him. May I borrow it?

What for?

I want to fill it with hindiyats and sell them in the street.

Take it, he said.

I went out and got the crate and carried it with me to the place near the Spanish church where they sold the fruit. I waited until the buses came in from the country. On top of each bus there were many baskets of hindiyats. They lifted the baskets down and the country women began to sell the fruit. I bought enough to fill the crate. And I put it on my head, and carried it down to the Calle de Italia where the café was. On my way the cactus needles kept falling down the back of my neck, but I did not know it until I got to the café. Then I found a lot of them sticking into the skin of my

106

back. I took the crate to the pump in the street and let the water run over the fruit. That way some of the needles washed off, and the hindiyats would be cooler for the people who were going to buy them. When I had them clean I went over to the wall and washed the sidewalk. Then I laid the fruit out in piles on the sidewalk. When the Jews of the quarter saw that I was selling hindiyats they all came and bought them from me, because they knew me and liked me better than the other fruit sellers. I bought better hindiyats than most of the others. Stone hindiyats they call them. The other boys gave eight or even ten of theirs for a peseta, but I gave only six. And I always sold mine before the others. The Jews used to say: The terrah sells the best hindiyats. They remembered me from the time when I had been a terrah and had taken their bread to the oven for them.

And I went on selling the fruit. Some days I made four rials, some days maybe three or five. And I was happy. The only hard part was carrying the crate full of fruit on my head from the Spanish church down to the Calle de Italia. But I got used to it.

When Amar the qahouaji saw that I was making money doing what he had told me to do, he said: Why don't you get a cart now? Fill it full of hindiyats, and push it through the street selling them. You'll make still more money.

No, I said. I'm doing well here. I'm making all the money I need. I'm better off right here.

You know best, he said.

And I stayed there selling them, until the season finished, and there was no more fruit to buy. Then I was back in the café again with no work, and no money either. Sometimes I got a job helping to empty the trucks that brought kachir wine from Meknes for the Jews.

I would sit alone in the café, thinking: See how many different kinds of work I've been doing. And yet I never have a job that goes on. I can't lift cases and bundles all my life. I've got to do something! I'm going to look around and see what I can find. Something that's easy to get hold of. Then I'll sell it, and I can have a pair of shoes and a shirt. And I began to listen carefully to the words the customers said to each other when they came in to drink tea and smoke their kif pipes. I would talk with them, and I would say: Why don't we two go somewhere and look around?

And the man would answer: No, no. You don't know how.

Don't worry about me. Don't think about me. Just take me with you.

But nobody would let me go with him. When they went to rob, they went by themselves. Some of them came in with wallets

107

full of money. Perhaps they had taken them from the tourists.

One of the men who used to come into the café was called Abdelouahaid. I wanted to go with him, and I said to him: Can't we go and look for something? I thought he might take me. Ahmed, he said. You don't understand. When we go out we have a special way of going out. Nobody can go with us because nobody knows how we do things.

Take me with you just once, I said.

If you came with me only once, he told me, we'd both be in jail fast.

It's better to stay in jail than this way in the street, I said.

You take care of your own life, said Abdelouahaid. But if you're going to steal, do it alone.

I stayed there in the café. I was thinking, and talking with them, and each day I spent less time looking for work. And finally I stayed the whole time in the café, and did not look for work any more.

There was a man, younger than the others, who used to sit in the café playing cards. He was a Riffian named Moreno. When he had no money he would sit there, and I would talk to him. Where do you work? I would say. He never talked about anything. What his work was or anything else. I said to myself: This one sits here all day. But at night he goes out, always. I'm going to keep talking to him.

One morning he was there in the café. Here you are, sitting here without a franc on you, I said to him. And I'm broke myself. Come on! Let's take a walk and see if we find something.

All right, he said. We went out together and looked all day, but there was nothing. Nothing to steal.

We went out many times together. We never found anything, but when we came back to the café we talked about what we had done and what we would do together. But Moreno never told me anything about the nights when he went out alone.

CHAPTER EIGHT

THE WIRE

ONE day in the month of Ramadan, Moreno and I went to Mogoga. We came to a warehouse. A French company had worked there. Now it was gone and the place was shut. We walked in front of the warehouse, and I said: We've got to see what's in there.

And he said: Let's go in.

And we went over and pushed against the door. We got hold of it and broke it. When the door was broken, I went in first and he followed me.

What's that?

Wire.

What's it good for? I said.

We'll take it. Then we'll find out what it's for.

I picked up a piece of it and looked at it. It was copper. And I said: If we're going to sell it, let's go now. We'll find a buyer. Then we can come back and get it.

Right.

We went out of the warehouse with a piece of the wire, and took it down to the Fondaq Waller. We showed it to a man there in the fondaq. He looked at it and said he would buy it from us. Good, he said. Tomorrow you bring it. We said we would.

The next morning we went at half past ten. We walked up to the warehouse and took out some rolls of wire. Then we carried them down and sold them, and got the money.

And there was another day. We went back to the warehouse in Mogoga and filled some sacks with rolls of wire and carried them outside. Moreno got a taxi and we filled it up and sent it to the Fondaq Waller. Then we went on bringing wire out and piling it by the gate. We took out all we needed for that day. I went across the street to the fountain to wash my hands. We were waiting for the taxi to come back so we could fill it up again. While I was at the fountain a girl looked out the window of the house above. She kept looking. Then she called to me.

What are you doing?

Nothing. Just washing my hands.

She came down to the door. Moreno saw her standing there, and he turned and ran. When he did that, she went in and called to her father. He was paid by the company to watch the warehouse. He came down.

What are you doing here? he asked me.

Nothing. I'm not doing anything. Just standing here.

Who took all that out of the warehouse?

I don't know.

The girl was saying: There was another one with him! He ran down that way!

When her father heard that, he started to run where she was pointing. I stayed where I was. There were many people passing

109

by because it was Ramadan. If Moreno had only stayed with me nothing would have happened. But he was running in the street at half-past ten in the morning. And the man caught him, and brought him back to where I was standing. A lot of people were there watching. Then the man called a policeman, and they came and took us both in a car to the comisaría, Moreno and me. We had told the taxi driver to go back to the warehouse, and he did. But all he found was a crowd of people talking in the street. The girl saw him and shouted: That's the man who was here with them! And the police took the driver to the comisaría too, and made me talk to him. Then they let him go.

The first night I was in a room by myself, and Moreno was in another room. You never know what time it is at the comisaría. Everybody had gone home except the guard. I think it was about nine o'clock. I called the guard and we talked a while. Then I told him: It's cold here. Wouldn't it be better if I went and stayed in my friend's room with him?

A little later he came and opened the door. Pass, he said. Go to your friend.

I went in. Ahilan, Moreno! Have you got a cigarette?

He said: No. I have kif if you want some.

But he had no papers, no pipe.

Wait, I told him. I know the guard. He might give us something. I went to the door and said: Agi, Si Mohammed, by your blessed parents. I want to talk to you. I need a cigarette.

Maybe you don't know it's forbidden to smoke? he said.

Either you have one or you haven't. It doesn't matter. There's no way I can make you do it.

He said: Here are two. You can't say I wouldn't give you tobacco.

I thanked him. Then I said: Look, Si Mohammed. Now I have cigarettes, but no matches. And he told me: Take the matches too, but don't call me again tonight.

I sat down by Moreno in the dark with the cigarettes and the matches. He handed me the kif. I emptied the tobacco out of one of the cigarettes and filled it with kif. I lighted it and smoked. After a while I gave it to him. When he had finished it he said: My mother's sick in Tettaouen and here I am in jail.

I said: If I get you out, will you take care of me?

Like a brother.

He knew I wanted him to bring me food to the jail now and then. But I asked him to do only one thing. I wanted him to get some clothes I had in the Café Mizmizi and take them to my mother's house and tell her he didn't know where I was. He said he would.

Tomorrow morning when they come, I told him, when they take us out to beat us up again, I'll do it for you. They'll let you go.

He said: Good. We went to sleep.

Early in the morning the police came. They pushed us out into the corridor and began to pound us with their fists.

Maybe this time some truth will fall out!

Good! Good! I cried. Wait!

They stopped. I said: This wire. I stole it. And this man came to work for me. He doesn't know anything. I was going to pay him for his work, that's all.

They let him go. After that day I never saw him again.

And I stayed four more days in the comisaría. They wrote out their papers, and they took me first to the tribunal to see the judge, and then to the jail at Malabata. I went in with some other prisoners. They searched us and took away our belts and our money, and put us into a room with about fifty others. Sit down, they said.

Three months later the judge called me to the tribunal again. They read out my name. I said I was there. Sit down, they said.

They called the guard of the warehouse and some other men. And when the judge read my name again I said I was there, and he said: Stand up. Did you steal this? I said: Yes.

What for? Why did you steal it?

I stole it because nobody wants to give me work. I'm a Tanjaoui and so everybody hates me.

You have to look for work if you want to find it, he told me.

I've looked a lot, but they always say come back tomorrow. And tomorrow there's nothing.

And he said: Good. You stole this. There was nobody working with you?

No, I said.

Sit down. He called the guard of the warehouse. This man stole from you. How much is this wire worth?

The guard said: Perhaps fifty thousand pesetas. The judge told him to sit down. There were two katibs and three other judges, and they began to talk together. When they finished they called my name and said to stand up again. The government condemns you to three years for robbery. For taking some wire. They told me I could say I wanted another trial in Rbat, and so I did.

And later they sent me and nine others to Rbat for a second trial. We went to the jail there and stayed today and tomorrow,

111

today and tomorrow, until one day they called us. They said to us: Tanjaouine will get their clothes together. Tomorrow you are all going back to Tanja. You're not going to get another trial.

What could we say? We slept there that night, and in the morning we took our things and went downstairs to another cell in the jail. We stayed there many days, waiting, and our papers did not come.

One day a guard came in and said: Tanjaouine will get up and go out into the courtyard to peel turnips. We went outside, and every day after that we peeled turnips and potatoes and carrots and took them to the kitchen. The food was very thin there. Never enough. But we got to know the cooks, and they let us take pieces of bread away with us.

There was hunger in that jail. Once I went up to the infirmary to see someone I knew who was sick, another Tanjaoui, a friend of mine. I went in and said to him: Allal, you have enough bread here, and the rest of them here have too. What's left over, leave it here by the door and I'll come up and get it.

The next day I went up to the infirmary and carried the bread downstairs with me. There was a guard there named The Turtle, with two stripes on his shoulder. He saw the bread in my hand.

Where is that bread going? he said.

I brought it from the kitchen.

Who gave it to you?

Somebody. I don't know his name.

He hit me in the face and began to kick me. Tell the truth! Then another guard called El Kebir came, and they beat me together. I said: This is a piece of bread I have with me, and I want to eat it. That's all.

No talking, The Turtle said. I'll have you put in the silon.

You have the power here. You can do what you want.

No talking! Get back in your cage! I went back to the cell with the other Tanjaouine. They did not let us out of it again.

One day they called me to the tribunal. They had written the papers so I could have the second trial in Rbat. I went to the court and told how I stole the wire. They sent me back to the jail and said they would call me again.

It was about seven months later when they came and told all the Tanjaouine to get their clothes, because they were going to another prison. I wanted to know where that was. They said it was in Dar el Beida. They carried us to the Dar el Beida jail. We went in. We did not know anyone in the place. Ten from Tanja, and we went into the cell. They told us to sit down, and then they threw each of us two old rags. They said they were blankets. There

112

was not enough room in the cell to spread the rags out and sleep. Everyone was on top of someone else.

Each cell had a cabran who commanded there. Our cabran had killed another prisoner. He was going to stay many years, and so the chief gave him command over the eighty men in the cell. But he had half the room just for himself. Only he and his friends could step over the line he drew on the floor. The others had nothing, no room to sleep. After we sat down we began to talk to each other. He told us to be quiet. Nobody was allowed to speak in that cell. We stayed there seven days. At the end of that time we went back to Rbat for nine days. That was when they told me my sentence. They took away a year from my term. Only two years instead of three. In the afternoon we went to Ain Moumen.

Ain Moumen is pink. It looks like a castle on the side of the hill. Inside it looks different. They took our clothes and searched them. They gave us work clothes and pushed us into a cell. After we were inside, they asked us: Which ones know how to do some sort of work? I said: I do. I have a trade. I'm a carpenter. That was not true. But I wanted to work. Another said he was a mechanic, and another an electrician. Three of us only.

They sent us to the workshop, and we stayed there and worked. A long time we worked there. It could be eight months or more. One day the government inspector of all the prisons, Beddou, visited the jail. He came into our cell. We were sitting there. He saw me. I was wearing a dirty shirt, and he asked me: Why is your shirt so dirty?

I said: I'll tell you. They don't give us enough soap.

Good. What's your name? I gave him my name. Very good, very good, he said.

After he had gone out and they locked the door, a guard called Beidaoui came and looked at me. That's very nice, what you did. Eh, Tanjaoui?

I said: He asked me and I told him how it was, that's all. There's not enough soap for everybody. It's not wrong to tell him that, is it?

Wait a little. When he's gone, you'll know.

In the workshop I always picked up all the little pieces of wood. I made charcoal with them so we could have tea in the cell. That afternoon I took back a big can full of pieces of wood. The cabrans walked with fan belts from car motors. They carried them in their hands. On the stairs a cabran came up behind me and began to hit me with his belt.

Why? What have I done?

He went on pounding me and I was crying: This isn't right!

113

This is a shameful thing you're doing. I only talked about soap.

I shit on your father and mother! You came all the way from Tanja just to tell us you want more soap?

If that was bad, forgive me. I asked him to forgive me and he beat me still harder. That night I did not eat. I was awake all night, and I cried. In the morning they called me. They told me I would have to work in the quarry. Not any more in the workshop.

But I'm seventeen. And I have a trade. Why do you put me in the quarry? I'll die there. I can't do it.

That's all right, they said. You've got to go.

I went to the quarry and began to work. Today and tomorrow, today and tomorrow, until they sent me to another jail called Kafeili, twenty kilometers farther south toward Mrrakch. They sent twelve of us. Kafeili is an even worse place where they send prisoners they don't want to see any more. The food was much thinner. It is better to die than go to Kafeili. In the morning you get some water with some flour thrown in, heated up a little. Nothing else. At noon, split-peas and water, or sometimes chickpeas and water. The law does not say that a prisoner always has to eat this way.

We ate our supper the first night, and went to bed. When I woke up in the morning I had red spots everywhere. I scratched all day.

What have you got here? I asked them.

Just bedbugs.

And you can't kill them?

The others laughed.

And in the room where they made the food not even a dog would go. But we were so hungry we ate everything with all the dirt in it. There was no bread. I had brought a little with me from Ain Moumen. But it did not last.

Every day we got up at five to go to work in the fields. Between sleeping and working we had no time to wash. There was no water to drink out there, and we went on working until eleven. We were always tired. At two o'clock in the afternoon they got us up again. It was hard to move then. But we went out and worked until five.

One day when I woke up I felt sick. I told the guard: I don't feel well. I can't go to work today. I asked him to call a doctor for me.

He said to me: So, my friend! You Tanjaouine come down here with only politics and ideas. Not with work in your heads!

I've worked since I came. I've never missed a day. But now I'm sick. I can't work. How can I work?

All of that is nothing, he said. You'll work whether you can or not. He called a cabran. The cabran came in and said: Get up and go to work. And he beat me with his fan belt.

I'm sick.

Get up!

Nothing. I could not get up.

Every morning for three days, after the other prisoners had gone out to work, he came and beat me.

I'm sick.

Get up!

A man who worked in the infirmary came in. One of the guards had told him there was a Tanjaoui there who would not get up to work. He asked him to look and see if I was lying or if I was really sick. The man who worked in the infirmary said to me: What's the matter with you, Tanjaoui?

I'm sick, I said. I can't move.

He looked at me and told them I was sick. He said to a guard called Boujendal: Get him out of here, Boujendal. Send him to the infirmary at Ain Moumen. You can't leave him here. If you do, he'll die with you. The guard said: Right.

In the afternoon a truck came. Boujendal said to me: You're going now. They carried me back to Ain Moumen. They put me in the hospital. The doctor came and wrote seven days of rest for me.

One day a package came from my family. Tobacco, ten packs, three pairs of pants and two shirts and two taguias to wear on my head. There was sugar and coffee too. Each day I took a little of what I had and gave it to one of the cabrans. They had been there many years and so they had command over us. I gave them my things. I thought that this way they would make less trouble for me. After that it was better for a while. Until the day when we had to make haystacks.

A man carried two sacks of straw, and he ran from one side of the field to the other. It was not heavy, but he had to keep running. One sack in front and one behind, and a guard on a horse shouting: Run! You'll never get it done! You've got to run!

How can a prisoner run with two sacks, one in front, one in back, and a man on horseback beside him? How is he going to work? I had two sacks of straw and I was carrying them. A guard was riding behind me on his horse.

Look out! I said. I may fall down. You'll ride over me.

He beat me with the belt and cried: Run! Run! Work!

If your horse steps on me, how can I work? I was running and the horse was running behind me. I thought: It's better to fall

115

down and finish with it. I fell down, and the horse stopped running. Abd el Krim, the director, was there in the field watching the work. He saw me fall, and he called to the guard and told him to leave me there. I got up. I swear by Allah, I said. Some day I'll tell them outside what it's like in here. I went on working without horses behind me. We ran until noon. Then I could hardly walk back to the jail.

We went out in the afternoon and began to pick beans. The same cabran came by and took some beans out of my basket and threw them on the ground. Then he called a guard on a horse and showed him five beans there. See what the Tanjaoui is doing with government property! Dogs like you have no shame. You leave beans behind.

I said: Look at my row. It's clean. The cabran began to hit me with a cane. The guard was on his horse watching. I called to him: You see this? I haven't done anything. How can this be?

Why are you talking to the cabran? he shouted. Don't talk! It's forbidden to talk. The cabran went on beating me. I was crying for a long time in the field while I worked. There was nothing to do but let him beat me.

Today and tomorrow, today and tomorrow, until it was almost time for me to leave. Perhaps two months more. My mother sent me a parcel with twenty packs of cigarettes and two thousand francs inside. I took two packs and one thousand francs and gave them to the guard. And I told him: Now I'm almost finished, and I want to rest a little before I go home. He said: All right. Tomorrow you can stay inside and work here.

Each day when the prisoners went out I started to work. I took a broom and swept out the room where we slept. Cell number sixteen. There were about seventy men in it. I scrubbed the floor and carried the dirty dishes to the kitchen and washed them. I took the bread from the kitchen to the room. In the morning I brought the harira and at noon I brought the food, and again in the afternoon. That was my work.

One day I was sitting in the room. The prisoners were out in the field and I was alone. A cabran came and called me. You, he said, come here. I went downstairs. Some Mrrakchi prisoners had arrived at Ain Moumen. The cabran gave me three of them. Take these three to the room, he told me. They went with me and sat down. In the afternoon when the cabran of number sixteen came he gave them their places. I served dinner and we ate. After dinner the men who had tea and sugar made tea and their friends drank with them.

And I was looking at a man who was sitting alone, one of the three from Mrrakch who had come that day. He was not drinking tea, not doing anything at all. Everybody was drinking tea and he was only watching. I got up and went over and sat down beside him. I said: Salam aleikoum. Aleikoum salam, he said.

Who are you?

I'm a Jew, he said.

You're a Jew!

Yes.

Do you drink tea?

Yes, I drink it. But it's a long time since I've seen any.

Good, I said. I'll bring you a glass, and you can drink it.

Thank you.

I went and made a fire in my mijmah, and brewed tea, and filled a glass and gave it to him. Here, I said. Here, maallem, drink it. When you finish, call me and I'll take the glass. And he drank the tea. When he had finished he called me. Here's your glass. Thank you.

In the morning after the prisoners had gone to work, the men from Mrrakch stayed behind because they had not been given work clothes. At breakfast that Jew had no sugar or anything. I made him a glass of tea and gave it to him. After that he got his clothes and went out to work. When he came back at noon he told me: This work I'm doing is too much for me. It's going to kill me. I told him: Be patient. Where have they put you?

In the quarry where Messaoud is, he said.

I'll talk with him when I see him, and say a word for you. I'll give him a pack or two. Maybe he'll keep away from you.

Many thanks, he said. May Allah repay you.

Eat and don't think about it any more, I told him. I'll do what I can.

I don't feel like eating, he said.

I went and made him some tea, and then I stayed talking with him, trying to make him eat. It made me sad to see him. A poor man, very quiet. After I had talked a long time, he started to eat. And when he had eaten he slept a little.

When the first siren blew, everybody got up and started out again to go to work. I went to look for Messaoud and found him. I told him: Messaoud, may Allah be with you. He's only a Jew. But he's an old man. He can't work. Don't give him so much to do. He can't. You can see that. A man who's used to working, yes. But he's very old to work. If you see him having trouble, let him alone for a while.

Messaoud said: Good, Tanjaoui. I'll do that for you. Messaoud

was a good man. He never beat us. Here are two packs of cigarettes for you, I told him.

No, no! he said.

Yes. Take them.

He took them. When the second siren blew, the men went
into the quarry. And the Jew went with them. Then Messaoud
began to treat him very well, because I had spoken with him.
That first day, when evening came, I asked the Jew: How's the
work now?

Much better, he told me. Thank you.

Three or four days later I went to the Jew and asked him if he
wanted to change places and live beside me. I said to the Moslem
next to me: Will you change with the Jew, and he said he would.
And the Jew came to live beside me. I said to him: You're from
Mrrakch and I'm from Tanja. All these people here, I don't
understand them very well. I don't get on with them. Now we're
here together. You not for very long, A month, you said. You
can be with me until you leave.

Good, he said. I agree.

So he stayed there with me and we ate our meals together.
We slept side by side, and whatever we did we did together.

One day his wife and son came to see him. They brought him
cigarettes, they brought him sugar and tea, and everything he
wanted. When they had gone he called me and said: Ahmed.
Take all these things. You know how to take care of them.
Put the cigarettes in the carton with yours. We both smoke.
When we want cigarettes we know where they are. Like this
we won't ever need anything. I said that was true. And I said:
If you trust me and want me to keep all this for you for later,
I will.

This isn't to keep for later, he said. It's for us two to use now.
You've always been good with me. We'll do it this way.

Good, I said.

We stayed together for a while, today and tomorrow, today
and tomorrow, until the day the trouble began.

Messaoud was a prisoner with a lot of power. The others
used to give him clothes and cigarettes. Then they did not have
to work so hard. He was a good man, because he never beat
anyone who gave him something. The others beat us anyway.
One day when I was working in the room Messaoud came in.
He was very angry.

I looked at him. Messaoud, what's wrong?

Nothing, he said. It's nothing.

118

No. Something's the matter.

Just let me alone, he said. So I did. And in the afternoon when the prisoners went out to work, two guards came and said to him: Get your clothes. You're going down to the silon right now.

And the rest of my things?

No, they told him. Leave everything. You've got nothing here now.

I'm sick, he said. The doctor gave me a paper that says I can't stay in the silon.

That's nothing, they said. They grabbed him and beat him on the top of his head and threw him into the silon with two blankets.

That night I asked another prisoner: What's the matter with Messaoud? What's he done?

He had a fight with Monsieur Joubert, he told me. Monsieur Joubert was taking a boy to his quarters to sleep with him. Messaoud tried to stop him.

Monsieur Joubert put Messaoud in the silon and told everybody that Messaoud was taking all the prisoners' food and cigarettes.

When Abd el Krim the director heard about it he went to see Monsieur Joubert and said: What is this?

Messaoud is always taking cigarettes from the men, said Monsieur Joubert. The director went down to the silon to see Messaoud. You've been taking too much from the men, he told him.

Messaoud said: I'm here because every night Monsieur Joubert takes a different boy to his room. He does what he wants with everybody in the jail. And you're the director and you don't see it. You don't know anything that goes on here.

Abd el Krim took Messaoud with him and went to see Monsieur Joubert in his office to ask him about it. It's a lie! said Monsieur Joubert. And he called in six or seven men, and each one said he had given something to Messaoud. One said: Five packs of cigarettes. Another said a shirt, another a thousand francs. Every man said: Yes, I gave it to Messaoud. Monsieur Joubert said to Abd el Krim: You hear? You're the director. You should hear this. What Messaoud says is a lie, that I take boys to my room. I wouldn't do that.

Messaoud cried: You have boys! This one right here you've had with you!

But the boy was afraid. He could not say he had been in Monsieur Joubert's bed. Messaoud went back to the silon.

He stayed there nine days and he would not eat anything they gave him. But he ate what I took him when everyone was

out at work. Every day I filled a can with coffee and tied bread
and butter on top of the can. When he had his walk outside in
the court I let the can down from the window on a rope. At the
end of the nine days when they took him out he was sick. They
put him in the infirmary. And the Jew and I were living together.

One day a prisoner came to see me and told me he was going
home. But he owed four packs of cigarettes to Messaoud. He
gave them to me. Here they are, he said. When you see him give
them to him.

I put them in the carton with the other packs. Everybody knew
the carton was full of cigarettes, Messaoud's, and mine, and the
Jew's. And so one morning at five o'clock I was in the kitchen
getting the harira for them. They opened up the carton and took
all the cigarettes except three packs. When I brought in the
harira, the Jew asked me to get him out a pack. I opened the
carton and saw it was almost empty.

I said to the Jew: Look. It's empty. And I went over to the
cabran and said to him: They've taken my cigarettes, and
Messaoud's, and the Jew's too.

He said: Shut the door. Nobody can go out until we see who
has them. We looked everywhere. We found them in the urinal
under a rag. Ay, Yimma habiba! I said. This is lucky! Messaoud
would have had nothing to smoke.

A cabran was in the latrine, and he heard me. Oh, you have
cigarettes for Messaoud? Messaoud ben Hammou? Monsieur
Joubert takes his cigarettes away from him. And you hide them
and give them to him behind his back?

I have cigarettes, I said. I'm not hiding them. And I told him
about it.

Good. Wait a little. You'll see.

He went to Monsieur Joubert. He told him: The Tanjaoui
gives Messaoud cigarettes.

Monsieur Joubert said: Call him. When I stood in front of
him he made me get all the cigarettes I had. I carried the whole
carton in and put it in front of him. There were twenty-one packs
of cigarettes, two kilos of sugar, four cakes of soap, three under-
shirts and two pairs of shorts. And he took everything out and
divided it among the men there, and told the guard to take me to
the silon.

I said to Monsieur Joubert: You're sending me to the silon,
and here's the man the cigarettes belong to. He's in jail and he's
not going to have anything to smoke. He's a Jew. No one's
going to give him even one cigarette. This thing you're doing is
not right. If you have to give cigarettes to the prisoners, give

120

them mine. Give them Messaoud's, too. If you're against him, give them his. That's between you. Don't give them the Jew's!

He would not listen to me.

I stayed eleven days inside the silon. On Fridays the qadi came to pray with the prisoners. And the director of the jail came with him. They were outside in the courtyard. I climbed up and called through a hole above the door while they were praying. I said: So this is the justice you have here! You take my cigarettes and give them to others, and I'm in the silon, and you send them to beat me! I've been eleven days in the silon! That's the justice I mean!

They said to each other: Leave him in there. He's a dog. He can't talk like that. So they left me there.

Every morning at ten o'clock they let me walk around the courtyard. One day I saw the Jew, and he told me he was going home. I said to him: So, good-bye, maallem. You've seen everything that has happened in this place. Forgive whatever needs to be forgiven. You know it wasn't my fault. They have the power. They do what they want.

Look, my son, he said. It's nothing. You were good to me long before my wife brought me cigarettes. It's not your fault.

Good-bye. Go with Allah.

He went away and I stayed there.

I had a blanket. I tore it into strips and made it into a rope. I hung it above the door with a noose at the end. Someone looked down from upstairs and began to yell: Look! The Tanjaoui's hanging himself!

I put my head in. They came and cut me down. Later I woke up in the infirmary. They put something in my nose.

When I was getting well, an old man said to me one day: If you do things like this, you only lose your life. How many other men before you have done the same thing! And it did them no good! They only died. You think somebody's going to be sorry for you? No. You only die. That's all.

I said to him: Thanks to Allah, nothing happened. I'm alive. But I don't want to talk, please.

When I could get out of bed, they sent me back to the silon. And I stayed there. And one day I was thinking: If I don't do something, I'll never get out of this place. So I decided not to eat any more until they took me out. In the silon they give you only bread. You can get water out of the latrine. That is all you have. That and kif. I always had kif.

The first day I left the bread they brought me. The second day I left it, and the third. I ate nothing. When the guard came, he saw the three loaves of bread, and he said: Why don't you eat, Tanjaoui?

I don't see anything to eat, I told him.

Eat, you son of a whore!

I won't touch it. I'll stay here until I die, and still I won't eat it, I swear by Allah.

He called the cabrans. This one doesn't want to eat.

He'll eat.

He kicked me. I'm already dead, I said. It doesn't bother me any more.

Another three days went by, and I left the bread. Then the director made them take me to his office. I could not walk by myself.

You came in here a long time ago, he said. All you've done is make trouble for us.

Trouble? They took my cigarettes and gave them away to everybody, and I said nothing. They sent me to the silon for no reason, and now they say I'm making trouble.

How much more time have you got here? he asked me.

Eighteen days more.

I'll let you work. Where do you want to work until you get out?

Work for eighteen days? I've had two years here and it's been bad all the time. That's enough. I need these eighteen days to get well. Be careful, or I'll be dead before I get out.

Good. Work in the garden until your time is finished, he told me.

Thank you, thank you, ya saadats moudir. And I went out of his office.

When the eighteen days had passed they called me. Get your clothes. You have to go now.

CHAPTER NINE

THE JOURNEY TO TANJA

THE next day they gave me five thousand francs and a paper that said I was free. There were seven of us who got out that day. We took our papers to a guard at the big gate. He looked at them and let us out.

I had a friend named Jilali, a prisoner they trusted. He worked outside and was free to go where he liked. The day before, I had said to him: Jilali, tonight's my last night here. Why don't you buy me some meat and some kif, and we'll have a little party tonight. Spend a thousand francs, and I'll pay you back to-morrow.

Jilali could not find any good meat, but he brought back two chickens instead, and vegetables, and a lot of kif. We had a good party.

When the seven of us were outside the gate, I said to one of them: Look. Can you lend me a thousand francs? I'll give it back to you in Settat.

What do you want a thousand francs for here?

I owe them to Jilali, I told him. I just want to pay him what I owe him. I'll give you my five thousand francs to keep until we get to Settat. Then I'll get change and pay you back.

Ouakha. He handed me a thousand francs and I gave him my five thousand.

I went to the house of one of the guards where I knew Jilali was working, and gave him his money. Thank you. May Allah bless your parents. Then I said good-bye, and the seven of us started walking along the highway toward Settat. It was only seven kilometers away. When we got there I took back my five thousand franc note and changed it, and paid the thousand francs to the friend who had lent it to me. Then I said good-bye to him. The others were already gone. I still had four thousand francs in my pocket. On my feet I had only a pair of broken sandals. And I went and bought a pair of shoes. I put them on and tossed the sandals into the street. A man walking by picked them up and put them on. His own sandals were even more broken than mine. Then he walked away holding his sandals in his hand.

I went on. I stopped a man. Where do the buses for Dar el Beida leave from?

You see where those buses are, up the street? The one that's full of people is going to Dar el Beida in a few minutes. If you want to go, hurry and catch it.

I ran all the way to the bus. There was a man wearing a leather pouch hung around his neck. He was standing in front of the door.

Brother, I said to him. Is this the bus that goes to Dar el Beida?

Yes, he said. I got in and found an empty seat in the back. I sat down and looked at the people inside the bus. The man with the pouch came and asked me where I was going.

Dar el Beida. How much?

Forty-four rials, he said. Two hundred and twenty francs. I paid him for my ticket. Some more people got on, and he went to the front of the bus to sell them their tickets.

I looked around the bus some more. In a little while I heard talking in the front. There were two women there. One was about eighteen, and the other was ten years older. The conductor was talking to them. They gave him their money. He was looking at it. Then he said: No. It's more than this if you want to sit here in front. This is first class here. What you've given me is only for second class. Now will you please go into the back of the bus and sit down?

No, they said. If we sit in the back we get sick. We want to sit here.

No! No! You can't stay here.

I was listening. I got up and went toward the front of the bus. What's the matter? I asked him. What do they want?

If they're going to sit here they've got to pay four rials more each, he said.

Here! I told him. Here are eight rials. I'll pay for them. Let them stay there.

Sit down, he said to them. You can stay. The boy back there has paid for you. He's given me the eight rials.

When the bus was ready to leave, the conductor came back to where I was. If you want to sit with them, there's an empty seat beside them, he told me.

Is that right?

Yes. Go on.

I got up and walked to the front of the bus. I sat down beside the older one. She started to talk to me. Where are you from, brother?

I'm from Tanja.

Where have you been?

I'm just getting out of jail. I was in Ain Moumen.

Poor man, she said to the younger one.

I wasn't the only man there. There are a lot of them in there. Most of them belong there.

I hope you never have to go back, she said.

Thank you.

Are you going all the way to Tanja today?

Yes, if I can, I said. I don't know.

We live in Dar el Beida. If you want to have lunch there at our house today, why don't you?

Yes! Yes! I said. Thank you. I'd like it very much.

I was very happy. Two years in prison. And the first day,

before I even get to my own town, here I am, invited by a woman! Because when a woman invites a man, it means something important. I was sure that I was going to have one of the two. Either the young one or the older one. The young one was just right for me, but I would have taken the other one and been happy.

The bus drove into Dar el Beida and stopped, and we got off. We started to walk, and I asked the older one: Where do you live?

We live at Bab Mrrakch, she said. I did not know the quarters of the city, or the streets, or anything.

Is it far to Bab Mrrakch? I said.

A little.

Let's take a taxi.

A taxi came by and I called to the driver. We got in and went to Bab Mrrakch. Along the street there were many people sitting on the sidewalk, selling mint. I paid the taxi driver. We got out and bought a bunch of mint. Then we walked to their house. When they got the door open, we went in and took off our djellabas. The older woman went out into the street to buy kifta for lunch. While she was gone the girl filled the mijmah with charcoal and made a fire. The woman came back with eggs, bread and kifta, and the two of them began to cook the meal. Then we ate.

When we had finished they brought the tray with all the things on it and we had tea. And we were talking about prison, and I was telling them what it was like inside, because neither of them had ever been. Now that we had eaten, I spoke only to the girl unless the older one spoke to me. We kept talking, and we talked about Tanja.

What is Tanja like? she asked me.

It's a good town, I said. And the people who live there are the best people you'll find.

Ah, brother! How I'd like to go to Tanja! It's too bad I don't know anybody there.

If you want to come to Tanja, I'll give you my address, and when you come, I'll take you everywhere and show you everything.

Thank you, brother.

What time is it? I asked her.

It's three o'clock.

I've got to go to the station now, I said.

We'll go with you.

We went out and walked to the railway station together, the

three of us. I went to the ticket window and tried to buy a ticket, but they would not sell it to me. There's no train now, they said. The three o'clock train has gone. There's not another until ten tonight.

Ouakha, I said. Then I told the two of them: Look, I'm going to stay here in the station and take the ten o'clock train.

It's still early, said the girl. Why don't we take a walk and look around? You haven't seen the city.

And we went out and walked through the streets. Soon a boy passed us and I saw that he was looking at the girl. She saw him too, and began to laugh. Ah! I said to myself. These are whores of Dar el Beida.

That was when I knew they were whores.

Do you know that boy? I asked the girl.

No. He's a neighbor of ours.

Why didn't you speak to him? Look, he's still there. Go and say hello to him.

She went over and talked with him a while. I don't know what they were saying together. Then he said good-bye to her and walked on. When she came back to me, I said: What was he saying to you?

Nothing, she said. He just wanted to know how I was.

Good. And tonight, won't I be seeing you?

Oh, she said. I don't know.

If you're thinking about money, don't worry. I have money. I'll pay you the same as I'd pay anybody else.

We haven't got that far yet.

Khlass! Don't try that with me! I told her.

The two were laughing together.

The train isn't leaving until ten, said the girl. There's plenty of time.

No. I'm not taking the train, I said. I'm staying with you tonight.

As you like, she said.

Good. I had more than two thousand francs in my pocket, and I thought it was a lot of money. We went to the market to buy some meat. We took it back to their house. Before they cooked dinner, they made a pot of tea, and we sat drinking it. The older one had not smoked that morning, but now she did. She and I sat talking while the girl cooked the food. We were talking about the world, and about the people in Tanja, and how they were better than the people in Dar el Beida.

I hope some day to go there, she said.

We ate our dinner. Then the older one said to me: And now are you going to stay here tonight or not?

Yes. I'll sleep here until morning, and then I'll go.

She went into another room and made up the bed there. Then she came back and said: Now I'm going to sleep in there, and you two can sleep here. The girl began to laugh and giggle. I took off my clothes and got into the bed. The woman turned off the light then, and the girl came and got in with me.

You see? I said. Now you're lying beside me. Isn't it better than when you were sitting a long way from me on the cushions, and you were only laughing? Now we'll have fun. And afterward we'll be comfortable and happy.

So we stayed there all night. In the morning the other woman got up and made breakfast. When she came into our room to wake us I was wishing it could still be night, so I could stay longer in bed with the girl. After so much time in prison, one night is not enough.

I got up and went and washed my face. When I came back, breakfast was ready. Then I asked the woman what time it was.

Nine o'clock.

I've got to go to the station. Do you want to come with me?

Yes, they said. We'll go with you.

We walked along the street talking. I was talking about the world, and they were talking about something else. Whatever I said, they talked about money. When we got to the station, the girl said to me: Brother, please. Haven't you got something for me?

How much do you want me to give you?

Whatever you like.

I'll give you a thousand francs.

That's enough for me, she said.

I took out a thousand francs and gave them to her. There you are, I said. Now, good-bye. What happened between us is over. Allah ihennik. God be with you.

I went into the station. At the ticket window I asked the man there: Have you got a train leaving for K'nitra?

Yes, he said. There's one at eleven.

How much does it cost to go all the way to Tanja?

One thousand seven hundred francs.

And I did not even have a thousand. I bought a ticket for K'nitra. I was thinking: I'll go as far as there, and then I'll go into the Amalat there and show them the paper. They'll help me get home to Tanja.

So I went to K'nitra. It was night by the time I got out of the

127

train. I began to walk around in the street. I thought: Tonight I'll stay here in K'nitra.

I walked some more. Then I went into the cinema. When I came out, it was after midnight. I had never been in K'nitra before. I knew nothing. I kept walking around, up one street and down the other, until four o'clock in the morning. Finally I stopped a man and asked him how to get back to the railway station.

You follow this street down all the way to the end. On the corner there's a policeman who'll tell you how to go from there.

I walked and walked. I found the policeman. Salaam aleikoum. Aleikoum salaam. Can you tell me where the station is?

Go down that way and keep going, and you'll see it in front of you.

I walked along. Four cars came down the street one after the other. When they got near I saw that they were jeeps. They stopped in front of me. There were police in all of them, and they all jumped out and came toward me. They had steel helmets on their heads. They were coming from all sides, swinging their clubs. Allah! I thought. They're going to kill me here tonight!

Stop! Come here! What are you doing?

Nothing. I'm on my way to the station.

The station! Hah! A few minutes ago you were with the others, and now you're on your way to the station!

I got out of jail yesterday, and I'm on my way home, that's all.

Let me see your papers.

I took out the paper they had given me at Ain Moumen and let him look at it.

Go on to the station, he said. Get out of here. And be careful we don't find you around here again.

I kept walking until I got to the station. I went in. The ticket window was shut. There were a few people sleeping on the benches and on the floor. Three or four were talking. A man was making coffee on a stove in the corner. I went over there.

Make me a cup of coffee, please, I said.

I sat down and drank the coffee. It was getting light. The trees outside the window were beginning to show.

Now it's day, I thought. I'm going back to town and find some breakfast. After that I'll look for the Amalat.

I walked all the way back to the town. The stores were opening when I got there. I bought some bread, a can of tuna fish, and two bananas, and then I began to look for a good place to have breakfast. There was a park with some palm trees in it not far away, and I went and sat there and ate. At the end of the park

I saw a long row of shacks. People were going in and out of them. I wonder what's down there, I kept thinking. I finished eating everything and lighted a cigarette. Then I got up and walked toward the shacks, and saw that it was a second-hand market. I shook off my shoes and carried them in my hand. I went up to a man who was sitting on the ground.

Do you want to buy these shoes? I asked him. And give me something to wear on my feet instead of them?

Those shoes you have in your hand? Where did you get them? You stole them, didn't you?

No. I bought them day before yesterday in Settat. I just got out of prison and I have no money to get home with. That's why I've got to sell them.

I'll give you a hundred rials and these old sandals.

What do you mean, a hundred rials? I said. I bought them for three hundred, and you're going to give me a hundred?

All right. I'll give you two hundred. He was looking at the shoes. But if you want the sandals, he said, you'll have to give me the socks you're wearing.

Good.

I took the socks off and gave them to him with the shoes. He handed me a thousand francs and the sandals. I put them on. Good-bye.

I spent the morning walking around, looking at the town. There were a lot of people standing in the street, waiting. I wondered what they were waiting for. I got hungry, and I began to look for a restaurant. I found one in a quarter they call Douar ed Doum.

What have you got to eat? I looked at the food in the kitchen and asked for some potatoes and a little meat.

Ouakha, said the cook.

I ate my lunch, paid two hundred francs, and went out again. I started to walk along the street. At the corner I looked down the other street. There were hundreds of people running and making a lot of noise. I turned to a man passing by. What's happening? What's the matter?

Haven't you heard the news?

No. I haven't heard anything. What is it?

It's a demonstration by the Ben Barka people. They've been breaking the store windows. Don't you live in K'nitra?

No. I live in Tanja. I thought: That's why the police stopped me last night. Where will I find the Amalat? I asked him.

Do you see that big building at the end of that street? That's it.

I walked down to the end of the street and went into the

129

building. Inside I began to ask everyone: Where is the oukil ed doula? Nobody knew, but while I was looking around I met three boys I used to know in Tanja. What are you doing here? I asked them.

The government is sending us to school here, they said. It pays for everything.

I told them what I was looking for.

Go upstairs and in the first door. They'll give you a ticket to Tanja, they told me.

I found a guard in front of the door.

Please. I want to speak to the oukil ed doula.

Why do you want to speak to him?

Just let me go in, and I'll explain it to him.

If you want to go in, you'll have to tell me what you're going to say to him.

I just got out of jail and I have no more money with me, and I want to see if he'll give me a ticket to Tanja.

We don't give tickets here, he told me. You'll have to go to the police station. Go there and see what they say.

All right.

I went back into the street and began asking people where the police station was. Finally I found it. I went in.

What do you want?

I told them.

Have you got your paper from the jail?

Yes.

Let me see it.

I handed it to him.

It says here they gave you five thousand francs when you came out.

Yes. They gave me five thousand francs. But it's two days, and I've spent them.

Get out of here! they said. Get there however you can. Go on. Get out!

I went out. What people! I thought. As if they were telling me to go out and steal again. Get there however you can! I'll go to the station and buy a ticket for Sidi Qacem, and see what happens there.

I went back to the station and bought the ticket. I waited outside on the platform, and after a while the train came. I climbed on and rode to Sidi Qacem.

When I got there, I said to myself: It's still early. I'll have a look at the town. I walked along the road from the station into the town. There were a lot of cafés and a cinema. And there were several circles of people listening to stories and music. I went over to a shack behind the crowd. It was a barber shop." There was room for one chair inside.

Brother, I said to the barber. Can you give me a drink of water?

He picked up the berrada and turned it upside down. There's no water, he said.

I walked on. Then I asked a woman in the street: Isn't there any water around here?

No. We have no water here, she said. They bring it from somewhere. I don't know where it comes from. Far away.

I thought to myself. No water in the place. I never heard of that before. I'm going over where the cafés and cinemas are. There must be water there. I'll ask inside in one of the cafés.

I walked over and looked around. Then I went into the biggest café and said: May I have a drink of water?

They gave me a bottle of water, but I could hardly drink it. It was dirty and almost hot. The taste was worse. The worst water I had ever drunk.

Ya latif! I thought, What a town! It's called Sidi Qacem and it has cafés and a cinema. And yet it has no water. How do the people live here?

I walked back to the station. I had seven or eight hundred francs left. I was hungry. In the station I bought some hard-boiled eggs and some bread. I walked back and forth inside the station while I was eating. Then I went and asked at the ticket window what time the train for Tanja left.

There's one leaving at half-past two in the morning, he said. It gets to Tanja before noon tomorrow.

How much is the ticket?

Eleven hundred francs.

Thank you.

I said to myself: Ay! An hour ago I had only seven or eight hundred francs, and now I've eaten and bought cigarettes. How am I going to get there? See how much they gave me, and now I haven't even enough to buy a ticket. All I can do is get on the train, and when the conductor asks me for my ticket I'll show him the paper they gave me at the jail, and tell him I have no money. Maybe he'll let me go on riding.

I kept walking around the station until half-past two in the morning. The train came in, and the man was shouting: Who's going to Tanja, Arzaila, El Ksar, Souq el Arbaa? Get in line.

Travelers get in line!

The people went out of the station one by one. Each man showed his ticket to the guard in the doorway before he went through. I had no ticket. But I still had the old ticket from Dar el Beida to K'nitra in my pocket. I got in line, and when I came to the guard I pulled out the old ticket and showed it to him. He let me through.

When we were all on the train, it started to move. The conductor came through the car where I was, looking at everybody's ticket. He came to me. Your ticket, he said.

I haven't got one.

That will be eleven hundred francs.

I had nothing. Even if I had given him my shirt and jacket, it would not have been enough.

Why did you get on the train if you have no money? he said.

Can I see the chief? I asked him.

The chief is a Nazarene, he said.

I want to talk to him.

You can't see him. If you don't pay me now, I'm going to call the soldiers.

The soldiers were there. They are always on the trains, like policemen.

Please take me to the chief, I told him. Afterward you can turn me over to the soldiers.

You're not going to pay? Then he called to a soldier. Come here! he shouted.

The soldier came down the aisle of the car. Look at this one! said the conductor. Here he is on the train, and he doesn't want to pay.

What's the matter with you? shouted the soldier. Why don't you pay?

Let me talk first, I told him. If it's a question of money we'll talk about that afterward.

We're not talking about anything, he said. Pay the man now or I'll take you to the room.

There is a car on every train with a room in it where the soldiers take prisoners and keep them until the train gets to a town where they can hand them over to the police.

I have no money to pay with. When we get to Arbaoua you can give me to the police if you want. But if there's a chief on the train, call him first, or take me to him, and see what he says.

He was looking at me. Where are you from? he asked me.

I'm from Tanja, I said.

Ah! Ah! You Tajaouine are always full of fancy ideas. It's too bad you don't have money, too.

It's a question of luck, I said. Every man has his own life and his own luck.

All right. I'll take you to the chief, and we'll see what he has to say.

May Allah bless your parents! I told him. That's a real favor you're doing me.

Get up! he said. I followed him through the train until we found the chief. He was sitting with some friends.

The Nazarene said: What's the matter?

I took out the paper they had given me at Ain Moumen and showed it to him. I got out three days ago, I told him, and I have no more money.

He took the paper and read it. But they gave you five thousand francs at the prison, he told me.

Yes, they gave me five thousand francs, but it's taken me three days to get this far, and this is all I have left.

I showed him the change in my pocket.

I said: I have a ticket with me. I showed him the ticket from Dar el Beida to K'nitra, so he would not think I had come all the way without paying.

But this time I didn't have enough money left, I said.

He gave me back my paper. Keep that paper, he told me. I don't mind if you ride. But I'm afraid that when you get to Tanja you're going to have trouble. You have to give your ticket to the guard when you go through the gate. They'll take you to the police station. You'll have to take care of yourself when you get to Tanja.

Thank you, I said. Just let me get to Tanja and I'll be all right. Don't worry about me. I'm not going through the gate where they take the tickets.

The soldier was listening. Ah, he said to me. You just got out of jail! So that's why your head is full of fancy ideas!

What ideas? If I'd had money I'd have paid long before you came and started to bother me. But you soldiers don't see any difference between one man and another.

I would not have dared to talk that way to the soldier unless the chief had been there.

You've got what you want, he told me. The chief's letting you ride free.

We went back to the other car. I was feeling good because of what the chief had said to me. I went on talking to the soldier, and sat down near him.

Look at him! said the soldier. The chief let him ride free, and now he thinks he's worth something. But his pockets are empty!

Yes, brother, I said. Would you have money if you weren't working? I'd like to see how much you'd have if the government didn't pay you.

That's enough words, he said. You Tanjaouine. You all think you're better than anybody else. And all you have is a wide mouth.

You're right, I said. I got up and went into another car, and found a wooden bench to sleep on. Sleeping, sleeping, while the train was on its way to Tanja.

When I woke up it was daytime, and we were at Hajra den Nhal. We kept going. There, I thought. I'm almost to Tanja. When we get to the beach I'll jump off into the sand the way the smugglers do. I can't stay here until we get into the station and have the police catch me.

The train was going along, and we got to the edge of Tanja where the tracks go along the beach. I said to the man standing near me: Allah ihennik, brother. Then I wrapped my jacket tight around my waist and jumped out. I landed on the sand. The train went by. At the back of the last car the chief was standing. He was smiling, and he waved at me.

I called to him: Gracias, señor! Then I walked from the beach to Bou Khach Khach, and started on my way to our quarter. Walking, walking through Tanja, until I came to my mother's house.

CHAPTER TEN

MERKALA

Aoulidi, aoulidi! Thanks to Allah you're here! May He never let you go back there again!

My mother kept talking, one word after the next, and she was happy.

It was all planned and written long ago, I told her. Whatever is written beforehand has to be gone through.

You have to do what is right if you want to live like other people, she said.

I want to live like other people, yes. I want to get married and have sons. I want to eat and drink and dress like other people. The day when I can do it will be the greatest day of my life. But how?

Wait. Just wait a little. Allah will help you. You have to be patient, she said.

Hamdoul'lah.

Hamdoul'lah.

I stayed on, living at my mother's house, today and tomorrow.

At first I did nothing. My mother's husband was busy buying sheep to sell for the sacrifice at the Aïd el Kebir. One day my mother said to me: You're not doing anything these days. Why don't you take care of your stepfather's sheep? At the same time you could watch other people's sheep for them. The Aïd el Kebir is coming, and you'll be wanting some money to buy clothes. Be a shepherd again for a while. That will give you enough to buy cigarettes with. You can eat here. And each man whose sheep you watch will give you a little money when the festival comes.

Ouakha.

And I began to take care of the sheep that belonged to my mother's husband. Each Thursday and Sunday there was the sheep market. When the people bought their sheep, they would bring them out to me to take care of for them until the day of the sacrifice. I sat watching them, and each day at noon I drove them to a field near the water-tap of Val Florida. I would fill a big basin with water from the cistern and put it in front of them, and they would stop eating and go and drink.

I sat in the sun watching them, and I was thinking. And often I thought of the Jew. I have known many people, Nazarenes, Jews and Moslems, but they were not like that Jew. If I live long enough, some day I want to go and look for him, I thought. And when I find him we can talk about the time when we lived together in Ain Moumen.

I had a dream one night. I was in the middle of a war, fighting. There were people all around me. We were fighting side by side. I looked at them, and I saw that they were all Jews. I could not understand why I was fighting on the side of the Jews. And I did not know who were the ones we were fighting against. I had a machine gun, and I was killing soldiers everywhere. I did not know who they were. I woke up, and thought about the dream. I could not understand it.

And I stayed that way. Some days my mother's husband gave me two rials, and some days three. I bought cigarettes, and I ate and slept at home. And the people kept bringing sheep from the market for me to take care of for them. One man would give me five rials, and another three or four or whatever he had.

One day when the Aïd el Kebir was only a few days away, I said to my mother's husband: Now the day is almost here. If you can give me a little money, I'll go down and buy some clothes.

All right, he said. Here's forty rials. And you go to all the houses of the men whose sheep you're taking care of, and tell them to pay you, too.

Ouakha. I took the forty rials to my mother and said: Will you keep this for me until I'm ready to go and buy some clothes? And this afternoon will you come with me and watch the sheep for me while I go to the people's houses to collect the money?

Yes, she said.

I took the sheep out. In the afternoon I watched my mother coming through the field and up the hill on her way to meet me.

Now I'm here, she said. If you want to go now, go on. I'll watch the sheep.

Be careful, they don't get mixed up with all the others.

Don't worry, she said. I'll take care of them. You just go.

I knew all the men who had given me their sheep, and I went to each one's house. When I found somebody at home I would say: Look. It's almost the Aïd now and I need money so I can buy clothes for it. If the man was home he gave me something, and if he was not, his wife would say: Come back tomorrow and he'll pay you.

I got a little money together. After a while I went back to the hill where my mother was sitting. When she saw me she said: What happened? Did you get anything or not?

Yes. A little, I said. But not all of it. Some of the men weren't at home. Tomorrow they'll give it to me.

The sun is setting now. We must take the sheep back to the house, said my mother.

We got them together by throwing stones at them. Then I drove them along. She stayed behind pulling up plants for the sheep to eat at night. After a while, when it was almost dark, she came to the house.

There's no water here, she said. You'll have to go out to the fountain and bring two pails full.

I took the pails and filled them. When I got back to the house her husband was getting home.

Aicha, he said. Is there any supper?

You went out early. You left no money.

Why didn't you tell me when I went out that you had no food in the house? Here, Ahmed, he said. Take this. Go and buy eggs and tomatoes.

I bought a half kilo of tomatoes and ten eggs and took them home.

136

Did you get any money from the others? my mother's husband asked me.

Yes. But not from them all. Not until tomorrow. Will you take care of the sheep tomorrow while I go and get it? And while I go to buy some clothes?

Yes. I'll watch them.

We ate our supper and slept. My mother was always the first one who got up in the morning. That day she made harira, and each one of us had a bowl of it and a piece of bread.

I said to my mother's husband: Let's take the sheep now so they can eat. And you can watch them while I go and collect the money.

We kept the sheep in a room of our house. I opened the door of the room where they were and let them run outside. Then I took them up to the place where they liked to eat. After a while my mother's husband came. Here I am, he said. Now you can go if you want to.

I went down the hill and knocked on the door of each house where they owed me money. Most of them gave it to me, and a few said they would not give any until the day of the festival. I put the money in my pocket and took it home.

Mother, I said. I've got the money now.

Spread it out here, she told me, and we'll count it and see how much you have.

I took the money out of my pocket and put it on the floor. My mother looked under her bed for the cloth she had wrapped my forty rials in, and brought it to me. Here's the rest, she said.

I was counting it.

There's a lot here. Do you know how much?

No, she said.

There's a hundred and twenty rials. I have enough to buy my clothes. I'm going now.

I went down to the city and bought a pair of shoes and a shirt and a pair of trousers. Then I took the clothes home and showed them to my mother.

Wear them in good health, she said.

The next day was the Aïd el Kebir. That morning I had only seven sheep to take care of. Two of them belonged to men who lived near us. They both came and led theirs away and sacrificed them. I took the five that belonged to my mother's husband and drove them out into the field, and sat with them. He had already taken the sheep that was going to be sacrificed and shut it in the house. He did not want the other sheep to be there when that one was killed, because it is bad for them to see it. I waited

137

with them until after the cannon had gone off. About ten in the morning is the time when the men go to the mosque and pray. Then they go home and kill their animals.

When I got back to the house, my mother's husband had already cut his sheep's throat. We grilled the liver on skewers with garlic and oil. It was good food, and it was the best thing of the festival.

After lunch I said: Now I'm going down to the town and walk around a little.

My mother's husband looked at me. You're going to the town? And the sheep are not going to eat?

I took them out this morning so I could have the afternoon free. Today's the festival!

He said nothing. I put on my new clothes and went out. In the town I walked around. I was nervous. It was early when I got home. I sat there a while. Then I went out to a café in the quarter and had a glass of tea and smoked some kif. Later I went back home to bed. That was the end of the festival.

And I went on taking care of the sheep for a while. My mother's husband was not earning much money then, and he began to say the same things he always said. Your son is not working. But he's eating. He's got to go out and look for work.

Once my mother said to him: Look. He just got out of prison. If you begin to shout at him, he's going to go and live in the street and start stealing again. Then he'll be back in prison.

I did not hear her say that. She told me about it later. But she was right. Many times when I went into the house I could see that her husband was angry and did not want to talk to me or even look at me. I said to myself: I don't know what to do about that man. If I were working I could give him money. But I'm not working. What can I do to help him? Here I just came back from jail, and he's already yelling at me. It's just bad luck, that's all. I'm going to go and live in the town again and see if it won't be better. I'll look in the street for work the same as before, and see how it comes out.

I said nothing to my mother. I went to the city to Mustapha's café, and began to live there. I was looking everywhere for work, but I did not find any. There were many others looking, too. About once a week I went up to see my mother. I stayed only a few minutes each time, and then went back to the café.

Today and tomorrow, today and tomorrow I lived there, always looking for work. One day Mustapha said: Look. You're hunting for work. But there isn't any. And you've only been out of prison a little while. I've got an idea, and it might come out right for you. That café of mine on the beach at Merkala. It's shut now for the rains. Why don't you go and live out there? You could be the watchman. I'd give you three thousand francs a month, and you could have your dinner every day at my house in Dradeb. It would be better for you than here. How does that sound to you?

Yes. Good. I said. May Allah bless your parents. It sounds like a good place.

But be careful that nothing disappears from there, he told me. He was thinking of the radio that Bouhoum had stolen.

I won't touch anything, I said.

There's wine and beer there, you know. And you leave it alone.

How many years have you known me? You know I don't drink wine or beer.

All right. Tomorrow we'll take your things out there.

That night I slept there in his café in the city. There were two other boys sleeping there, too. This was my last night there, so I said to them: I earned four rials today, carrying a crate to a warehouse. I'm going to buy some food so we can all eat.

I went and bought tuna fish and bread and oranges. Now let's eat, I said. From today to tomorrow is a long way, and no one knows what can happen.

After we had finished eating, we were lying on the floor smoking. One of the boys said to me: You're going out to Merkala to be the guard there?

Yes, I said. It'll be a little better there. It's outside the town. If you eat, nobody sees you. If you don't eat, nobody sees you. In the country nobody knows whether you eat or not. In the city everybody is watching. If you have nothing to eat they laugh at you.

Yes. It sounds like a good place, he said.

Al Allah! I said. It's better to go out there than go to jail. If I stay here I'll be back in jail in a little while. I'm going out to the beach there with one thing in my mind. That Merkala and jail are almost the same thing. I've been in jail. I can stand it out on the beach.

I knew that Merkala was a hundred times better than prison, but I did not tell them that. We went to sleep.

It was morning. When Mustapha came, he said: Ahmed, have you got everything ready to go?

He had his motorcycle outside. I carried my things out and we got on and rode away.

It was winter, and the sun was very bright that day. When we got to the beach at Merkala there was a watchman inside the café. Mustapha said to him: Azouz. This is the new watchman I'm leaving here in your place. Give him the keys, and I'll show him where to put his things. And you take everything of yours out now.

I went in, and Mustapha began to show me around. This is full, and this is empty. The other watchman was busy picking up his clothes and boxes.

And Mustapha said: Good. I'm going now.

I'll be going now, too, the watchman said. I'll bring a cart back and take away my things.

I said good-bye to them, and then I went back inside and began to look around. What a café! I was thinking. Everything is old and dirty.

I went outside and saw the ocean. The waves were breaking on the beach in front of the café. The beach was small, and there were high cliffs and big rocks at each end. I found a ladder that went up to the roof. I climbed up. The roof was piled with papers and garbage and pieces of wood and broken chairs and tables. Everything that was no good had been taken up to the roof and left there. I looked all around the beach. There was not a person anywhere. Only the big rocks and the cliffs.

And I stayed there. Sometimes the wind blew. I used to lie there at night when the cherqi was blowing, and I would listen to it. The wind, the ocean, and the rain. I would lie on my bed and smoke a cigarette, and I would be listening to the ocean hitting the cliffs of Merkala. Brromm! Then it would be quiet a minute, and then it would hit again. Brromm!

And I thought to myself: Ah! This is why he can't get anybody but me to stay here. I would hear that rain and wind, and the ocean pounding. And I would think of how little money I was getting. But I thought: People say if you want to get honey you can't be afraid of the bees. Here is where Allah has put me. I'll stay here. Something else will happen. I'll get better work later, if that's the way He wants it.

Sometimes the moon was bright and the sea was calm. And only the frogs were shouting in the dark. Qrrr! Qrrr! They lived in the swamp behind the café. Everything else was quiet. And the moon was so bright that you could see a white ship far out at sea. I had a mat and a blanket. I would climb up onto the roof and spread them out. And I would make tea and carry it up there and drink it. Then I would lie down and smoke a cigarette, and look between the rails at the beach in the moonlight. I would think of what Merkala was like in the rain and the wind, and how different it was when the sea was calm and the moon was shining.

I thought: When the wind blows, it's so strong you can't climb up here to the roof. You can't even go out of the café.

When the cherqi started to blow I would close all the blinds at the windows. It was dark inside after that. It was like the end of the world, inside and outside.

At first I had no friends at Merkala Nobody knew me. Sometimes men walked along the beach, on their way to go fishing, but I did not speak to them, and they did not come near the café. At noon each day I went to Mustapha's house in Dradeb and ate. His wife would give me the food. He was not there. I would eat and then I would go back to the beach.

At Ain Moumen I had met a boy from Tanja named Rubio. I had known him since we were small together. One day he came along the beach and I saw him. We talked a while.

I come by every day, he said. Each morning Rubio had been walking by the café to go fishing and look for wood, and I had not seen him.

After that I saw him every day. In the afternoon he often brought a stack of wood with him on his back. Sometimes he had some fish in his basket.

One day I said to him: Where do you bring the wood from, Rubio?

From the forest at Agla, he said. Why don't you come with me some day? All you ever do is sit here. You can sell it to the bakers for their ovens. Come in the morning early when I go out, and pick it up. Make a good stack of it and bring it back. The baker by the garage at Dradeb will buy it. You can make a little money that way.

Yes. Tomorrow morning when you come by, incha'Allah, call me, and I'll go with you.

The next morning about half-past six, Rubio came along the beach and began to call: Ya, Ahmed!

I was already up. I always got up at daybreak because I liked the smell of the air there very early in the morning. It was best when the sea was calm.

Are you ready? Let's go, he said.

Wait. I have to get a rope. There was a pail inside that I used for drawing water from the well. It had a rope tied to its handle. I took it off and hung it over my arm. All right, I said. I've got an ax here. Shall we take it?

We're not going to bring big wood. You don't need it. We can break it. It's dry.

We walked along the rocks above the water, at the bottom of the cliffs. It was a long way. We came to the quarry.

141

I'm going to stay here and fish, Rubio said. You go on and get your wood.

Where do I go?

Under the fence over there. Climb up the mountain past those Nazarene houses at the top of the cliff. You can see where the forest begins. The wood's in there. You just go in and pick it up. If I don't get any fish, I may come up later.

Ouakha. I climbed through the fence and began to go up the side of the mountain. When I was high up, I looked down and saw Rubio sitting on a rock down below. I went on. There were some women from the country sitting at the edge of the forest when I got there. I went inside where the high trees are, and began to pick up sticks and branches, until I had a stack of them. It was big, but not as big as the ones the women carry into the market. I tied the load up and put it on my head and began to go back down the side of the mountain.

When I got to the rocks by the water where Rubio was sitting, he looked at the pile of wood.

I've brought it, I told him.

That's not much wood. You saw how much I brought back.

Yes, but I'm just beginning. This is the first day. I'll learn, and later I'll be able to bring more. Are you going back now?

Yes.

Have you caught anything?

He opened the basket. There were two or three small fish at the bottom. Nothing, he said. The ocean's no good today.

If you'd gone and got a pile of wood, you could have made some money, I told him. It would have been better than fishing.

Yes. It would have been better.

We started to walk back over the rocks, until we got to Merkala. We went into the café. I put the wood on the floor, and I sat down.

I'm tired, I said. I'm going to wait a while before I take that wood up to the baker's.

I'll show you how to sort it and pile it straight, so the baker will buy it, said Rubio. He put the sticks together so they made a neat stack. After that he bound the stack with the rope, tied the ends of the rope around his shoulders, and put his head into a noose he had made. He tried to lift it up from where he was sitting on the floor.

Help me up.

I pulled him up off the floor with the wood on his back. Then he took it off and put it on the floor again.

Now do it the way I did it, he told me.

No. Later, I said. I sat down again.

We talked a while, and then I picked up the wood and put it on my head.

Do it the way I did it, said Rubio.

Not now, I told him.

And we started out for Dradeb with the wood. When we got to the baker's, Rubio said to him: Do you want to buy a stack of wood?

Who's selling it?

Rubio pointed across the street to me.

How much, boy?

What you always pay, I said.

Two and a half rials.

For such a big stack? I said. Is that all?

I put it on the floor and he gave me the money. I put the rope over my arm and gave half a rial to Rubio. He had no money to buy cigarettes. With the other two rials I went to the Soussi's store there and bought butter, sugar, tea, and half a loaf of bread. Then I went back to the café and lighted a fire with some of the wood that I had saved out of the stack. I made tea and had my supper.

I had a piece of awning to sleep on and part of an old blanket to cover me. I had brought them from the café in the town.

And so I began to bring wood from the forest every day. I learned to carry it on my back like other people, instead of on my head. It was easier that way. I did not have pains in my neck afterward. Only a little pain in my back.

One day Mustapha came to the café and said: Ahmed, we've got to tear down that wall up on the roof, and build a new one.

I knew that wall. It was half a meter thick and built around an iron frame.

We'll need men who are used to working in a quarry, I told him. That wall is thick. We can't use ordinary workmen.

You worked in a quarry at Ain Moumen, he said.

Yes, with a gun pointing at me.

Then I said: If you're going to get somebody to help me, get Rubio. He worked in the quarry at Ain Moumen, too.

All right. Bring him and put him to work.

He comes by in the evening. I'll tell him.

Mustapha went back to town. The sun had gone behind the mountain when I saw Rubio coming around the bottom of the cliff on his way home. He was carrying a stack of wood on his back, and he had his basket in his hand.

Ahilan, Rubio! I called. Did you get any fish?

No. One or two.

He came over to the café.

There's work for you here.

Do you mean it?

Yes. If you want to work, come tomorrow and help me tear down the wall upstairs.

I'll be here.

Early the next morning Rubio came. We took two sledge-hammers and went up onto the roof. Then we began to pound the wall. When lunch time came we went downstairs and Rubio brought out half a loaf of bread. I cooked some potatoes and tomatoes. And we ate. We sat and smoked two cigarettes each afterward. Then we went back to work, and pounded the wall until five o'clock. A little while later Mustapha came.

Look at that work! he said. You've taken all day to knock down that little piece of wall?

If you think it's easy, here's the hammer. Try, I said. You'll see how it goes.

No, no. That's all right. You've got money?

No. I haven't. Nothing. I need some.

What? This is the first day you're working, and you want to be paid already?

What is it? Do you think I have money hidden away? You think that's how I eat? Maybe I go and get a little every day? No, I said. It's not like that. At breakfast time if there's anything to eat, I eat. If there isn't, I don't. And the same at night.

Ouakha. He gave us each seven rials. When I saw them in my hand, I said to myself: Aha! This work is better than carrying wood. It's easier. You don't get pains in your back from this, or thorns in your feet. And you don't sweat so much either. Now Allah has given me good work. I'll stay and do it, and perhaps some day He'll give me something even better.

CHAPTER ELEVEN

ZOHRA

WE went on tearing down the wall for many days. Pound-ing, pounding, until it was almost summer. One day Mustapha came and said to me: Here we are at the beginning of summer. I've got to open the café now. We'll have to leave the rest of the work until next winter. I'm going to bring a Nazarene and his wife out here to cook the food and serve the drinks. They'll come every morning and go home at sunset.

He brought a man named Antonio. And his wife was called Inez. They had been married many years. We would talk together. They were good people.

The sun was very hot now, and people began coming to the beach. The café was open. They came and sat on the terrace in the shade and drank Pepsi Cola or coffee or tea. Many of them wanted water to wash with after they had been on the beach. Mustapha would tell them: We have no water here. But I would get them water from the well. And I got to know many people.

There was one girl who came every day to swim. Sometimes she came with her family, and sometimes she came alone. I wanted to know her, but I could not find a way to speak to her. Finally one day I said: Good afternoon. She looked at me. That was all. Then every day when I saw her coming I went out and said something to her. It's a fine day. Are you going swimming? She never answered.

If you talk long enough to a girl, some day she will answer. And one day she spoke to me. Each day we talked a little more. She asked me where I lived and what sort of work I did, and I told her.

I eat and live and work right here in this café.

You stay here alone at night? she asked me.

Yes, I said. Are you married?

No. I'm not. I'm divorced.

Listen to that! I said. Here you are, still very young, and you're already divorced. Why did you get divorced from your husband?

We were always fighting, she said. He was never happy, and neither was I. So we got divorced.

I see. And when are we going to take a walk or go to the cinema or somewhere?

I can't. My mother might find out.

How's your mother going to know? Is she brighter than you are?

Some day, maybe, she said.

You know where I am, I told her. I'm the watchman of Merkala day and night. You know where I live. But if you want to meet me somewhere else, tell me, and I'll meet you wherever you say.

Some day I'll tell you where, she said. And now I have to go. Good-bye.

The next day she came to the beach earlier than usual. Good morning, she said.

You came early today.

It's the best time of day.

145

Do you want some coffee? I still haven't had mine.

No, thank you.

You've got to have some! If somebody offers you something early in the morning, you can't refuse it.

Ouakha. Give me a glass of coffee.

But you know something? A glass of coffee costs fifty francs here.

She laughed. I gave her a chair and she sat down on the terrace in the shade. I went inside to the kitchen. There was a glass of coffee ready for me. I said: Señora Inez, will you make another glass, please?

Another glass? Who's it for?

For a girl outside.

She laughed. Ah, Ahmed! So now you're looking for a girl, are you?

That's the way the world is, isn't it? The girl is for the man and the man is for the girl.

She made another glass of coffee. She spread butter on some pieces of bread, and gave them to me.

I took the tray outside through the garden to the room where I slept. Then I went and told the girl: Zohra, come in here.

No. It's shameful to go in there, she said. I can't go in.

I'm not a lion. I'm not going to eat you.

After a while she came in and sat down. Here's the coffee. Here's some bread.

She ate a small piece. That's enough for me. I'm full.

As you like. I can't make you eat if you don't want to.

Then she said: Now I'm going out and sit on the beach.

Aren't you going to swim today?

No. I don't like to swim if there are people in the water.

You have to come on Monday or Tuesday, then, I told her. You know which days the beach is full of people. All right. Go and sit on the beach. But if you want to have lunch with me here, tell me now so I can get it ready.

No. I've got to go home for lunch.

She went out onto the beach and sat down by the big rocks. Every few minutes I would go outside and look to see if she was still there. At lunch time she came by the café. Now I'm going, she said. Good-bye.

The next day instead of coming in the morning, she came late in the afternoon. The sun had already set. There were not many people left on the beach. I said to myself: I wonder why she's coming so late. I went outside, and she came over.

Good afternoon, she said. Can you give me a glass of water?

Here I've been waiting all day to see you, and now that you're here you think I wouldn't give you a glass of water?

I was looking at her.

Well, give it to me, she said.

I got a glass and filled it. Here. Drink. Why did you come so late today?

I just felt like coming now, that's all.

Do you want to take a walk or maybe go to the cinema?

I'm afraid my mother will find out.

Is it shameful if she knows we went to the cinema?

Yes.

Good. Then we won't go to the cinema. We'll take a walk.

All right.

Wait. I'll put the tables and chairs in and lock up the café. Then we'll go.

I carried everything inside and swept the terrace while she sat in a chair outside the door of my room. Then I locked the café. Are you ready? I said.

We went up the valley to the highway. Then we walked under the big trees to the Spanish cemetery, and climbed up to the park of Sidi Boukhari. It was night then.

This is a nice garden, I said.

It's too bad we haven't time for it, said Zohra.

Another day maybe we will.

I've got to go home now, she said.

Yes. I have to go back, too. There's no one watching the café.

We kept walking, past the Spanish consulate and then behind the Italian school, until we were up on the Marshan, near Zohra's house. We stood in the street there.

How many people are there living in your house? I asked her.

Myself, my father's wife, and my father.

So you're like me! I said. Your father's wife is not your mother?

Yes. That's right.

When are we going to meet again?

The next time I come to the beach I'll tell you.

Good-bye. I'll be going now, I said.

Good-bye.

I went down to the beach, lighted the fire, and made tea. Then I cooked my dinner and went to bed. In the morning I did my work. I was waiting to see Zohra, but she did not come in the morning or in the afternoon. Four days went past, and I did not see her. Something's wrong with Zohra, I thought. I wonder what's the matter. Perhaps her family saw her with me and beat her.

The fifth day went by, and still she did not come. When it was twilight I locked the café and climbed up to the Marshan to the street where Zohra's house was. I did not walk by the house, but I stayed always where I could see it. It had one window on the street. I walked back and forth for more than an hour, but there was nobody. Then once I looked over and saw Zohra leaning out the window. I stayed where I was. She made signs with her hands, and so did I.

What's the matter? I was saying to her. Why didn't you come? What happened?

She made signs. I'll see you at the beach and tell you about it. Go away now. Later. Go on.

Be sure you come.

Yes, yes.

I went back to the café. She'll come one day soon, I said to myself.

I thought about Zohra that night. I was alone and there was only the noise of the ocean outside. And I was still thinking of her when I got up. I put the chairs and tables out on the terrace. Then I drew water from the well and gave it to all the plants. By the time I had finished my work the sun had come up. I made some tea and took it out and sat on the ground under the fig tree drinking it. I drank the tea and looked at the ocean. And then I saw Zohra coming along the road alone.

I got up and went to meet her. This time she was not afraid to come into my room. She sat down in a chair by the door. It was still early, before the time when Antonio and Inez were supposed to come.

Why did you stay away so long? I asked her.

You've got to tell me something, she said.

What do you want me to tell you? Say it.

Do you love me?

Of course, I said. Of course I do.

But why? What for?

For whatever you like. For everything.

Do you want to marry me?

Yes, I said. If you don't mind the way I live.

We'll see. Later.

Yes. Think about it, I told her.

I will.

And today I'm not going to see you? Or tonight?

She began to laugh. Stop! she said.

148

Khlass! Don't laugh. My heart has been waiting a long time now for you. What are you going to do? Are you going home now or later?

Why?

You don't know why I'm asking? I told you once. I don't have to tell you again, do I?

She laughed. I'm going over to the beach and sit a while. Then I'm going home.

You're going home? Don't forget to come back later, then.

If I come back, what are we going to do?

What everybody does.

Ouakha.

But don't lie to me. Come back. If you're coming, I'll get dinner for both of us. Afterward I'll take you home.

I can't come down here alone at night, she said.

All right. If you can't, then when the daylight is finished I'll shut the café and climb up and get you. I'll wait until you come out of your house, and then I'll follow you. There won't be anything to be afraid of.

All right.

Be careful of your family, I told her.

Yes.

She went across the beach and sat down. Antonio and Inez came and began to do their work. A little before lunch time I went into the café and asked Antonio for a lemon soda. I took the bottle and a glass out to Zohra on the beach. The sun was like poison and the sand was very hot.

Are you thirsty? Here's something to drink.

I went back to the café. A little later she walked by in front of the terrace.

Good-bye, she said.

Don't forget, I told her. I'll be there in the street.

Yes.

In the afternoon I went to the Soussi's store and bought a lot of bread, six eggs, half a kilo of bananas, a kilo of oranges, and half a kilo of tomatoes. I took it all back and put it in my room.

At sunset Antonio told me: Bring in the chairs and tables now. We've got to go.

Why don't you go now? I said. I'll take everything in after you've gone.

They went home. I put the furniture in and swept the terrace. Now I'm going up to get Zohra.

It was already half-dark. I locked the café and went out. Then I thought: Here I am on my way to see Zohra. And I haven't

149

even started to cook dinner. I'll leave it, and cook it when she's with me. It'll be more fun that way.

I was climbing up the steps through the village. There are no lights in that quarter. I could not see very well. There was a girl at the top, coming down the steps toward me. I was not sure whether it was Zohra or not. I looked, and I thought it was.

I'll just stand here, I thought, and wait until she comes down. She kept coming until she got down to where I was.

Ah, Zohra!

Ay! she cried. You frightened me!

Why? I said. You came out just at the right time.

You're alone at the café?

I'm always alone there. You know that.

I thought there might be some man there. Some friend. Somebody.

You know I wouldn't do that to you.

That was the first time I put my arm around her. We walked that way down the steps until we got to the valley. And we walked the same way along the road to the beach. There was no moon. It was very dark, but I knew every stone and tree along the way. When we were passing the well she said: It frightens me, this place where you live.

The ocean was hitting the rocks.

No, I said. For me it's better than any other place. There's nothing to be afraid of here.

We got to the door of my room by the garden. Go in, I said.

It's dark in there.

Don't be afraid. Go on in. I'll light the lamp.

I had to pour in alcohol first. After a while it was lighted.

Take off your djellaba, I told her. Don't be ashamed.

No. I'll leave it on.

No, no. Take it off. We've got to get dinner, you and I.

She took off her djellaba and hung it up. I was looking and looking at her. I walked over to her. I took hold of her and kissed her.

You know what we're going to do now? We're going to make a glass of tea and come back here and lie down a while. Then we'll get a good dinner.

Ouakha. When a man and a woman are lying in bed together, nothing matters. Not even hunger, she said.

Now, I told her, you can wash the dishes. I'll get some fresh water from the well for the tea.

I filled a pail and brought it back. I lighted the alcohol stove and started to heat the water. She was sitting on the bed.

While we were waiting for the water to boil I sat beside her and kissed her. Then I made the tea and we sat kissing while we drank it.

You know, I said. If a man's dying, farting won't save him. This isn't enough for either one of us. Let's pull back the blanket and get into bed. After that we'll make dinner.

Whatever you like, she said.

But she wanted to even more than I did.

Get up and sit in the chair while I make the bed, I told her.

I got the bed ready and took off my shirt and trousers. Then I got into bed.

Take your clothes off, I said.

No. It's shameful.

There's no shame. Just you and I are here.

She took off everything but her serrouelles, and got into bed, and I was kissing her.

What? I said. You've still got your serrouelles on?

Then she took them off, too.

Make yourself comfortable, I told her. Lie back. Like this.

Here I am, she said. Everything's yours.

This is the way I've been wanting to see you, I said.

In about five minutes we got up and washed. Then we cooked dinner. After that we made tea.

While we were having tea, Zohra said: It's late. I've got to go home.

Before you go, I told her, let's get into bed again for a while. And then I'll take you home.

Ouakha, she said.

After we had finished, she got up and washed. Then she dressed and put on her veil and her djellaba. And we walked back up to the village on the Marshan. When we got near her house I told her: Don't forget what you said.

I'll see.

Good. I'm going now. Later we'll talk about it.

I went back to Merkala.

Five days later she came down to the beach.

I've talked about it with my father's wife, she said. And she told me I had to ask my father. She doesn't care whether I get married or not.

Did you ask your father?

Yes, I told him about you. He said he didn't know who you were. He said you were just a watchman on the beach. He said you were no good. And I said: How do you know he's no good? How can you know that, unless you've lived with him? What am

151

I going to do?

I don't know, I said. I told you how I live and how much I earn. I haven't hidden anything from you.

Money doesn't matter. What matters is living together, the two of us, she said. I can work, too. We can both work. If only my father will let us.

We'll see what happens.

I'm going home. I don't feel like talking now, she told me. Good-bye.

A few days went by. One day a small girl came to the café asking for me.

Which one is the watchman here named Ahmed? I want to talk to him.

What do you want of him? I asked her.

There's a woman who wants to see him. He's supposed to go to her house.

Where's the house?

Up in the village on the Marshan, she said.

Then I knew it was Zohra. I thought something must have happened. I said to the little girl: Shall I go with you now?

Yes.

I put on my jacket and we started out for Zohra's house. When we got near it, the little girl told me: Wait here. Then she went to the door and knocked.

Here is the man named Ahmed, she said. He's come.

Someone said something to her, and she came and told me: Come.

I went over to the door. Zohra was standing there.

Ah, Zohra! What's the matter?

Come in. Come in, she said.

I went into the house. She was there with her father's wife. The woman's face was angry. I held out my hand, and she did not want to take it. She sat down far away from me and nobody spoke. What's wrong with her? I thought.

Then Zohra said: This is the man I was talking about.

Yes? said the woman. Good. That's nice.

I was thinking: She's talking like a Nazarene. She's just saying things because she has to. She doesn't mean anything she says.

I've got to go now, I told her. Thank you.

My son, if you're going, go, she said. And anyway, we all know who you are. You work for Mustapha. You're the watchman of Merkala. You're nothing.

Yes. Maybe, I said.

I went back down to the beach. But now I could not work the

way I had before. I was thinking: I don't know how all this is going to end. I dreamed every night. Good things and bad things. Sometimes when I woke up I was crying. But no one heard me. There was only the ocean.

One day I was sitting on the ground in the sun outside the door of my room. All at once a woman walked up to me. It was the woman who was Zohra's father's wife.

Were you looking for me? I asked her.

Aren't you the man who came last week to our house?

Yes. I am. What is it?

Are you coming up and have dinner with us tonight?

Are you inviting me?

Yes.

Ouakha. When people invite you, I said, even though you have to go all the way to Baghdad, it's a short distance.

After you've finished your work, when the muezzin calls the aacha, come up.

Yes. When I finish I'll come.

Good-bye.

When she was gone I was very happy. Now they're going to give me Zohra! Something beautiful to look at always! We can live here in the café together. I can build on a room. We'll make a good life together.

That evening I put on my best clothes and started out to the Marshan. I got to the house and knocked on the door.

Who is it?

Ahmed.

Come in. They opened the door. Inside were Zohra, her father, her father's wife, and a young man. I shook hands with them all. Then the woman sat down, and I sat beside her. Zohra's father sat on the other side next to the young man. Zohra was making the tea at the end of the room. The young man was dressed like a Nazarene. His clothes were expensive.

After each one had a glass of tea in his hand, we began to talk. We were talking about the world. Then the man who was dressed like a Nazarene said to Zohra: Is this the man you're going to marry?

Yes. He's the one, if it's written, she said.

I hope you'll be happy, he told her.

I turned to him. Yes, I said. Incha'Allah!

Then the woman pointed across the room at the young man and said to me: Now you see what a good husband Zohra's going to have! Did you think she was going to marry the watchman of Merkala?

153

In front of her daughter she was saying: Now you see who my daughter's going to marry, and what sort of man he is. A professor, a teacher. He teaches people how to read. And you know what I'm going to say to you?

No. What? I said.

You're not going to see Zohra any more. And you're not going to follow her in the street either.

Is that all? I said. Is that what you invited me here to tell me?

I got up. Good-bye, I said. Excuse me. I said good-bye to all of them, and went out.

I went straight to the café and slept with my clothes on. When I woke up it was morning, and I saw that I had not undressed. I took off my suit and changed into my work clothes. Then I put the chairs and tables out and swept the café the same as always.

I kept looking out the door to see if Zohra was coming. No one. While I was working, Antonio and Inez came with the food from the market. We drank coffee together. People began to come into the café for drinks.

I was thinking: I'm going up to the village and walk through Zohra's street. Maybe I'll see her somewhere.

A little later I climbed up and began to walk up and down in front of her house. I did not see her anywhere. I went back down to the café. Mustapha was there.

Where have you been? he said.

Just up the road.

You'd better stay here and do your work.

I don't know what I'm doing.

Why not? What's the matter with you?

Nothing. Nothing.

Do your work. That's all. Stop thinking about the whores. You'll see. Some day they'll drive you crazy.

You're always after women yourself. I'm no different from you.

You're worse, he said. Pay attention to your work.

I'm doing all I can. Don't worry about my work.

Every day I would climb up to the village, but I never saw Zohra.

One day Mustapha said to me: Listen. I brought you here to work, and you're not doing it. You work a little in the morning. As soon as Antonio comes, you go off and leave him here.

I'm sorry. I don't know what I'm doing.

If you're going to do your work, do it. If you're not going to, tell me now. I want to know. If you don't want to work, you can leave.

I'm going to work, I said.

But every day I had to go and look at her house. I had to, no matter what happened. I always thought she might come to the window. See what I'm like now, I thought. I don't even know what I'm doing until I'm already doing it.

Mustapha went on shouting at me that I went away every day and left Antonio and Inez alone. He would come into the café and find me talking to myself. Who are you talking to? he would say. What's the matter with you? And I would tell him: I'm not talking to anybody.

I think you've eaten tseuheur again, he said. Some whore has put a spell on you.

One day he said: All right. You're finished working for me. Put your things together and get out.

It was true that I did not know what I was doing. I packed up my things. There was nowhere to go but back to my mother's house. I went and began to sleep there again. Every morning I went to the village on the Marshan and sat on the steps across the street from where Zohra lived. I thought that if I could only see her for a minute in the window, I would go home and be happy. But I did not see her.

I left each morning without eating anything. Why do you go before you've eaten? my mother would say.

I'm not hungry.

In the afternoon when I went home she would ask me: Do you want to eat?

No. I've eaten, I would tell her. But I had not eaten. Sometimes she would get me to take along a piece of bread with me. Some days I could not eat at all. I smoked cigarettes and drank tea. At night when I was asleep I talked aloud.

Why do you talk in the middle of the night? my mother asked me.

Talk? I don't talk.

One day an old woman who was a friend of my mother's came to see her. My mother told her: My son speaks alone in his sleep. And he always goes out into the street without eating. I don't know what's wrong with him. I don't know whether he eats in the street or not.

The old woman said: He's probably having trouble with some woman.

I don't know, said my mother.

Yes, the old woman said. Take your son to Sidi Hassein. Buy two black roosters and give them to the fqih who sits at the entrance to the tomb. He'll kill them for you. And you'll see what will happen.

155

When I went back home that day, my mother said: You've got to go with me to Sidi Hassein. She did not tell me anything about the old woman.

You go alone, I told her. It's better if I don't go with you.

Every day you spend all your time walking around in the street doing nothing. And then I ask you just to go with me to Sidi Hassein and you don't want to. You won't even do that much for me.

All right, I said. I'll go with you.

The next morning we made a lunch to eat in the country. Then we took a Zeriah bus out to the foot of Sidi Hassein. My mother was carrying the two black roosters by their feet. Sometimes they made a noise. I did not even wonder why she was bringing them. I was only looking out the window. When the bus stopped, we climbed up between the big rocks and the cactuses until we were on top of the hill. Then we made a tent out of my mother's haik, and sat inside it. After a while my mother got up. She took the two roosters and went out.

Where are you going? I asked her.

I'm going over to the tomb, she said. While I'm there, you look for some wood to make a fire with. Then when I come back we can eat.

I got the wood and made the fire. My mother came back. After we ate we made tea. We sat there until late. The air smelled good up there. There was a strong wind.

The next morning I slept very late. When I woke up I jumped out of bed. I saw the sun in the sky. What's the matter with me? I've never slept this late. I dressed and went into the next room.

Do you want some breakfast? my mother asked me.

Yes. I'm hungry.

She made me a glass of coffee and gave me a loaf of bread. Here. Take it.

After I had eaten I wanted to go down to the town. If you have a hundred francs, I told my mother, give them to me.

Here you are. I took the hundred francs and went into the town. All day I walked in the streets, until late in the afternoon. Then I went into the cinema.

Afterward, when I came out, I went to Mustapha's café in the city.

Ahilan, Ahmed! Mustapha said. How are you? Are you working or doing nothing?

Nothing.

How do you feel? What about coming back to Merkala to work?

Yes. I'd go back. You know whether you want me or not, I told him.

Good. Tomorrow, if you want, bring your clothes down. I'll be there.

It was three months before summer would begin. I went back to Merkala. Mustapha paid me the same as before, and I ate at his house every day.

We've got to finish a lot of work inside the café, Mustapha said. I want to make a counter for the bar and build some bathing cabins on the roof. And it's got to be finished before summer comes.

One day it rained very hard. I was sitting inside the café. A truck drove along the road above and stopped. It was full of bricks and cement. The men in the truck threw everything out onto the road on the other side of the swamp. Six workmen had come with them to help with the work at the café. I was helping them carry everything. For each load we had to go down the bank into the swamp. We had to wade through it and climb up again. The day was black, and it rained all the time. The mud was deep and soft everywhere, Up and down, up and down, through the mud and water, until we had everything inside the café.

The next day Mustapha came with the builder, and they talked about what they were going to do. I began to work with all the others. Mustapha paid us all the same. By the time we had the café ready, it was almost summer.

One day I went home to see my mother. I found an old woman sitting with her. When I went in they were talking about me. The old woman was saying: And what happened after Sidi Hassein? How is your son now?

He's much better, said my mother. He's working at the same place as last year.

They stopped talking when I went into the room. It was only then that I knew what had happened. Yes! I thought. That's when I forgot about Zohra. When the fqih killed the two roosters.

Summer came and Mustapha opened the café. The days were hot. There were more people on the beach than there had been the year before. One day I saw Zohra walking by on her way to sit on the sand. I turned my face away so I would not see her. She began to come every day. She even came into the café to get drinks. I would put my hands into my pockets and walk out whenever she came. And I would go back in only after she was gone. I never spoke with her again.

CHAPTER TWELVE

ZNAGUI

ONE day Mustapha came to the café. Ahmed, he said. My wife is sick. I need a girl to come and work in my house for a while.

I don't know any girls, I said. Why don't you look for one? If you like, I'll look too. And maybe between us we can find a maid for you.

We'll look.

If I meet some woman I know who has a daughter, I'll talk with her, I said.

Ouakha.

Then Mustapha went to the city, and he did not mention it again.

When he had been rebuilding the café, there had been six men working there every day. One of them was an old man named Cherif Bou Ralem. He lived in Mstakhoche and had a large family. I did not think he would be able to do the work because he was so old, but he was still strong.

One morning early while I was asleep, someone began to knock on the door of the café. Daf! Daf!

I got up. Who is it?

I opened the door. I saw a Nazarene standing there. He was my age.

Sbhalkheir, he said. Good morning.

What is this? I thought. How can a Nazarene be speaking Arabic like that?

Good morning, I said. Who are you?

I'm the Cherif Bou Ralem's son, he said.

What? That's a surprise. You're the son of the Cherif Bou Ralem? Look at him and look at you. You don't look anything alike.

It's the way it is, he said. He's my father.

Good. I was sure you were a Nazarene. Come in.

I gave him a chair and he sat down. And I went into the kitchen and lighted the fire. Then I put the water on to boil. I made tea and took that to him with a dish of olives.

Here's your breakfast, I told him. We stayed talking a long time. His name was Farid. When Antonio and Inez came, he went on to the beach to swim. Later his mother and one of his sisters came with food. The girl was about fourteen years old. They ate together sitting on the sand. After his mother and sister had gone back home Farid played ball with some others on the beach. At sunset he came into the café and had a glass of tea with me.

Your sister's young, but she's already very pretty, I told him.

All girls are pretty at that age, he said.

Is she working?

No. My older sister works in the city.

You know, I said. Mustapha's looking for a girl to work in his house. His wife is sick. Do you want your sister to work?

Yes.

Why don't we ask Mustapha if he'd like to have her?

Yes. It would be better for her than sitting in the house all day.

I'll ask Mustapha. And you speak to your mother about it.

Ouakha, said Farid.

We left it that way. I spoke to Mustapha. He said he still needed a girl at his house. A few days later Farid took his sister to Dradeb, and she began to work with Mustapha's wife there.

One day Mustapha said to me: I've found a painter to paint the café.

Who is he? I asked him.

A man named Znagui. He used to be a boxer. Now he paints houses.

Is he coming today?

Yes. At five this afternoon.

Znagui came. Salaam aleikoum.

Aleikoum salaam, said Mustapha. They went in. Mustapha showed him all the work that had to be done. He wanted him to whitewash the walls and paint the doors and tables and chairs. After they had talked a while they came out and went up onto the roof. Then they sat at the end of the terrace and began to speak about money. Mustapha said: I'll give you thirty thousand francs.

Forty thousand, said Znagui.

No. I can't pay more than thirty.

All right. But give me half now, and the other half when I finish.

No. I'll give you ten now and twenty when you finish.

Ouakha, said Znagui.

I've got no money with me here, Mustapha said. Come home with me now and I'll give it to you. Then he said: Allah ihennik, Ahmed. Znagui's going to buy whitewash. He'll bring it in the morning and start work.

159

Mustapha took Znagui away with him on his motorcycle.

The next morning I got up earlier than usual. I thought: I'll finish my work now, and be ready for Znagui when he comes. When I had done all my work I had my breakfast. Then I took a chair onto the roof and sat there waiting for him. I sat and sat, and Znagui did not come. At half past two in the afternoon I was hungry. I'm going up to Dradeb to Mustapha's house and eat lunch.

I went to Mustapha's house. The door was always open then because his wife was expecting me. I went in and sat down.

I called to Mustapha's wife: Here I am! She came in and shook my hand.. Then she went up to the roof. Farid's sister was washing clothes in the kitchen up there.

Seudiya, take Ahmed's lunch down to him.

Seudiya brought the food and put it on the table.

Don't you want to eat with me? I asked her. Sit down and eat.

No, thank you, she said. I've eaten. Eat in good health.

She went out.

Then I called Mustapha's wife. That girl is very pretty, I told her.

Well, marry her, she said.

I would if she wanted to.

But she's young.

She'll get older. We're in the world. Everything changes.

I ate and went back to the beach. I sat there all afternoon, and Znagui never brought the whitewash.

When night came, I made a fire in a pail I kept in my room, and left it outside until the charcoal was burning. I kept looking for the light of Mustapha's motorcycle on the road. I took the pail inside and put the kettle over it. Later I drank tea for a long time. Znagui did not come, and neither did Mustapha.

The next day I got up early again. Today Znagui will surely come, I was thinking. And I started to wait for him again. At noon he still had not come. A little later I heard Mustapha's motorcycle up on the road.

Where is he? said Mustapha. Where's Znagui?

I haven't seen him. You said he was coming yesterday. I've waited all day yesterday and half of today, and he still isn't here.

What!

That's right.

The son of a whore! He's taken the money and gone and got drunk.

Do you know him? Does he get drunk?

Mustapha did not answer. I've hired a robber. The son of a whore!

I don't know him, I said.

I'm going to look for him, Mustapha told me. Do you want to come with me?

Yes. Let's go.

We got on to the motorcycle and went in to the city. Beyond the Avenida de España on the beach was the factory where they packed the tuna fish in tins. We left the motorcycle in front of the factory and walked behind it to the sand dunes. In good weather there were always many men lying in the sand there, drinking bottles of wine. Mustapha knew a lot of them, and he spoke to them all. Have you seen Znagui? Finally one of them said: Yes. I saw him yesterday in a cantina. He was drunk.

We went back to the motorcycle. Mustapha said: Let's go to the Fondaq ech Chijra and look around. We rode to the gate of the Fondaq and went inside, but Znagui was not there.

For several days Mustapha and I went through the city looking for him. In cantinas, in whorehouses, in cafés, in bars. Then Mustapha met a friend who knew Znagui. He's gone to Sebta, he said.

Yes. He's gone there to get drunk on my money. When he comes back, we're going to have a talk together.

One afternoon a few days later I was at Merkala sitting in the café with Mustapha's family and some friends of theirs. We were waiting for Mustapha to come from the city. The women had brought their children with them, and the children were playing in the sand. We were laughing and drinking tea and Pepsi Cola. Soon we heard Mustapha's motorcycle coming along the road. We looked and saw someone sitting on the seat behind him. Mustapha's brother got up and went around to the other side of the café. Then he began to call to me.

Ahmed! Come here!

What is it?

Come here! Look! Mustapha's got Znagui with him. He's caught him.

In a few minutes Mustapha came in with Znagui. Znagui was limping a little. Salaam aleikoum. Everyone was saying good afternoon.

How are you? I said to Znagui. You've come early to paint the café! After ten days. Ten days we've been looking for you.

Mustapha said to his family: You see? You see what he's done to us? It's summer. We wanted to get the café painted fast. And look at it! It's not even begun yet.

Mustapha's brother was talking to Znagui. It's too bad that you did this. The café could have been all finished by now.

Znagui was saying: But I was in Sebta, and I had business there, and somebody stole my wallet, and everything was very bad.

And why didn't you come back then and tell me? said Mustapha. We could still have worked instead of having to look for you all this time.

That's all past now, said Znagui.

And what are you going to do about it? said Mustapha. Are you going to paint the café or not?

Yes. I'm going to paint it. I'll do it fast. But you'll have to give me another ten thousand francs. I have no money.

Mustapha shouted: I swear you won't get another guirch! And if you don't paint the café I'll take you up to the comisaría and your family will be in the street!

Ouakha, said Znagui. I'll get hold of some money and buy the whitewash, and come tomorrow.

You'll be here tomorrow? said Mustapha.

Tomorrow morning.

Mustapha said to the others: You've heard what he said. And we all told Znagui: Yes. Don't act like a child. Come and paint the café and be finished with it.

Znagui said: I give you my word. I'll come and start the work tomorrow morning.

Mustapha and Znagui rode away on the motorcycle. And the people stayed a little longer on the terrace talking. Then they picked up their baskets and clothes and went home.

Allah ihennikoum.

Allah ihennikoum!

I ate my dinner and went to sleep. In the middle of the night I woke up. Someone was pounding on the door. Daf! Daf! Daf! Daf! And I was very sleepy, and I did not even know which door it was. I got up and looked through the window. All I could see was the light of a flashlight outside. I said to myself: I don't know who's here with a flashlight. And I'm not going to open the door. Then I heard voices saying: There's nobody here. Let's go.

After they had gone, I opened my door a crack and looked out. I saw a jeep up on the road. I did not see the men. That's a police jeep, I thought. What do they want with me? Somebody's probably gone to the police and told them that the smugglers are using Merkala again. They want to search the café and see if there's anything here. I have nothing to hide. They can look if they want to.

I went back to bed and slept until morning. Antonio and Inez came, and we drank our coffee and did our work. A little later Mustapha came.

Hasn't Znagui got here yet? he said.

I haven't seen him.

We talked a while. While we were talking a police jeep came down the road and stopped. An inspector and a policeman and a driver came down to the café. Salaam aleikoum.

Mustapha, will you come with us to the comisaría?

Yes, he said. Yes, if you want me. Why?

A man there says you and your watchman brought him here. He says you tied him up and beat him.

What? I tied somebody up and beat him?

Yes, said the inspector. The watchman too. Then he spoke to me. Look. You just tell the truth and nothing will happen to you. We won't even put you in jail. Just tell the truth.

Yes, I said. Whatever I've seen I'll tell you. Why not? Why are you asking me all this?

He said: Last night you and Mustapha brought a man here to the café. Then you tied him up and beat him. He's badly beaten. He can hardly walk.

Yesterday a man named Znagui came here, I said. But it wasn't at night. There were a lot of people sitting here. They saw him. He went away before they did.

All right. Now we'll go to the comisaría.

They took us in the jeep. When we got there they began to ask Mustapha many questions, and he was telling them the story of how he gave the money to Znagui, and how we had been looking everywhere for him.

And when I found him I took him to the café, Mustapha said. And I was talking to him. I said: Don't you think it's shameful for a man to do what you've done? My family were there, and they were talking to him too. And he said he'd buy the whitewash and bring it this morning and start work. And I told him when he finished I'd give him the other twenty thousand francs. He came with me to the café on the motorcycle, and he was already lame. Everybody saw it.

The police said: He wasn't lame when you took him to Merkala. You tied him up, the two of you. One of you had a club and the other a knife. And you beat him.

One of the policemen said to me: You'll pay for this, you son of a whore! Watch this!

He hit me twice in the face with his fist.

So you like to kidnap people and carry them off to Merkala

where there's nobody to help them? You like to beat them? You like to kill them? Criminals!

I said: Yes. You're right. We like to kill people. We're criminals. A man gives ten thousand francs to another man, and that one goes off and spends it getting drunk. Then we ask him to do his work. Of course, we're criminals. He took the money, and now he says we beat him.

Come and look at him, said the inspector. You want to see him? See if you can go on lying after that.

I went with him into another room. Znagui was there. His face was black with bruises, and one foot was bandaged. I was looking at him. Allah! I thought. We didn't do this. But nobody's going to believe us. I try to keep away from trouble. And trouble follows me around, looking for me. And now it's caught me.

The inspector said to Znagui: Is this one of the men who did it?

Yes. He tied me up. And the other one, Mustapha, beat me with a club. And while he beat me this one had a knife in his hand. And he said if I yelled he'd kill me.

I did? I did that?

Yes. You did that to me, he said.

I turned white. I thought: See how a lie can come out of the sky and hit you.

All right, I said to Znagui. Say whatever you like.

The inspector hit me in the face. You won't get out of this, no matter what you tell us, he said.

That's all I have to say, what I've already told you. I can't say any more than that. Now stop hitting me. I'm already beaten. Can't you see that? I do everything I can so I won't have to come here to the comisaría and be hit by you. If you're going to call me a criminal, it would be better for me to go out and steal right now. Then at least you'd have a reason to hit me. And I wouldn't have to stay alone at Merkala winter and summer for a hundred francs a day.

The inspector took me to a bathroom. We went in. All right. Take off your clothes, he told me.

Am I going to take a bath?

Yes. We're going to give you a bath.

I took off my jacket and my trousers and my shirt. Then I took off my undershirt and my shorts. I stood in front of him as naked as when I came from my mother.

Here I am! I shouted. I'm ready for the bath. I wanted somebody else to hear. The inspector looked down the corridor.

No, no! Put your underwear back on, he told me. Not that kind of bath.

You said to take my clothes off.

Another policeman came in. Put your clothes on, brother, he said. What's the matter with you? Put them on.

The inspector walked away.

He said to take them off, I said.

You aren't ashamed? Put your shorts on.

We kept arguing. Then Mustapha came to the door. Why don't you get dressed, Ahmed?

I put my clothes on. They wrote out the papers. And they locked us into a room there. When night came, Mustapha pounded on the door. A policeman came. What do you want?

I want to speak to Azouz, the Frenchwoman's son, Mustapha said. The Frenchwoman's son was one of the policemen who had arrested me many years ago when I had the kif with me. At that time he was just a policeman. Now he was an inspector.

The Frenchwoman's son came to the door.

Look, said Mustapha. It's very cold here. We have to stay, I know. But we can't sleep on that wet concrete floor without something to lie on. Couldn't you let me send home for a blanket?

The Frenchwoman's son knew us both, and he said: Yes. That's all right, Mustapha.

A boy who was a qahouaji from the café across the road was bringing tea and coffee into the comisaría for the police and for us. The Frenchwoman's son sent the qahouaji in to see Mustapha.

Listen, said Mustapha. Will you go to Dradeb and ask for my house? And when you find it tell my wife please to give you a blanket for me. And tell her to send some kif and some food.

The boy said he would do that. When he came back he had everything with him. And he brought Mustapha's mother, too. She began to tell the police: My son has done nothing! And he's lost his ten thousand francs. And on top of that now he's going to be sent to jail! All for nothing!

Mustapha was talking to her. Don't worry about it. It's nothing. You go home and don't think about it.

The blanket the boy had brought from Mustapha's house was very large. It had many metres of thick wool. He had bought it in Mrrakch. We folded it in half and spread it on the floor. Then we lay on it and began to smoke kif. After a while that room in the police station was another place. It was like a wedding. It had many bright lights and music was playing. We ate our food and smoked our kif and talked and laughed. Each one filled four or five cigarettes with kif and smoked. And it was almost as if we

165

were not even there. After a while we began to sing. And we forgot all about the comisaría.

Once Mustapha said: There's no justice in the world.

What difference does it make? I said. I had the kif in me. I was happy.

And finally we went to sleep. In the morning we got up. At nine o'clock they called us. They began to read us the reports they had written about us. After they had read each one, they asked us: Do you agree? Is that what you said?

We said: Yes. And both of us had to sign our names in Arabic at the bottom of the paper. Znagui signed his paper, too. Then they said to him: You go home until we call you.

They put us into a jeep and drove us to the Mendoubia. A judge started to talk to us. So you tied a man up and beat him, he said.

Mustapha told him: None of that is true, sidi. It's the opposite. That man took my money and ran away with it. I looked for him everywhere. Then when I found him, he did this to me so he could keep the money and would not even have to paint my café. Now the café will be shut and I'll be in jail and there's no watchman. Somebody may break in and steal everything. How do I know?

We can't do anything about that, said the judge. We can only punish people who disobey the law.

Do what you have to, then, said Mustapha.

They took us to the prison in the Casbah. When we went in, the guard said: Take everything out of your pockets and give it all to me. We took out our money and other things, and handed everything to him. I had a pack of kif with me, and I kept it in my hand while I was giving him my things. He made a list of everything and gave us back our cigarettes. Then he looked at my hand. What's that in your hand? Open it.

I opened my hand. It's only enough kif for two pipes, I told him.

Why didn't you give it to me? he shouted. I ought to hit you. But there are too many people watching. You carrion! He took the kif away from me and sent us upstairs to cell number ten. There were some friends of ours there.

What are you doing here? they were asking.

It's nothing, said Mustapha.

They had plenty of kif there, and so we smoked anyway. When the guard came around, he told us: Put it away. Hide that pipe. Where is the boy who just came in a little while ago?

I went to the door. He said: Come out.

He shut the door and we stood in the corridor. Here, he said.

Here's your kif. Another time leave it in your pocket. Don't try to hide it in your hand where I can see it.

Thank you. May Allah bless your parents.

Then he opened the door and I went back into the cell.

Why did he call you? said Mustapha. What did he want?

He just wanted to talk to me, I said. I could not tell him in front of the prisoners.

A few days later, a lawyer came to speak to Mustapha, to see if he wanted him to speak for him in the tribunal.

I don't need a lawyer, Mustapha said.

The lawyer talked a long time to him. Then he said: So you don't want me?

If you did speak for me, how much would you charge? Mustapha asked him.

Give me twenty thousand francs, and the case will come out the way you want it.

All right, Mustapha told him.

If he had not said that, we would have stayed a long time there in the prison. The lawyer did his work with the judges, and in another week or so they called us to the court.

The judge asked me: Are you the watchman working for this man?

Yes.

How much do you earn a month? he said.

I told him: Three thousand francs and lunch every day.

Good. You tied up this man and your employer beat him?

I explained to him everything that had happened. And I said: Now the café is empty with no one to guard it, and we're in jail. That's the only truth.

The judge said to us: You must have fought in the German army, you two. You gave that man a very bad beating. You must have learned that kind of thing from the Germans.

Yes, yes, yes, said Mustapha. We must have been in the army with the Germans. Perhaps we were.

You can see what's written in the report, the judge told him.

I know. He says what he says and we say what we say.

But what you say is all lies, said the judge. All right. Sit down now.

After a while he said to me: You can go now and wait in the jail. Your sentences are not ready yet. We'll call you later.

We went back in the police truck to the Casbah. The next day Mustapha's mother came and said: You're getting out. Tomorrow you'll be free.

And the next day they called us to the tribunal again. They

167

gave us three months' probation and twenty thousand francs fine each.

If you have any more trouble you'll have to pay us the three months of jail, too, they told us.

Ouakha, sidi.

They took us back to the prison and we got our things together and went out. Mustapha's mother was outside at the gate waiting for him.

I'm going to take my mother down this way, said Mustapha. You carry the things and meet me at my house.

He went with his mother through Bab Haha, and I carried the clothes and things the short way through Zanqa Touila.

I was carrying the djellabas and trousers and jackets, and a big basket full of pots of food. And I had a sheepskin over my shoulder. Mustapha's mother had brought it to the jail for him. I went along slowly. When I got to the Medersa Guennoun a man called to me. I looked at him and knew he was from the secret police.

Come here. Where are you going? What have you got there?

Just clothes.

Put everything on the ground, he told me.

I threw the sheepskin down and piled everything on top of it. A lot of dust came up into our faces.

What's the matter with you? he said. Go slowly. Look at all the dust you're making.

He looked at the things.

Today was a good day for you, he said. Pick it all up. We're going to the police station.

I was thinking: I can't even get out of prison without going to the comisaría!

Where did you steal all that? he said.

From the jail in the Casbah.

I ask you a question, and you laugh at me?

I swear I'm bringing them from the jail.

Whose things are they?

Mine and Mustapha's.

What Mustapha?

The one who has the café in the Calle de Italia. We were in jail together.

Get out of here! he told me. Hurry up!

Why didn't you say that earlier? I thought. I picked everything up, and went to Dradeb. I left Mustapha's things there. Then I went to my mother's house.

Thanks to Allah you got out, she was saying.

You see? And I only told the truth, too.

Allah gives every man what he deserves, she said.

I've got to go to the café now. Give me my clothes.

Already?

Yes.

I took my things and carried them down to Merkala. Mustapha's brother was living in the café. He had been the watchman there while I was in jail.

Ah, Ahmed! How are you? Is it all finished?

Yes. And we're out. But we have to pay twenty thousand francs each.

Don't worry about that, he said. Mustapha can arrange that. You won't have to pay.

We did not have to pay. A few days later Mustapha brought two painters from Sidi Bouknadel to do the work. They painted fast, and I helped them. We had it all done quickly.

CHAPTER THIRTEEN

THE HOUSE OF THE NAZARENES

MUSTAPHA'S wife was feeling better. She began to come down to the beach every afternoon. Seudiya was still working there for them, and she came with her.

I was always talking to the girl. I told her how pretty she was, and this made her laugh. Each day I would joke with her, and ask her if she did not want to be my wife.

When summer was over, Mustapha came and said to me: Now it's time for me to get rid of Antonio and Inez. But you'll stay on the same as last year. And you'll eat at my house in Dradeb the same as you did then.

Ouakha.

I stayed at Merkala by myself again. Every day I went to Mustapha's house, and Seudiya always served me my lunch.

One day there was a very strong sun. It was a fine day, like spring. I was sitting on the beach near the water with the workmen who were building a road there. We were eating our lunch. A yellow car came down the road and stopped. A man got out. He stood pissing. He had a beard. The car was full of boxes and valises, and there were crates strapped on top of it.

One of the workmen said: Ahmed! Look at that car! Look at the dust on it. The driver can't even see out. Why don't you go over? Perhaps they'll give you work washing the car. I think they're foreigners.

I don't know.

Go on. Go on. Maybe you'll get something.

All right. I went across the beach and started to climb up to the road. There was someone else sitting in the front of the car. The man got in. Then he drove away before I could get up the bank.

Bad luck! I thought.

I went back to the beach. Nothing, I said.

Another day you'll get something, the workman said. We did not talk about the yellow car again.

When night came I went to the café and made tea. I was thinking: Those Nazarenes must be going to live here. If Allah wants me to have work with them, He'll send them back here sometime.

Three or four days went by. Then one afternoon I saw a Nazarene walking down the road toward the beach. He climbed down the bank and cut in front of the café to walk on the sand. I was sitting on the roof looking down at him. After a while he turned around and came back. When he got nearer I thought: I wonder if that's the one with the car. I'm going down and ask him where he's from. That Nazarene wasn't brought up in this country. Look at that beard he has!

I went downstairs and stood on the terrace. Then I said: Hola! Hola!

Do you speak Spanish?

I speak a little Italian, he said.

Italian's like Spanish, isn't it?

We spoke in Spanish. Sometimes he understood and sometimes he did not.

Where are you from? I asked him.

From France, he said.

Where do you live?

I'm here with a friend. We have a house on the mountain here. Up there. We just rented it. We're going to live here.

When he told me that, I said to him: Don't you need somebody to work there with you? Maybe to paint the house or something?

We have a Moslem working there. He's helping me and my friend paint the house. We don't need anybody now.

I see. Good. But remember, please, if you need anyone later I'd like to work for you. You can pay me whatever you like.

Not now. But I'll see later. I'll speak to my friend, and we'll see. Good-bye for today.

Good-bye, I said. Don't forget. If you need anybody, I'm

170

always here. You can find me.

I'll see.

He walked on. I went into the café.

One day a week or so later I looked out of the window and saw two men coming down the road toward the beach. When they got near I saw that one of them was the Frenchman I had talked to before. The other was younger and had no beard.

That must be the friend he was talking about, I thought. I've got to watch and see what they're going to do now.

When they were in front of the café, the older one said: Hola! I called to him. Come over here!

They stood talking together for a minute. Then they came over and shook hands with me.

Do you like tea? I asked them. Would you like some?

The older one said: Yes. It might be nice to have some.

Come in. And they went into the café. It was closed for the winter, but I brought them out some chairs, and they sat down. I offered them cigarettes. They had their own. I looked for an ash tray for them, and lighted the fire. Then I made tea.

This tea is wonderful!

Yes, yes!

Moslems always drink tea like this, I told them.

We talked a long time, about where they had been and what work they did and how they lived. The younger one said: Some day you'll see what sort of work we do.

Incha'Allah.

The older one said to his friend: This is the boy I told you about.

We have a man painting there now, said the younger one. When he's finished we'll come and tell you. There might be work for you then. We'll let you know.

Thank you.

Then they said: We must go.

It's dark now, I said. I'll walk with you as far as the highway. As far as the Soussi's store.

I went up the valley with them to the store. Then they climbed up the mountain road to their house. I went back to the café very happy. Now Allah has given me good work, I thought, and I won't have to stay here forever.

One afternoon I saw the yellow car coming down the road toward the café. When it stopped, two men got out, and I saw that they were the two Frenchmen. Then I knew the yellow car was theirs. The younger one came running down to the café.

Ahmed!

171

Is that your car? I asked him.

Yes. It's ours.

You came down here to the café in the car once, a long time ago, and went away again without getting out?

Yes. That was when we were looking for a house to live in, he said. Can you come with us now in the car? You can see where our house is. Then tomorrow morning you can come to work.

I put on my jacket and went with him to the car. The older one was sitting there. Hola!

And we drove up to their house on the mountain. The older one knocked on the door. A Moslem came and let us in. He was whitewashing the walls. In one room there was a painting almost as long as the room, with a great many people in it. It looked like a whole city. The older Nazarene saw me standing in front of it. It's not finished yet, he said.

The younger one pointed to the man who was whitewashing the walls. He's almost finished. Now you can come and work. Do you want to eat here or at home?

Whichever you like, I said. If you want, I'll eat here.

Then you eat here, and we'll give you three hundred francs a day. You'll work from nine to two.

Good, I said. I knew their food would be better than what I ate at Mustapha's.

I went back to Merkala that night and slept. In the morning I climbed up to their house.

Buenos días, Ahmed. The younger one let me in.

Buenos días. We always spoke in Spanish. The Nazarenes did not know any Arabic.

Come out to the workshop with me, he said. He took me through the garden to a big room that was full of wood and pieces of furniture.

You see? This is our work. We make tables and cabinets and screens for people.

He gave me a small piece of wood with a curved line drawn on it. Can you cut along this line? he asked me.

No. I don't understand that kind of work, I said.

We'll give you something else to do. He brought out a tray full of many different kinds of hinges and screws. Put all the ones that are alike together, each kind in a different box, he told me. Later you can learn how to cut the wood.

I worked a while with them, and soon I knew how to cut wood the way they wanted me to. And I went on learning. I cooked their lunch for them every day. Each morning when I got to the house they were asleep. And they slept in the same bed. Once I

172

said to them: Is that a good idea, for two men always to sleep in one bed?

They laughed. The younger one, Marcel, said: Yes. Why don't you sleep with us, too? That would make three.

No. It's better for two, I told him.

They were always joking with me like that. One day Marcel came into the kitchen and told me: Look! Today I'm going to make the lunch. You go upstairs and get into bed with François. He's waiting for you.

No, I said. It would be better if you went up.

Their house was full of plants and paintings and statues. They ate all their food from wooden plates. Everything they had was made of wood. Their trays and bowls and spoons and forks and dishes. They had a big bed in a room upstairs. They would paint pictures and hang them on the walls around the room. Then they could see them from the bed. They liked to stay in bed.

Today and tomorrow. One night I was sitting in the café, and I was thinking: Here I am working at Merkala, and there's always rain and mud. Those Nazarenes are going to stay here. I have good work with them. I ought to look for a room somewhere and rent it. Then I can finish with this café for good, and rest a little. It would be better not to stay here any longer.

And one afternoon when my work was finished and I went down to the beach, I found Mustapha there.

Mustapha, I want to talk to you.

What is it?

I'm working for the Nazarenes, you know. And the money I earn with them is enough for me. I'm going to look for a room and go and live in it. You'll have to find another watchman for the café.

Where am I going to find a good one?

We could ask Farid's brother Abdallah.

Do you know him well?

No. I've met him here with Farid a few times, I said. But you can talk to him, and see how you think he would be. It's your café. If I bring somebody and he steals or does something, you'll blame me. It's better if you get your own guard.

Good, he said.

A few days later he brought Abdallah down to Merkala. I'm going to try him, he told me.

Yes, I said. Let him stay here a while. I've got to look every afternoon for a room.

I went to see my mother. I thought she might know where I could find a room.

173

Mother, I need a room where I can live alone. Now I'm working and I can save a little money. Maybe later I'll have enough to buy some clothes and get married.

Al Allah! It would be better for you if you could.

You don't know where I can find a room?

Wait until your stepfather comes. He might know about one.

Good. I'm going up to Mstakhoche for a while. I'll be back.

I did not want to see my mother's husband. I thought I would go down to Merkala after I had looked around Mstakhoche, without going back to my mother's.

I climbed up the hill and went by the reservoir to the top of Mstakhoche. As I passed by a shack there, I saw Farid sitting inside. He called to me.

Ah, Farid! I said. What are you doing in there?

We're just sitting. Nothing else.

What is this shack?

A café. Haven't you ever seen it before?

No. I see a shack. I don't see any café.

It's a café! Come in and have a glass of tea with us. You're welcome to come in.

No. I've got a lot to do. Thank you. You don't know whether there's a mahal around here somewhere?

The master of this café owns the whole building behind here. The third mahal is empty. I think he wants to rent it.

Who is he?

An old man named El Haddane.

How much does he get for it?

Twenty rials a month.

Yes. I can pay that. Could we go and look at it?

Wait. I'll go and see if he's home.

Farid went across the street and knocked on the old man's door. I was watching. His wife came and opened it.

What do you want?

I want to see El Haddane, he said.

El Haddane came to the door.

There's a boy here who wants to rent your mahal. The one that's empty.

What did you say?

A boy. He wants to rent the mahal.

What?

I went over. What's the matter? I asked Farid.

He's deaf. He doesn't hear. He hears only the things he likes.

Yes. I know deaf people, I said.

El Haddane said: Where's the boy?

174

Here he is.

Ah! he said. Salaam aleikoum!

Aleikoum salaam.

So, my son. You want to rent the mahal?

Yes, if it's for rent. Can you open it so we can look at it?

Wait. He went in and got the keys. Then we went with him to the mahal and he opened the door.

Look, he said.

I went in. It was so dirty you could not see it. What's been living in here? I said. People or donkeys?

People, he said. People were living in here.

It's not possible, I told him. Haven't you ever white-washed the walls?

Why should I whitewash them if somebody's going to come and get them dirty right away? You can whitewash them if you want.

I spoke to Farid. Will you do it for me?

Yes. I'll whitewash your walls.

I took out a thousand francs and gave them to El Haddane. Give me the key, I told him. And make me out a receipt.

Tomorrow I'll give it to you.

Then I gave two hundred francs to Farid. Buy a little white-wash and cover the walls with it. It'll look better that way. But before that we'll get some soudani and burn it. I want to get rid of some of the bedbugs.

I went to the bacal and bought fifty grams of powdered red pepper. Farid's house was down the street. He went home and got a mijmah full of hot coals. When he came back we blew on the fire with a bellows until it was very hot. We stuffed rags and papers into all the cracks in the walls so that the smoke would not be able to get out. Then we put the mijmah inside the mahal and poured the red pepper onto the hot coals. We ran out of the mahal and shut the door.

For a half hour or so we sat talking in the café, and then we went back. I got a broom and began to sweep the bedbugs into piles. You see how many there were? And I was going to live here in the middle of them.

All these rooms here have bedbugs, Farid said.

Why don't the people do this?

They don't even know the bedbugs are there.

Look, I said. Here's the key. It's late. I've got to go. You white-wash the mahal, and tomorrow I'll come back.

The next day I went up and found Farid working there. We talked a while. He went on spreading the whitewash. Then he said: See how it looks now.

It's a little better, I said. Better than the filth that was there before.

I gave him four hundred francs. Excuse me for asking you to do the work, I told him.

I don't want to be paid, said Farid.

No. No. Take it. You've worked, and you've got to take it.

I put the key into my pocket. Do you want to come with me? I'm going to get my things out of the café at Merkala and bring them here.

All right.

We walked down to Merkala. Mustapha was there, sitting on the beach.

I've come to get my things. I've found a mahal.

Good. Whenever you like. I'm still your friend, you know, even though you did leave your work.

Then I went to the house of the two Nazarenes and said to them: I've rented a room. All my things are down at the beach. Could you come in your car and help me move them to my new place?

Yes, of course, Ahmed, Marcel said. I've got to go to the post office. François, you take Ahmed with you and get his clothes. Meet me afterward at the post office.

And François drove me down to the beach. Farid was standing on the terrace. I'll help you, he said.

We began to carry the things from the café up to the car. There was a mattress and a reed mat, and clothes and pots and plates. Farid carried the mattress on his head. François was looking at him. He began to say to me: Where does he live? Have you known him long? Does he work? Wherever Farid went, François looked at him.

When we had put all the things into the car, François said: Is that everything? There's no more?

No.

Does your friend want to come with us?

Get in, I told Farid. Come on. I put him in the middle of the seat, between us. And we drove up to Mstakhoche. The wind was blowing. François kept looking into the mirror while he was driving, and combing his hair. And then the wind blew it the other way again. Now and then he spoke to Farid.

We drove as far as the shack that was a café. Then we took everything into the mahal and left it there.

I'll see you tomorrow, François said to me.

I thanked him for helping me. He drove away.

Farid, I said. Let's go into the café next door and have something. I've got no fire in my room.

We went to the café. Farid told the qahouaji: Make us two glasses of coffee with milk.

There's no milk, said the qahouaji. This isn't a city café. You can have tea or black coffee.

Tea, I said.

For me too.

I went out and got some bread and tuna fish, and we ate it with the tea. After a while I was sleepy.

I'm going to bed.

Good night, Farid said.

If you want to come to my mahal, come on.

Another night I'll come.

Each morning I went up to the mountain to the Nazarenes' house. I would knock at the door, and one of them would open it. Buenos días.

Buenos días. I would go in. Do you want your coffee in the dining room? Sometimes they came downstairs for breakfast and sometimes I took it up to their bed.

They would show me my work for the day and leave me alone to do it. They would get dressed and do their own work. At lunch time I would ask them what they wanted to eat. Then I would go down the road to the Soussi's store and buy the food, and make their lunch. They were both good to me. It was like living with a family. We were all happy doing our work. And we ate at the same table, and talked and laughed together.

One day when we were eating, Marcel said to me: That big tunnel beyond Merkala, where the water runs into the ocean. Why do the people go inside of it? What are they doing in there?

I don't know, I said. Probably they're having fun with each other. Haven't you ever gone inside?

Yes. I went in once. And I found a very nice boy in there.

You liked him?

A little, he said.

That's between you two.

And you, he said. Don't you like boys?

No, I don't. Girls are better.

We always talked together like that while we ate.

One day they got a big order for furniture. We were all very busy in the carpenter shop. And I was buying the food and cooking the lunch and cleaning the house and washing the clothes. Marcel came to me and said: We've all got too much work in this house. Can't you find us a maid? She can do all the

177

other things, so you can spend all your time in the shop working with us. How much do you think we should pay a girl like that?

I don't know. If I can find one for you, you'll have to talk to her. I'll see if I can bring a girl here, and then you talk to her.

That afternoon I went to my mother's house. Mother, I said. We need a maid up there at the Nazarenes' house. But I don't know where to find one. A girl we can trust. They live there and work there, and we can't have someone who's going to take things.

Yes, you're right, she said. There's a girl here in the quarter. Poor thing! She was married, but now she's divorced. And she has a little girl. You could take her there. I think she'd do the work well.

You know her?

Yes. I know her.

Tomorrow morning, incha'Allah, I'll come by here. You bring her here and I'll take her up with me.

The next morning I went to my mother's house and found the girl there. Look, I said to her. You'll come and work, and they'll pay you. But you won't touch anything. If you want something, you'll ask for it. Even if you find money somewhere, you pick it up and leave it on a table where the Nazarenes will find it.

Yes. I know, she said.

What's your name?

Khaddouj.

We went together up to the house on the mountain. Marcel opened the door and went upstairs. Khaddouj was waiting in the road. I took her into the kitchen and made the Nazarenes' coffee. Then I carried it upstairs to their bed.

The girl you wanted is downstairs in the kitchen.

Good, they said. When we come down we'll talk to her.

I went down and started to work in the carpenter shop. After an hour or so they came down. Buenos días, they were saying to Khaddouj. She spoke a little Spanish. I went into the kitchen. Listen to what they say, I told her. How much they're going to pay you and when you come and when you go home.

And I told Marcel: Talk to her. She understands.

They talked, and Khaddouj said: Good. Good.

And we worked together in the shop, the three of us, and Khaddouj cleaned the house and washed the clothes. The work went well and everybody was happy. We never found anything missing.

One day the two Nazarenes told me: We're going to a party today. You'll have lunch alone. Here's the money for Khaddouj.

Eat your lunch and go home.

They came back early, before I had left.

How was the party? I said.

It was wonderful! They were happy. Marcel gave me five hundred francs that day.

When I got to Mstakhoche I saw Farid standing outside the shack where the café was. I had five hundred francs in my pocket, and I invited him to go to the cinema with me.

Come into my mahal, I said, and have something to eat with me first.

Good.

I made him some eggs, and we went into the town to the cinema. Afterward we walked back up to Mstakhoche.

Why don't you stay with me tonight? I said. My house is your house. We're neighbors now.

Yes. We're neighbors, Farid said. Good night. Then he went home to bed.

CHAPTER FOURTEEN

FARID'S SISTERS

FARID's aunt lived in the mahal next to mine. There was only a wall between us.

And besides Seudiya, he had another sister named Aicha. She was two or three years younger than I was. The girl used to come to see her aunt. First I got to know Aicha, and then I knew the whole family.

One night we were sitting in the aunt's mahal, drinking tea and talking. Farid's mother was there, and his aunt, his brother Abdallah, Aicha, and another sister who was only a little girl. Seudiya was still living at Mustapha's house in Dradeb, working for him and his wife.

I turned to Farid's mother and said: Cherifa, is your daughter Aicha going to get married or not?

When Aicha heard this, she began to laugh.

Yes, said her mother. She's going to get married.

Who are you going to marry her to? I asked her.

She did not answer.

I went on talking. If you like, I'll marry her, I said.

Everybody was laughing.

Yes, said her mother. If you like her, I'll give her to you.

179

Good, I said.

We talked a while. Then Abdallah said: I'm tired. I'm going home to bed.

Yes, I said. So am I.

We said good night, and I went into my mahal. While I was getting undressed, I heard Farid's aunt talking. She was saying to Farid's mother: Why not? If he wants to marry her? Why not let him have her? You won't find a better young man for her.

Farid's mother said: We'll see. We don't know yet how things are.

I could not hear any more. I got into bed and fell asleep.

One day Farid and I went to the city together. I bought a lot of food. When we were on our way back from the market I said to him: Look. If you want to come and bring your family to my mahal tonight for supper, you're invited.

Do you mean that?

Yes. You're all invited. I'll make the food and take it next door to your aunt's, and we'll eat there. Tell your brother and your mother and the others.

The Cherif Bou Ralem always stayed in the country with his cows until late at night.

Ouakha. I'll go home and tell them. I'll be right back.

We got to Mstakhoche. I went into my mahal and began to work on the food. A little later Farid came. I made tea and we sat talking while the food cooked. When it was all ready I said: Go and get the others. I'll knock on the wall and tell your aunt to open the door.

Tan! Tan!

What is it?

It's me. Get ready. They're coming.

I'm ready, she said. They can come any time.

Farid came back. Take the dishes, I told him. I'll carry the tray.

They all came in. The mother, Abdallah, Aicha, her sister, and a little boy who lived in the quarter. We were saying: How are you, and how are you? There were eight of us.

While we were eating we talked. Farid's mother said: Think of it! I have two daughters, and they're both working. And I have two sons and neither one of them works.

Some day Allah will give your sons work, too, I told her. There's no hurry. Then I said to Farid: How is it? Are we going to be brothers-in-law?

He laughed.

What are you laughing at? It's nothing shameful. People get

married every day. Moslems and Nazarenes. There's nothing to laugh at. It's not a sin to get married.

I don't understand anything about all that, he said. My mother's here. Speak to her. Or speak to my father.

We're just talking, I told him. We haven't got any further than that.

It's none of my business, Farid said.

I turned to Abdallah. And you, Abdallah? What do you say?

It's for you and her to talk, he said. If she wants to and you want to, why not?

You hear, Farid? I said.

No. I don't hear anything. You have to talk to my father, he told me.

We finished eating. The water was boiling. Farid's aunt made the tea and we drank it. Then I said: I'm sleepy. I've got to go to bed. Allah ihennikoum. We'll talk again about this some other time.

A few days later I was at my mother's house, talking with her. You know, mother, I said. I've got something to tell you. I'm going to get married.

What! Who is it?

A girl in Mstakhoche.

Whose daughter?

The Cherif Bou Ralem. The man who goes sometimes with your husband to the Souq el Fhem. It's his daughter.

Yes. He has daughters, she said.

Do you know them? Have you seen them?

Yes. I've seen them. I don't know them. But if you like one of them, it's for you to decide. All I want is for you to be happy.

Today and tomorrow I was going to the Cherif Bou Ralem's house. I would take food and money and give it to his wife. And Farid always came to my mahal for tea. We were all friends.

The two Nazarenes went to Portugal. They had been gone for two weeks. I was sleeping in their house while they were away, so that no one would break in at night.

It was Sunday, and I was waiting for them to come back. I had no money at all. I said to myself: Here it is Sunday, and they're not back yet. And I've got no money. I needed money to buy food with. And I wanted to give some to Aicha's mother.

I went to the house of another Nazarene who lived higher up on the mountain. He was a friend of Marcel's. I asked him if he would lend me two thousand francs until Marcel came back from Portugal. He handed them to me and said: Pay me when you can.

I thanked him. I went into the city and bought a lot of food in the market. I took it home and divided it in two. One part for me and one part for the Cherifa. I put the food into a basket and went to their house. All the men of the family and a lot of others from the houses around were there, digging a ditch.

I saw Farid. What are you doing? I asked him.

We're putting in a pipe to carry away the shit, he said.

Ah, good! Is there anybody in the house?

My mother's there. Knock on the door.

I rapped on the door, and the Cherifa came and opened it. How are you, Ahmed?

I handed her the basket of food. I've got to go.

Thank you. Thank you.

Good-bye, Farid, I said. May Allah help you with that work.

I went to the mahal. I thought: I'll go into the city again and watch a film. Then I'll go up to the mountain and see if the house is all right.

I changed my clothes and went into town. There in the Calle San Francisco I met a friend who lived in a mahal near mine in Mstakhoche. He was selling candy.

How are you? he said. Have some candy.

No. It makes my teeth hurt, I told him.

Come here and talk, at least, he said.

Why? Is there news? Has something happened?

Come here. Come closer. Take a piece of candy.

No, no. I can't.

We've got a wedding tonight in our quarter, he said.

A wedding? Whose?

Bou Ralem's daughter.

He knew I wanted to marry Aicha. I said: That's enough. It's not true. I know it's neither one of his girls. Which one's getting married?

I swear there's a wedding tonight at the Cherif Bou Ralem's house.

Which daughter?

The older one. Aicha is her name.

It's a lie!

You'll see. Tonight you'll see if it's a lie.

But I just came from their house. They didn't say anything about it. It's impossible. I saw them all and talked to them. They didn't even mention it.

I did not believe it. The man kept saying it was true. I said to myself: I won't go to the cinema. I'll go back to Mstakhoche and cook my dinner and sit in my mahal and wait and see.

When I got back to the mahal I found the door next to mine

open. Good afternoon, said Farid's aunt.

Good afternoon, I said.

Nobody came. I did not hear anything.

Nothing's going on.

I had my tea. When it got dark I thought: Now I'll make dinner and go up to the Nazarenes' house. It's late.

After I had eaten, Farid's aunt knocked on my door.

Good evening, Ahmed, she said. Don't you want to go to my sister's and sit with the other men for a while?

What's happening? Why are they sitting there?

Aicha's getting married tonight, she said.

What? I cried.

That's right. If you want to go and sit with the men, come with me now.

What men? Who are they? I asked her.

My brother's coming from the mountain, and there's the whole family and all the neighbors.

I haven't time to sit with them, I said. I have to go to work now.

Sit a little while. You can go later.

No. No. Thank you. I can't.

She went out. I sat a while smoking and drinking tea. A little later, someone knocked on the door.

Who is it?

It was Aicha's mother. How are you, Ahmed?

All right, thank you.

Here's a little food from the party.

Look, I said. You can see with your own eyes that I've just finished eating. I handed the food back.

It's shameful! she told me. You can't give me back my food when I'm standing here in your mahal.

All right, Cherifa. Leave it there.

She set the food on the floor.

Sit down, I told her.

No. I can't. My house is full of people.

People? What's going on in your house?

We're having a wedding.

Whose wedding?

My daughter Aicha's.

I thought we'd talked about that long ago, I said. I thought you said you were going to give her to me. I thought she was going to wait until I had a little money.

You had bad luck. That's all, she told me.

I was thinking: What people these are! They promised me I

183

could marry Aicha. It was all understood. But it's better this way, without her, if this is what they're like. I'm lucky to be outside that family.

The Cherifa went next door to see her sister. I walked around the quarter and sat for a while in the café there. Everybody was talking about the wedding. See how shameful they are, they were saying. They've done it again. Ahmed isn't the first. They promised her to the garbage collector, and then they wouldn't let them marry.

I went to the mountain, to the Nazarenes' house. When I got to the store on the corner at the bottom of the road, the Soussi said, Those Nazarenes have come back.

I climbed up to the house. They were standing there outside the door, waiting for me. I had the key.

Here he comes! said Marcel. The car was full of valises. I carried them in. Then I told Marcel: I have no money.

We're tired, he said. Tomorrow we'll talk about it.

I went back to Mstakhoche and slept.

A few weeks went by, and I stopped thinking so much about what the Bou Ralem family had done to me. But if I met any of them at the fountain they would not speak to me. Even Farid looked the other way. One day I met him in the street.

Listen, I said to him. Why won't anybody in your family talk to me? What's the matter?

Nothing. I've got nothing against you. I don't know about my family.

Ever since the wedding, none of them will speak to me. What is it? Your aunt lives next door to me. She won't even look at me. What's the matter with all of you? Your sister's married. She married somebody else, that's all. Why are you angry with me? It's all past.

After that we were friends again.

About the time Aicha married, her younger sister Seudiya stopped working for Mohammed, and came home to live. She was getting older.

One day Farid's mother said to me: Why were you so angry when Aicha got married? Look at Seudiya. She's prettier and younger. If you want her, we'll give her to you cheap.

Ouakha, Cherifa, I said. Seudiya's something I like too.

If you want her, you can have her.

I went to see my mother. You know, mother, Aicha's married.

Yes. I know all about it, she said.

But now her mother says I can have Seudiya, the younger one. That's the beautiful one.

That's the one, I said. You must go and see her. I like her.

Ouakha. I'll go up on Sunday.

I'll be there, waiting for you. Come to my mahal.

On Sunday morning my mother came.

Sit down, I told her.

No. I have a lot to do at home. I've come to Mstakhoche just to see the girl. After that I must go home.

We went to the Cherif Bou Ralem's house. My mother knocked and Farid's mother came to the door.

Good morning. Come in. Our house is yours.

Yes. I've come, said my mother. But I can't stay. I have to go soon.

She went in. I went back to the mahal.

After a while my mother knocked on the door.

How do you like her? I asked her.

She's prettier than the other, she said. Wait. I'll speak to your stepfather. He'll talk to the Cherif, and we'll see how much they want for her. Don't forget to come tomorrow and see me.

Good, I said.

The next day I went to see my mother again.

What happened? Did your husband speak to the Cherif?

That Cherif is crazy, she said.

Why?

You know how much they're asking for that girl?

No.

First they want fifty kilos of flour. Then they want a sheep and ten litres of oil. And twenty kilos of sugar. And you have to buy her a haik and wedding slippers with gold on them. And a pair of shoes for every one of the family. And her grandmother wants a pair, too.

That's very good, I said. With a few more pairs they could have a rugby team. Do people get married so their family can open a store?

I said that to your stepfather, she said.

This afternoon I'm going to Farid's house myself and talk to the Cherif Bou Ralem, I told her.

I climbed up to Mstakhoche. Abdallah was in the street.

Is your father home?

Yes.

I want to speak to him for a minute, I said.

Go and speak to him.

I went to the house and knocked on the door.

Ah, Ahmed! Come in.

How are you, Cherif?

185

Sit down. What is it?

I came to talk a little with you.

Yes. What about?

Are you going to give me Seudiya or not? I asked him. Are you going to make it easy or hard for me?

No. It won't be hard, he said. If it's written that you should have her, you'll get her.

I want her. But how much are you asking?

Let me see, said the Cherif. A sheep, a sack of flour. He went on telling me all the things I would have to buy. And you'll have to pay for the almeria to carry her in, and the rhaita players, and the drummers. And a pair of shoes for me. And a pair for Farid. And a pair for my wife. And a pair for my mother.

Yes? And if I haven't got the money to give you all those things? We can't get married?

That's the way it is, he told me. I'm just telling you the price. There's a man in Oued Bahrein who'll give it. If you can pay for her, you can have her. If you can't, he can. That's all I have to say.

Yes. Well. Good-bye, I said. I can't talk any more.

And I went away. I was thinking: I don't have to get married. It's not worthwhile trying to marry a girl who's going to cost that much. If I've got to beg in the street to be able to have a wife, I'd better stay single. Allah will send me someone some day.

CHAPTER FIFTEEN

OMAR

For three or four months everything went well in the Nazarenes' house. Every morning before the sun was up, I would go to the beach at Merkala to swim. After that I would climb up through the orchards to the house on the mountain. Khaddouj always waited in the road until I came. Then I would knock and they would let us in. We would work until afternoon, and I would go back to the beach or take a walk in the country. The Nazarenes were happy. Their work was going well and they were making money. They got more orders from other countries, and sent more things away.

One day Marcel said to me: Ahmed. Now you've learned how to do this work. We need another workman here to help us. Can you get one for us? You could show him how we do everything. We could get more work done each day.

Ouakha, I said. That boy we saw one day at the beach. He's

not working. If you want him to work for you, I'll ask him.

François said: Oh, yes! I remember him. Bring him to see us. How much are you going to pay him? I asked him.

The same as you, he said.

I'll bring him tomorrow.

That afternoon when I finished my work, I went to Farid's house and knocked on the door. His mother opened it.

Ah, Ahmed! How are you?

Is Farid there?

No. He's in the city.

When he comes back, tell him to come to my mahal.

What is it? Is anything the matter?

No. The Nazarenes I work for need another man. I thought maybe Farid could come and work with me there.

Good. Good. May Allah bless you!

I went to my mahal. A little later Farid knocked on the door. When he was inside he said: What is it?

Nothing. The Nazarenes want another man. They asked me if I knew anybody. I said: Farid. And they remembered you. They told me to take you up to their house. But you won't make much there. Three hundred francs a day. From nine to one. The same as the maid.

Ouakha.

That's all I wanted to tell you. I'm going to bed. If you want to stay here and sleep with me, stay. If you don't, go home.

Good night, he said.

Before I was up, I heard someone knocking on my door. I got up and saw Farid. I let him in and gave him breakfast. Then we walked out to the mountain. Khaddouj was waiting in front of the door. We all went in and sat in the kitchen. I took coffee up to the Nazarenes. They were playing records and reading books in their bed. After a while they came downstairs.

Ah, good morning, Farid, they were saying. And François kept looking at Farid, the same as he had done on the beach. The Nazarenes talked a while in French, and while they were talking François did not stop looking at Farid. Then he spoke to Farid in Spanish: What sort of work do you do? Are you married? Where do you live? We were all talking and laughing.

After a while we went to the carpenter shop. The Nazarenes told me: You show Farid how to do the same work you do. And I showed him that day. In a few days he understood how they wanted the work done.

One morning when we got to the house, Marcel told me: When you bring the coffee upstairs, I want to talk to you.

I made the coffee and carried it upstairs to their bed. Look, Ahmed, Marcel said. Now you understand the work here very well. We want to give you more money. If you like, we'll pay you five hundred francs a day now, and you can have breakfast here, too. Only you'll stay until four in the afternoon. Is that all right? And your friend Farid. We'll pay him four hundred francs a day. And he can have his breakfast and lunch with you here.

Good. I'll tell him.

I went downstairs. Do you know something? I said. Then I told him what Marcel had said.

When Marcel came downstairs, he had cut his trousers very short with the scissors. They were like a bathing suit.

Why did you do that to your trousers? I asked him.

I just thought of it.

Then I said to him: I've told Farid what you said, and he's happy.

Today and tomorrow we did our work, and each one was satisfied with the others. Farid came to work with me in the morning, and left with me in the afternoon. François could never talk to him alone.

When the Nazarenes had first come to Tanja, they had stayed at home nearly all the time. They would drink wine in the sala upstairs and play music on the guitar. Now they began to go to bars at night. They would get home very late. This was the time when they began to have bad habits.

One day François came to the carpenter shop. He said to me: This noon you and Farid are going to eat lunch alone. Marcel and I have been invited by a boy who lives in Hasnona.

Who is he? I said. Who has invited you? Where's he from?

He's a Tanjaoui. He works for the government or something. He's from a good family. Everyone knows his family.

Do you know him? I said. I was surprised. I did not think they had any Moslem friends.

Yes. We know him a little.

Do as you like, I told him. I don't know anything about it.

They said good-bye and drove away in the car. About three o'clock they came back.

Did you have a good lunch? I asked them.

Yes, yes.

What did you have to eat?

Ground meat and squash, said Marcel. Something like the food you gave us the other day.

Did it taste good? I said.

Yes. Very good.

I don't know, I thought. I wonder if it was really good.

I said to him: Every man has his own fate to follow.

After a while I forgot about the Moslem who had invited the Nazarenes to his house. We went on working and swimming. Then one morning when I was cutting wood in the carpenter shop, François came in.

Listen, Ahmed, he said. Wash your hands. We're going in to the market and buy some food. The Moslem who invited us to his house is coming to lunch today. We've got to make a good meal for him.

Is that right?

Yes. He's coming.

The Nazarenes dressed. I put a basket over my arm and we got into the car and drove down the mountain into the city. We bought a lot of food and took it back to the house. Then I began to cut the vegetables and cook the lunch. After a while the Nazarenes said: We're going now to Hasnona to get our friend.

Good. When you get back, lunch will be ready, I told them.

I stayed in the kitchen with Khaddouj, stirring the food in the pots and getting everything ready.

I called to Farid.

What is it?

We've got a guest today.

Who?

A Moslem.

Do they know him?

They say they do. I don't know.

Just get lunch ready for them, said Farid. Don't worry about them.

Soon the Nazarenes were blowing the horn of the car. They wanted me to open the door for them.

I went and opened it.

They said: Here's the friend who invited us to his house that day.

The boy was tall. He had dark skin. He came in with his hands in his pockets. He took out one hand, and I shook it. How are you?

His trousers were very tight over his legs. He had a white shirt, but the collar was almost black with dirt.

I said to Marcel: Lunch is ready. They sat down at the table in the dining room. I went out to the carpenter shop and called Farid. He came in. We all sat down together. And while we were eating, I was looking at the one the Nazarenes had invited.

I was thinking: It's impossible. That one invited them to his

189

house? The sandals he has on his feet aren't worth fifty francs. He invited them? Never!

And François was always touching him on the shoulder and saying: What a good friend he is, this Omar.

Yes. He's a very good friend, I said.

After we had eaten, I made coffee and took it into the dining room. We sat there drinking it. Then François said to me: Marcel and I are going to take Omar home. You and Farid can go on with your work. We'll be back.

They drove away in the car. Farid went into the carpenter shop to work. I carried out the dishes and spoons into the kitchen. After that I went and began to work with Farid.

What do you think of the one they invited? I asked him.

Do you know him?

I never saw him before. They told me he lived in Hasnona. They said he's from a good family.

Maybe it's true, he said.

I wonder.

We did not talk any more about it.

Today and tomorrow we worked. But the Nazarenes were not living the way they had been living before. In the beginning, when I would get there each morning, I would take them their coffee, and they would come downstairs and work in the carpenter shop until lunch time. And after I went home in the afternoon they would go on working until dinner time. But now, after they drank their coffee at breakfast time, they would go back to sleep. They would get up at noon and leave our money for us. Then they would go out, and we would not see them again until the next day. And sometimes they were shouting at each other for an hour or more.

One day when they had been arguing, Marcel came to me and said: Ahmed. I'm going to Portugal for two or three months. When I come back, if you can get a passport, maybe you can go with me there afterward. We can work there the same as here. François wants to stay here. I'll be back. Maybe you can get a passport.

Incha'Allah!

Marcel packed his clothes.

I was not happy to see him leaving. I knew that the work would not go on very much longer once he was not there.

The next morning we put all his valises into the car. Marcel was thanking Farid and me for the work we had done for him. We said good-bye. François drove him down to the port and he got on the boat for Spain.

Then François came back to the house. He took out his money and paid us. You can go home now, he said.

It's still early, I told him. It's not even noon.

That doesn't matter, he said.

Good.

Farid and I put on our jackets and went out. Adiós.

Adiós.

The next morning I went up to the house. Khaddouj was sitting outside the door.

Good morning. Have you knocked yet?

No. Not yet.

Let's wait until Farid gets here. Then we'll knock.

We sat there for a while, and then Farid came walking up the mountain. I got up.

Tan! Tan! Tan!

François came down and opened the door. He had nothing on but his shorts. We went in. He stayed in the kitchen while I began to make the coffee.

When you've got the coffee ready, just put the pot on the table in the sala upstairs, he told me. Don't bring it into the bed-room.

I made the coffee and took it up to the sala. Here's your coffee, I said.

How many glasses did you bring? One or two?

One.

Bring another glass.

I went down and got another. I took it up and put it with the first glass. Then I went downstairs into the kitchen. I heard François go and get the coffee and take it into the bedroom. There were voices talking.

It's none of my business, I thought. Let him manage it.

We worked for a while. Then François called to me. He was standing in the stairway.

Look, Ahmed, he said. There's a Moslem up here who wants to leave. Shut the doors so Farid and the maid won't see him.

Who is it? I asked him.

The boy who invited us to his house in Hasnona, he said.

Ah! I thought. So that's who it is.

I said: Oh! We've already seen him. You don't have to hide him. What for? He can come down and talk to us. We're all the same. Everybody does what he pleases in life. No one will think anything about it.

I don't mean you, he said. I mean the others.

It doesn't matter.

François began to laugh. He was happy to hear what I was saying.

I went back to the carpenter shop. In a little while Omar came downstairs with his hands in his pockets, and his broken sandals on his feet.

Good morning, brother, I said.

Good morning.

Come over and sit down with us.

No. I have to go. I have some work to do, he said.

François came in with the keys of the car. Come on, he said to Omar. To Farid and me he said: You go on with your work.

Today and tomorrow we did our work. François never came any more to the carpenter shop except to sit for a minute and talk with us. He did not work any more at all. One day I said to him: What's the matter? You don't look happy the way you did before. Your face looks different.

He laughed. Maybe it's because I've shaved off my beard.

What is it? I said. Why are you thinking so much? If a man's going to do something, he does it. He doesn't sit and think about it. You're not working any more.

I'm a little nervous now, he said. It's nothing.

Another day he called to me. Look. Now we don't have much work to do. You'll have to tell Farid that we can't keep him any longer. Marcel's in Portugal and I'm here alone. The four of us are going to live here now. You and I and Khaddouj. And Omar. He's coming to live here with us.

You know best, I told him. You're the one who gives us the money.

Here, he said. Pay Farid and tell him he won't be working here any more.

He gave me four hundred francs. I went to the carpenter shop and handed the money to Farid. Wait for me, I told him, and I'll leave with you.

I told François: It's time for me to leave now. He gave me my five hundred francs. Farid and I went out.

In the road I said: Farid. You've got no more work with us now. But perhaps Allah will send you something better. Wait a while. Now Marcel's gone to Portugal, and this other one's coming to live here. So there isn't enough money. If he needs you again, I'll let you know.

Ouakha, said Farid.

The next morning I went up to the mountain. Khaddouj was not waiting in the road for me. I thought: I wonder what's happened. This is the first time she hasn't been here waiting.

I knocked on the door. It was Khaddouj who opened it.

Ah, Khaddouj! When did you come in?

A while ago, she said.

Who opened the door for you?

That boy. That Moslem.

I see.

When I got to the kitchen, they had already drunk their coffee. I thought: Ya latif! This house is going to fall to pieces fast!

I made coffee for myself. Then I went to the carpenter shop and began to work. About noon François came downstairs.

Ahmed. You don't have to work today any more. Nor Khaddouj either. I'm going to pay you and you can go home. My friend and I are going to Hajra den Nhal. It's in the country.

Good.

He paid us, and Khaddouj and I went out.

The next day I climbed up to the house. Khaddouj was waiting outside. When I knocked, François came to let us in.

Make two glasses of coffee and bring them up to the bed, he said.

I made the coffee and took it upstairs. They were lying in the bed. The sheet was over them.

Good morning, I said to Omar.

Good morning.

There was a table on each side of the bed. I put a glass on each table and went out.

At lunch time I said to François: What shall I get today for lunch?

Wait and I'll ask the boy what he wants, he said.

Ask him.

Omar was upstairs talking to Khaddouj. François called: Omar! Omar! What do you want for lunch?

Oh, anything.

No. You have to tell me.

Ah, said Omar. He came to the top of the stairs. Let's ha beefsteak, peas, eggs and tomatoes.

François gave me five thousand francs. Here. Bring what said he wanted.

I went and bought it all and took it back to the house. V I was cooking the food, François and Omar came into the kit

Cut the meat into small pieces and put it on skewer; François. You have to do it over a charcoal fire. Omar v that way.

I went and made some skewers first, because there v any in the house. I cut some wire into pieces and st through the meat. Then I made a fire. They stood watching me. When the food was ready, they went into the dining room and began to eat. I stayed in the kitchen broiling more meat for them.

After we had all eaten, François said: We're going out. If you want to go home, go on.

Good. He paid me, and I left.

I was walking through Dradeb. The yellow car came up behind me. They waved to me. Adiós! Then the road was full of dust.

I thought: That house! I don't know what's going to happen. Every day things get worse there. What it was like in the beginning, and what it's turned into! But I'm in it. There's nothing I can do. I'll stay, no matter what happens.

Each morning when I got to the house, Khaddouj was already inside. Omar let her in. They were always together.

One day I knocked on the door. Khaddouj opened it. Omar was standing in the kitchen. He was wearing pyjamas. And she was making coffee.

Good morning, I said.

I was looking at her and at him.

It's a fine day, isn't it? I said.

They laughed. When the coffee was ready, they began to drink it.

And for me? I said. No coffee?

You can make it yourself.

I made my own coffee. Then I went out and started to work. I was thinking about what was happening in the house. We always left the dishes on the sink shelf for Khaddouj to wash. She washed them as soon as she came in the morning. But now she began to leave them. Wherever she was in the house, Omar was always with her. She laughed and talked with him the whole day. When I would go into the kitchen to get lunch, I would find everything dirty. Each day I would say to her: Khaddouj. When you come in the morning, wash the dishes first. That's the first thing. Then if we need something, we'll find it clean.

But she would say: You're not the one in charge here. The Nazarene is.

Yes, I know, I said. It's the Nazarene's house. But he's always telling me everything is dirty, and then I have to wash the things myself. But do as you like. It's not my business.

And that was the way things were going.

After he had drunk all the coffee he wanted, Omar came out the carpenter shop and sat down. Well, my friend, he said. ow's the work going? Have you got any kif in your pocket?

No. I haven't. But if you want some, I can get it for you.

We talked for a few minutes. Then he called to the maid: Khaddouj!

What is it?

Come and sit down with us.

I'm busy.

Leave your work a while. Come on. What's work? It's like the wind. It's nothing.

She came out and sat down in a chair. I went on working.

Khaddouj. Are you going to get married? I said.

Who am I going to marry?

Omar.

Yes. I'd marry Omar, she said. If he wanted to.

I knew that each time François was out of the house, Omar would try to get Khaddouj to go into François's room and lie on the bed. All day long he followed her around the house, kissing her and touching her.

Of course Omar wants to marry you, I told her.

Omar laughed.

We heard François coming downstairs. Khaddouj jumped up.

Sit down, I told her. Don't be afraid.

No, no! she said. And she went to the kitchen.

François came in, and I told him: Omar has a girl friend now.

What girl friend are you talking about?

Khaddouj.

Ah! He laughed once. Then he sat down in the chair where she had been sitting. Omar put his legs up and rested them in François's lap, and François held on to them with both hands. He moved his chair nearer to Omar's chair, and then he put his arms around Omar's neck.

It's nice to sit that way, isn't it? I said to him.

Ah! he said. It's wonderful! Everybody likes to sit this way.

Every man has a body to do what he likes with, I told him.

One day François said to me: Omar and I are going to Hajra den Nhal. You'll have to sleep here in the house while we're gone. We'll be back on Tuesday.

Ouakha.

I thought: What are they doing, going again to Hajra den Nhal? There's nothing there but a few mud shacks.

Here's fifteen hundred francs.

They packed their things and drove away. On Tuesday they came back and blew the horn. I let them in.

They went into the dining room and began to talk. Every time I went through the room they stopped talking. Then they would begin again. I saw that they did not want me there. I said: Here's

195

the key. I'm going now.

Thank you, Ahmed, François said.

Nearly every day Omar wanted to eat in restaurants. Perhaps once a week I cooked lunch for them. Most days François would pay me and tell me to go home. But he did not give me any lunch, or any money for lunch.

One day François left me my wages and went out for lunch with Omar. I was making the meal in the kitchen. Khaddouj was ironing.

I said to her: Do you want to eat with me?

If I don't even eat with your master Sidek Omar, why should I eat with you? You only work for him.

Ayay! I said. How far up you've gone in the world! You're very fine now, aren't you? I paid for this food myself. I'd be crazy to give it to you. I swear I won't give you anything. When one o'clock comes, put on your haik and go home. You can eat your own food. I invite you to eat with me and you say all that!

Khaddouj put on her haik quickly and went out. She slammed the door very hard.

I made my lunch and ate it. Then I went back to the carpenter shop. About four o'clock I heard the car-horn blowing, and I went to open the door.

We went all the way to Hajra den Nhal for lunch! said François.

I looked at his face. I saw that his eyes had changed. Something had happened to them. They were half-shut, and he looked very happy. He looked more than that. He looked almost crazy. He and Omar came in and sat down in the dining room.

Ahmed, François said. This love I have for Omar is the greatest love I have ever had in my life.

Yes?

Por Dios! he said. Omar is the best man I've ever known.

That may be, I said.

Omar was laughing. Here, Ahmed, he told me. Take your money and go home. We'll see you tomorrow.

Good, I said.

I thought: People say it's better to have no life at all than a life full of holes. But then they say: Better an empty sack than no sack. I don't know. This is something new, a Moslem giving orders in a Nazarene's house. I don't know how it's going to come out, all this.

The next morning I got to the house and began to knock. I knocked until Khaddouj came to the door. I said: Good morning. She did not even look at me.

196

Listen. I said good morning to you once. I'm saying it again. Good morning.

She sniffed in her nose. But she did not say anything. What a stupid woman, I thought.

Good morning, I said to François.

Ahilan, brother, said Omar.

Is there anything new? I asked him.

No. Make us some coffee.

After everybody had drunk coffee I went to work in the shop. Omar came in. He had a cigarette in his mouth and his hands in his pockets. He began to walk back and forth in the carpenter shop, talking about how much money he had, and how much more he was going to make, and how many men he was going to have working for him.

At lunch time Khaddouj spoke to me. She said: Give me my money.

I always got the money from François and paid her when she left. But this day I said: I'm not in charge here. You said so yourself. Ask your master for your money.

She went to François and said: Please pay me. I'm finished for today.

Yes, said François. Omar will pay you. He's the one who has the money now.

Omar put his hand in his pocket.

How much does this woman get? he said. He knew as well as we did, but he liked to do it this way.

I said: You know how much. Two hundred francs. How long have you lived here? In all this time you still don't know how much she earns?

He gave her the money.

It's after one, I said. Aren't we going to eat today?

No. We're not eating here today, François said. We're going out.

Then give me some money so I can buy some food. I have no money left, I told him.

Go down to the store and see if they'll give you something. Tell them to put it on my bill.

You'll have to go with me, I said. The Soussi's not going to give me anything if I go alone.

All right. We'll take you in the car as far as the Soussi's.

We drove down to the store. Listen, I said to the owner. This Nazarene says he wants some food, and he'll pay you later.

Yes.

I took some eggs and bread and a can of peas. I was working in the shop at four o'clock when they came back. I said to François: I'm ready to go.

François said: Omar. Pay him, please.

Omar put his hand into his pocket and pulled out a great pile of bills. How much do we owe you? he asked me.

I thought: Ah, the baby's really spoiled now. He's got forty or fifty thousand francs there.

You know I get five hundred francs a day, don't you? I said to him.

He had plenty of change, but he took out a ten thousand franc note and handed it to me.

Give me change, he said.

I haven't any. If I had nine thousand five hundred francs in my pocket, I wouldn't be working here. I've been in this house a long time. You've been here only two months, and you've already got all the money in the house.

Are you surprised? What did you think I was going to do?

François was there, but he did not understand what we were saying.

Spend your money in good health, I told Omar.

Then François gave me five hundred francs, and I went out. I was thinking: That house! It's getting worse every day and it's going to go on getting worse. The kitchen used to be full of vegetables and fruit, and it was clean. Everybody used to work. Now there's nothing. Khaddouj doesn't work. François never comes into the carpenter shop.

Time went by. Whenever I spoke to Khaddouj about the dirt, Omar stopped me. Leave her alone! he would say.

One day I said to François: Look at this house! You see how filthy everything is? The girl does nothing. We can find another who'll work the way she should.

I don't know, he said. Omar will know what to do. I'll ask him.

I see.

I did not speak to Khaddouj any more about her work. Every day she did less and less. She would come in the morning and make coffee. After that she would sit talking to Omar until it was time for her to go home. He always had his hands on her, and often I saw him kissing her. Sometimes they were alone in the house. Omar said they used the bed in François's room.

I would sit working in the carpenter shop, and I would think: Nothing's ever going to be right again here. But I'll stay and see how it all ends.

When we looked for something, we often could not find it. Everything was disappearing from the house. François did not care. Even his watch was gone, and his clothes, and a blanket from his bed. He only said: It doesn't matter.

One morning when I got to the house, there was a big pile of cloth in one room. Marcel had sent it from Portugal to put on the chairs they sold. I saw Khaddouj holding up a piece that was about eight meters long. Later I went into the room. I looked for that piece and saw that it was not there.

It was here, I thought. And now it's not. I'm going to see where it is.

I went into the kitchen and looked in the corner under Khaddouj's haik. The piece of cloth was there.

I'll leave it there. I won't say anything to her.

I waited until one o'clock. Then she said: All right. Now I'm going.

Wait, I said. Don't go yet. You've got to bring down the dirty clothes so they can be washed tomorrow.

She went upstairs. I called to Omar. Come here. I want to show you something.

What is it?

I said: You know whose haik this is?

Yes. It's Khaddouj's.

I opened it up. The cloth was still there.

You see? She's taking it with her.

No, no, he said. She wouldn't do that.

Watch and see, I told him.

We left it the way it was, and I went back to the carpenter shop to work.

Khaddouj came back downstairs with the clothes and left them in the other room. She put on her haik. Then she went to Omar and said: Pay me. I'm going.

She said good-bye to me and went out of the house.

She's gone, I said. And she's taken it with her.

I went to François and told him: That girl we have here is stealing. If you don't believe it, I'll call her so you can see with your own eyes.

Is that true? he said.

You'll see if it's true or not.

I went out the kitchen door into the garden. Then I opened the lower gate. She was going down the road. I called to her.

Khaddouj! Khaddouj!

What is it?

The Nazarene wants to speak to you.

What for?

Just come. He wants to say something to you.

199

She came back. François and Omar were sitting in the carpenter shop. I said to her: Take off your haik.

Why should I? She was sweating. Her face had turned yellow. Take it off. That's all.

She took off her haik, and there was the cloth underneath. We unwound it from around her body.

Look! I said. This is the one who's been taking everything out of the house.

No, no! I never took anything until today, she was saying.

It doesn't matter, said François. Perhaps she needed it.

Why didn't she ask for it, then?

Let her have it, he said.

I told him: Whatever happens in this house now, it won't be my fault. If you miss something, don't come and ask me where it is.

Khaddouj put her haik on. She said to me: What did you get out of it? You're just a chkam. An informer!

Then she went home with the cloth. After that she stole things every day. I never said anything again. It did not matter to me any more what she did. The house got dirtier and dirtier, and there was less and less in it. François would ask me where something was, and I would say: Why do you ask me? I told you long ago what to do about it.

He would come and say: Why are all my clothes still dirty? And I would tell him: I don't wash the clothes. I work in the carpenter shop.

After that, François and Omar began to take Khaddouj out for rides in the car. They would go and spend the day together on the beach at Achaqal. François knew that Omar liked her and had slept with her.

One day he said to me: Look, Ahmed. I haven't got much money. I can't afford to pay for two men and keep you and a maid too. You'll have to stop working in the carpenter shop and do the work in the house. And you'll have to tell Khaddouj that she won't be working for us any more.

Ouakha. I'll wash the clothes and clean the house. But I won't tell Khaddouj. You have to do that.

All right.

Later Omar called her. Khaddouj!

What?

The Nazarene says he can't pay you any longer. So you won't be working here any more. If we have work again, we'll tell you.

He handed her a thousand francs and she went out. At the door she said to me: Now you're happy, aren't you?

Yes. Very happy, I told her. May Allah keep you out of this house forever! But it's not your fault. It's my fault for bringing you here in the beginning.

Afterward she told everyone that I had made her lose her work.

CHAPTER SIXTEEN

THE MASTER OF THE HOUSE

THE three of us went on staying in the house. François, Omar and I. Sometimes Omar paid me my wages. Some weeks I had to follow him wherever he went before I could get my money.

I went to François once. This isn't what we said it would be when I first came to work here. I'm not getting paid for my work. I'm supposed to get lunch here every day. There's never any food. And there's no money to buy any, because Omar won't give it to me. And I don't earn enough money to save it from one day to another and pay for my food the next day. I'm not eating. You've got to pay me every day.

Omar pays you every day.

When I ask him he puts his hand into his pocket and pulls out a bundle of money. Then he says he has no change. I've got to know. Who am I working for? You or Omar?

You're working for both of us.

But who's the head of the house?

Omar, he said.

I see. Good. Now I understand everything. You're not the master. It's Omar who's the master. Whatever Omar tells me is what I should do. Is that it?

Yes. That's right.

One day François got some money in the mail. Tomorrow's Sunday, he told me. Omar and I are going to Hajra den Nhal to see his family.

His family lives there?

Yes.

I see.

I was thinking: So that's why they always go to Hajra den Nhal! But if his family lives in that place, they haven't even enough to eat!

We'll pay you for today and tomorrow, and shut the house up and take the key with us. You'll come back on Monday.

On Monday I went up the mountain and knocked. Daf, daf,

daf, daf, daf! They opened the door. There was a high pile of dirty clothes to wash. I put them all into the laundry tub and started to wash them. The underwear was filthy. I did not touch it.

Omar came into the laundry. I said to him: I'm a Moslem and you're a Moslem. I used to work here and earn my living and eat my lunch every day. Now I'm not getting what I should be getting. Neither the money nor the food. What you're doing to me is shameful! Why are you doing it?

What do you expect me to do? What do you want?

You've got all the money there is. When the Nazarene wants a pack of cigarettes he has to ask you, and you buy them for him. I'd still know you were here, even if you weren't quite so bad. Just let us live the way we lived before. What you do with the Nazarene's money doesn't matter to me. But I've got to eat and live the way I was doing before. I can't live like this. The rest of it's not my business.

Don't come to me about anything, Omar told me. Talk to the Nazarene you're working for.

Yes, I said. You're right.

Every time any money came for François, Omar took all of it. We would live for a few days. Then Omar would say: There's no more money.

Later François would come to me and say: Look. We have no money. Now you go home and stay there for a few days. Then when we have money, you can come back again.

But how will I eat?

You'll eat somehow.

I would go to Mstakhoche and sit there eating bread, and one day they would come in the car and take me back to the mountain. Then there would be a lot of work to do, because everything was very dirty.

One day at lunch time François said to me: Today we're going to eat at home, in the house.

Ah! Gracias a Dios! I said. It's a long time since we've eaten here.

I went out and bought the food. On the way back up the road I stopped at the café and bought a packet of kif.

I cooked the food, and we ate our lunch in the dining room. Afterward I made coffee and brought in three glasses. I took a cigarette with a filter in it and emptied the tobacco out of it. Then I filled it with kif. I lighted it and began to smoke.

Soon Omar said: You're smoking kif?

Yes. Do you want a little?

Good. Give me a cigarette.

I filled another cigarette and gave it to him.

François said: What are you smoking? Kif?

Yes.

Give me some. I'll smoke with you. It always makes me feel better.

Omar gave François his cigarette. François smoked a little and gave it back to him. I made some more cigarettes and gave them to Omar.

Neither François nor Omar was used to smoking kif. They drank cognac and whiskey instead. After a few minutes, Omar's head was full of kif.

He said: Brother, this kif is good!

You see? I told him. You see how strong it is?

François put his head in Omar's lap and stayed that way.

Look, brother, I said to Omar. Tell me the truth. By your father, you've got to tell me what you gave this Nazarene to eat. How did you make him this way? What did you give him that time when you went to Hajra den Nhal? Tell me the truth.

I gave him a donkey's tongue, he said.

Are you telling the truth?

I swear!

Where did you get the donkey?

There was a dead donkey outside the village in a field. We cut off its tongue and its ears.

What did you mix it with? What sort of food did you put with it?

We just put it with the other meat, he said.

Do you know how to do that? I asked him.

What do you think? You think I don't know how?

You did a fine piece of work there, I told him. You changed him into another man. It's wonderful, what you did!

What are you talking about? said François. I want to hear.

We're just talking about the world, I said. It's nothing.

Their heads were full of kif and they began to hug each other. Then Omar said: Ahmed. I'll pay you and you can go home.

Ouakha. He gave me my money and I went home. As I walked along the road I was thinking: I never knew you could give a man a donkey's tongue and change him that way. It's probably true. His mother must have known how to do it, and she put tseuheur in with the tongue. It's lucky he's still alive. I thought of the time I was hanging by my feet in the hospital.

Another day François went to the post office and found a letter from Marcel.

Marcel's coming back. He's on his way from Portugal now, he said. I hope he gets here soon. I've got to pay the bill at the Soussi's. And now they've cut off the water. I have a lot of bills to pay. The food bill is very big.

Why don't you keep your own money? I said. Then you could pay all your bills yourself. Now you spend more money than you make. How are you going to pay any bills that way?

Each one does what he wants in life, he said. That was what he always said when I talked to him. It always made me angry.

Yes. Do as you like, I said. Then I said the same thing in Arabic. Amel li brhiti. That was all there was to say.

A few days later he told me: Today I'm going to the port to get Marcel.

When Marcel knocked on the door I was very glad to see him. How are you?

Ah, Ahmed! And you? How are you? How's the work? Have you learned anything new?

Yes. A little, I told him.

Marcel opened his valises and took out four shirts someone had given him. They were not new, but they were not yet torn.

I brought you these from Spain.

Thank you. Thank you very much.

I put the shirts in another room and went on working. When it was time for me to leave, I went to François and said: May I have my money? It's five days you owe me now.

I can't pay you today, he said. I can give you five hundred francs, if you like. And that's all.

Marcel gave you a lot of money.

Yes. But I have a lot of bills to pay. I'll pay you in a few days.

All right. Give me the five hundred francs.

Marcel came into the room. François, he said. I'm going to sleep at the hotel. You've got your friend here.

That's a good idea, said François.

A few days later Marcel said to me: Let's go into the town and buy a lot of food in the market, and make a meal the way we used to.

Yes, I said. Whatever you like.

François got the car keys. I took a basket. Omar did not want to go. The three of us went into the city and bought food. François and Marcel talked a lot and laughed together. I did not know what they were saying. We bought everything and went back to the house.

You make the food, Ahmed, Marcel said.

I stayed in the kitchen cooking the food. When it was all done,

I called to them. If you want lunch, it's ready.

While we were eating, Marcel said to me: François has found a good wife now. You're supposed to give a wife nice clothes and good food. And then you take her out and show her to other people. He has a fine wife. And she's happy to be with her husband.

We were laughing. Omar was trying to laugh the same as the rest of us. But he could not laugh.

Marcel went to Mrrakch. François took him down to the station in the car. When he got back to the house, I said to him: Now Marcel has left you money. You can pay me my wages. It's still twenty-five hundred francs you owe me.

I'll ask Omar if we're going to the bank today, he said.

When he asked him, Omar said: No. We can't go today. We'll go tomorrow.

Tomorrow, I said. That's because you have enough to eat today. If you're not going to pay me, I'll go now and try and find something to eat somewhere. But tomorrow you'll surely pay me?

Yes, yes, said François. We'll cash a check and pay you.

The next day when I got to the house I did not feel well. I had had no dinner the night before. And no breakfast that morning. Omar came to the door. The first thing he said was: Make me some coffee fast.

You can make coffee, I said. Make it with your own hands. Or don't you even know how to do that?

Ayay! he said. You're feeling good this morning, aren't you?

I'm the same as always, I told him.

He ran upstairs to François and said: I told Ahmed to make the coffee and he wouldn't do it. He told me to make it myself.

François came down. Why don't you want to make our coffee?

Who is Omar? Why should I make coffee for him?

Who am I? said Omar. I'm your master. I pay you your wages. I keep you alive. You work for me.

You keep me alive? To me you're worth one piece of shit! Then I said it in Spanish to François: Para mí este hombre vale una mierda, nada más!

No, no! No, no! Don't talk that way to him! François was almost crying. I don't want to hear another word. I can't stand any more! If you don't know how to talk, Ahmed, you can leave the house. That's all!

Pay me and I'll go now, I told him. Why should I work for you?

I'll pay you now, he said. And he took out two thousand five hundred francs and gave them to me.

Thank you, I said. Now I'm going.

I went out and walked down the road. Then I heard someone running behind me. Ahmed! Ahmed!

It was François. I stopped walking, and he caught up with me. Come tomorrow morning, he told me.

If you want me to come, I'll come.

I went back to Mstakhoche.

The next day when I got to the house, Omar opened the door for me. I said good morning to him, but he would not answer. It doesn't matter, I thought. His good morning doesn't mean anything anyway.

I went into the kitchen to make the coffee, but there was no coffee. I asked François for money to go and buy some. He said: Ask Omar.

I went to Omar.

I have no money for coffee, he told me.

As you like, I said. I had coffee at home before I came. Then I began to wash the dishes. After a while François came downstairs.

Isn't the coffee ready yet?

I told you there wasn't any in the house. Did you give me any money to buy it with?

And I told you Omar would give it to you.

It's nearly an hour since I asked him, I said. But he hasn't given it to me yet.

All right. All right, he said. Then he went to Omar and told him: Come on. Let's go to the city and have coffee somewhere on the Boulevard.

Then I knew they had done it this way so I would not drink coffee at their house any more. It did not matter to me.

When Marcel came back from Mrrakch he stayed only a week or so, and then he went to Paris. After that there was almost no work for me. François would send me home for a week at a time because he did not want to have to pay me. When I went back to work, it would be for only a half-day, and then I would have to wait again. Each month there was less work, and I earned less money. I stayed in Mstakhoche and waited.

What can I do? I thought. There's no remedy for this. What's written has to be gone through to the end. If you give a man a donkey's tongue and maybe its ears too, how is he going to have any head left for his work or anything else? Nothing's going to matter to him. His mouth will be open and his eyes half-shut, that's all.

One day François said to me: I'm going to England for a while.

Everything will be in charge of Omar. You'll stay and work for him in the house. You'll get half a day's wages every day. Three hundred francs.

That's not very much, I said. But it's all right if I really get it. Who's going to pay me?

A Hindu who lives in Vasco da Gama. He can read and write. He'll keep the accounts and pay you every day. You'll have to go to his house to get the money.

François was busy getting ready to leave for England. Those days Omar did not leave him by himself for a minute. He followed him everywhere, all over the house, talking to him. He did not want him to go.

To me Omar said: I swear by Allah he won't get out of here!

To François he said: Now you're going to leave me all alone.

Don't worry, Omar. You'll never need anything. You'll have whatever you want. And so will Ahmed. And I'll come back with a lot of money.

One night François came in the car to Mstakhoche and blew the horn outside my mahal.

I went out and said: Buenas noches. Come in.

Yes, he said. I just want to talk a little with you.

We went inside.

Now we can talk if you want, I told him. What is it?

I'm going away. Soon, he said. And now you're going to be working for Omar. But you'll have time to look for some other work, too. You know how to get on in the world by yourself.

And Omar? I said.

I'm leaving money here. He can get fifty thousand francs at the bank every month. He needs much more than you do. You're used to living without money. You can always keep alive.

Maybe. We'll see, I told him.

I have to go now. But will you give me your word that you'll work every day for Omar?

Yes.

And you won't quarrel with him?

No.

François went out and drove away.

The next morning Omar came into the kitchen. I was scrubbing the floor. He looked very worried. I knew it was because he did not want François to go.

And now he's going, he said.

Can't you stop him? Isn't the donkey's tongue working any longer?

Omar cried: He won't get out of my hands! I'll keep him here.

I swear he won't leave this country!

But you're not even sleeping with him now, I said. You give him a donkey's tongue and then you won't go to bed with him. One day he's going to find somebody else.

You watch, he said. He'll stay.

A few days later he came to me. Listen, he said. I'm going to get married. I've found a girl and I'm going to marry her. But now I need a lot of things for the wedding.

Why don't you speak to François? He'll get them for you.

You think he will?

They were talking together all the time, every day. I would hear Omar telling François: I need everything for my wife. I need a house and furniture, and all sorts of things. How am I going to get it all with the little money you're leaving me? Marriage is the most important thing in a man's life.

François would say: Even if you get married, you'll still always come to sleep with me?

Yes, yes, said Omar.

One day when they were talking this way, François said: I'll tell you what we'll do. I have two hundred thousand francs. I was going to use it to go to England. I'll give that to you. And then you'll have enough.

Good, said Omar. Now we'll go and look for a house, and I'll show you the girl I'm going to marry.

Yes, said François. But I'm still afraid. If you marry that girl you won't come any more to my house.

No, no. I'll come the same as always. I give you my word.

They went and looked for a house for Omar, and they found a good one.

You can live here, said François. This house is right for you. And everything that's in my house I'll give to you. And whatever you need, I'll buy it for you. That way you'll have everything you want.

Good.

One day François told me: Ahmed. We're going to empty everything out of the house and take it to another house.

What house? I said.

Omar's. You know he's going to get married. And I'm going to stay here in Tanja.

I see.

We began to carry all the furniture from the house on the mountain up to the Marshan, where Omar was going to live. I saw François taking all the wood and the machines and tools from the carpenter shop.

Why are you taking those things? Does he want them, too?

Yes. He's got two houses. One's going to be a carpenter shop. That way he can make a little money.

Ah, I said.

We kept filling the car at one house and emptying it at the other, until there was nothing left in the house on the mountain. Then we went to Souani to have a lot of mattresses made for Omar.

Another day François and Omar went and bought trays and rugs and pots and many other things that had to be in Omar's house. When everything was ready in his new house, Omar said: Now I'm going to have the wedding.

The night of the wedding François took Omar to a bar and they got drunk. Then they went to another bar, and then to more bars. After that they went to the Café Hafa and sat in the garden. Omar's friends were already at the house. Omar was telling François: I'm going to keep giving it to her all night. And François was crying.

Then Omar told him: You've got to take me to my house. I've got to get married now. They were both very drunk. François took him in the car to the house on the Marshan and left him. Then he went to his hotel.

Two or three weeks went by. I was working at Omar's house every day until one o'clock. I did not see his wife. Sometimes Omar was not up by one, and then François paid me. It was better than it had been, because I got paid every day.

One day when François came to see Omar, he told me: I'm going to look for a house near this one, where I can live. Then I'll be near Omar, and he can always come and see me.

Do as you like, I said. You know more than I do.

If you hear of an empty house in this quarter, let me know. If I find one, you can work for me, too.

Ouakha. And I began trying to find a house for him. There were many houses, but they all cost more than François wanted to pay. He wanted a very cheap house.

One day he came in his car to my mahal in Mstakhoche.

I've rented a house in Mtafi, near Omar's house. Let's go and buy some whitewash and paint. Then you can put it on the walls and doors for me. First let's go to the house, and I'll show it to you.

We drove to Mtafi.

Is this the house you've rented? I said. How are you going to live in a house without any water, or any bathroom to wash in?

I like it that way. You can bring water from the fountain every morning.

Yes. But you don't know how to live in a Moslem house. You're a Nazarene. You've always had water. The rooms are so small you can't sit in them.

I have no money, and this house is cheap.

Your family is always sending you money, I told him. But you never have any.

He never liked to hear this when I said it to him.

This house won't do for you, I said. It's a house for poor Moslems.

It's all right until I can get a better one.

We began to go every day to the Joteya, to buy second-hand things for his house. He would buy things that were so old he could not use them. He bought old lamps, and six broken crates to sit on. And he bought some old curtains that were torn. He had many pictures that he had painted, and he hung them on the walls.

That's all I need, he said. The house is full.

But you've got no bed to sleep in.

I'm going to the second-hand market and buy a mattress stuffed with straw. That will be enough for me.

You had a wonderful bed in the other house. And now Omar's got it, and you're going to sleep on straw.

That's what I like. It will be better, he said. I sleep better on the floor.

Ouakha. We went and bought an old straw mattress. When we got it back to the house I dropped it on the floor.

Soon you'll be a Moslem, I told him. You'll be sleeping on a mat the way I used to in the café.

Each man lives his life the way he wants to, he said.

He moved into his new house, and I stopped working at Omar's. I went to François's house and worked each morning, until one o'clock.

One day Omar and I were sitting upstairs in François's house, smoking. We heard a car drive up. I went down and opened the door. François had a very dark Moslem with him. I had known him when I was a boy and we lived in Emsallah. We had played in the street together. But I had never seen him since.

Salaam aleikoum, he said.

Ah, brother, how are you? I said. How have you been, Mseud?

Go upstairs, François said to him.

We all went up.

This is Omar, my friend. And this is Ahmed. He works for me.

210

When I went downstairs, François came down with me, and began to talk.

This boy is going to do a little work for me here in the house, he told me.

I see. Do you like him?

Yes. Very much.

Good.

Now you go to the bacal and buy food, and we'll have lunch.

Allah! What a day! I said. It's a long time since we've eaten together. We've never had a meal in this house.

Yes, it is a long time, he said. But now we're going to.

After lunch François took Mseud out in the car to the beach. I sat down again and said to Omar: What do you think of that one who was here?

Nothing, he said. It doesn't matter to me who he brings here. I've got money now, and I've still got the Nazarene. I told you he wouldn't get away.

Why did he bring him? I said. You told him you were going to go on sleeping with him. I don't believe you're sleeping with him any more. And that's why he's got that one with him.

I'm going to leave my wife at home in bed and come down here and sleep with him?

Do as you like, I said. But Mseud's going to put you out of here some day. Wait. You'll be in the street.

That one's going to put me out? What do you mean? You know I own half of everything the Nazarene has. Whenever he gets any money, I'll always get half of it. You know that!

I know he did you a big favor. You didn't even have enough to eat for one night. You got more money from him than you've ever seen in your life. He paid for you to get married, and got you a good house. And you still say you have half his money?

He's done nothing for me, said Omar. Everything I got from him I got in spite of him. He never gave me anything because he wanted to. I got everything by myself. I worked hard to make him give it to me.

Yes. You're right, I said. Moslems never think anyone has been good to them. You're not the only one who thinks the way you think.

And you? he said.

I think he's always been good to me. He's done many things for me. And I'll never forget all those things. I thank him for what he's done for me. The two of them came here, and they were good people. You're the one who ruined the house and separated them. You're the one who brought François here to live in this

211

house that hasn't even water. But wait. Watch that one who came today. See what he's going to do to you. You'll see it with your own eyes, what's going to happen.

I went on working there in the house with François. Some days Omar came for a while. François brought Mseud to the house whether Omar was there or not. And he took him in the car to the beach, and to all the bars and the cinemas, and left Omar sitting there in the house. Each week he spent more time with Mseud.

Then Mseud began to come and stay all night with François. Every two or three nights he would come and sleep on the mattress with him. One morning the car stopped in front of the house. François and Mseud got out. Mseud had all his things with him.

What's happening? I said. Is that one going to live here?

Yes. He's going to live with me the same as Omar used to.

Good. You like him that much?

Yes. I like dark boys.

Sometimes Mseud and François talked together like friends, and sometimes they argued. But they were always together.

I said to Omar: You see? What did I tell you? By Allah, that black one is going to put you out of here yet. You've got no more bread in this house. That was long ago, the time when you were in charge. Not any more!

CHAPTER SEVENTEEN

MSEUD

Now Mseud lived in the house. He and Omar were not friendly. Sometimes they got angry and shouted at each other. When that happened, Omar would not come back to the house until François went to get him

Then François would say something to Omar, and Omar would shout at him.

One day François and Omar were having a long argument. When they had finished, I said to Omar: What's the matter? What's it all about? Why are you always fighting?

He wants me to sleep with him. He won't give me any money unless I do.

If you don't want to sleep with him, it's simple. Don't come any more to the house, I told him. Mseud sleeps with him every night, anyway. What good are you to him? He's right. Sleep with him, or go and look for your living somewhere else. Nobody tells you to come here.

Half of everything he owns is mine. He's not going to get away from me, said Omar.

Yes, I said. Half of everything's yours. Yes. I remember a day in the house on the mountain. François told me that you were the master of the house. But that was a long time ago. You've got nothing left here now.

Today and tomorrow, Omar kept coming to the house, but François never spoke to him. He spoke only to Mseud and to me. He would say: Mseud. What are we going to have for dinner tonight? And Mseud would tell him all the things he wanted to eat.

I always paid for my own food now, because François did not give me anything. Once in two or three months he would invite me to have something to eat.

One morning I went next door to the store and bought some tea, sugar and bread. I took it back to his house and had my breakfast. When François got up, he sent me back to the store to get food for him.

The Soussi said: Yesterday the black one told me not to give anybody any more food unless they paid for it. Only the Nazarene and the black one.

Why? I said. It was shameful that he did not trust me. Who gives the orders, the Nazarene or the azzi?

I can't give you anything.

I went back to the house. Mseud was asleep on the mattress. He was naked. I woke him up.

Listen. Did you tell the bacal not to give anybody any more food?

Yes, he said. The Nazarene said we were losing too much money.

If he's losing money, it's not on me that he's losing it. I went to get the breakfast for you and him, not for me.

François came in. What is it? What are you talking about? I've got to know.

Nothing. Mseud can say it.

Mseud said: Didn't you tell me to ask the bacal not to give anybody any more food?

Yes. I did.

I said to François: Then why did you send me out just now? You knew he wouldn't give me anything. Send Mseud. He's the only one who can get something.

I was only thinking of Omar, said François. He's been getting

213

all his food there without telling me. Now I have a lot of money to pay.

Then he said to Mseud: Tell the bacal to give Ahmed things the same as always. Go with Ahmed now.

I went out to the store. Mseud was behind me. He said over my shoulder to the Soussi: The Nazarene says to give Ahmed our breakfast. I got the food and took it back to the house.

You see? I said to Mseud in the kitchen. I got the food in spite of you. I know one thing. If you're working in a house that has other Moslems in it, you'll never have any peace. Only trouble.

Don't go on talking, Mseud said. I'm not listening.

A little later Omar knocked on the door downstairs. I went down. Good morning. You slept late, I said.

Why should I come early? he said. There's nothing to do here.

You remember what I told you a long time ago? You can fly high in the air for a while. But afterward you come down. This is what happens when Allah gives a loaf of bread to a man who doesn't know how to eat it.

Don't worry about me, Omar said.

You'll see everything in a little while, I told him.

Isn't there any coffee?

Yes.

Make some, he told me.

Omar went upstairs. I made two glasses of coffee for me and Omar. I took them upstairs and sat down with the others. We were talking. We talked about women and men and other things. Then François said: You know what we're going to do?

What's that? I said.

We're going to find out who has the longest one. You or Omar or Mseud.

Yes? How are you going to find out? Are we all going to take off our pants right here?

No, no! You don't have to take anything off, he said. I know a way.

How?

Let me see your hand.

Here it is, I said.

He bent my middle finger across my hand. Then he did the same to Omar, and then to Mseud.

Mseud and Omar are the same, he told them.

They were laughing.

But which of the two do you like better? I asked him.

I like them both, said François. But Mseud is better than anybody else.

That's fine, I said. Go on having a good time. But I wonder where it's going to take you.

Each one does what he likes.

Yes. I know. You always say that. This isn't the first time. I've got to do my work now, or I won't get anything done today.

You can clean the house and do the dishes while Mseud and I go out for a ride. We'll be back at one o'clock.

Ouakha.

When they were on their way out, I said to Omar: Are you going with them?

I knew he was not going.

I'm going home, he said.

François and Mseud drove away, and Omar went out. I swept the house and scrubbed the floor. I put the sheets and blanket straight on the mattress. Then I went three times to the fountain and brought back three pailfuls of water to clean out the latrine. It was dark in there. There was only a hole in the floor, and the smell was very strong. In the mornings before I cleaned it, the smell filled the house. Sometimes I had to go up on the roof so I could breathe. It was like a street latrine. I could smell it outside the front door before I opened it. This was because they did not go into the room. They used the walls and the floor of the room next to it.

When I had finished all the work, I sat and waited for François to come back and pay me. At two o'clock I thought: He said he'd be here at one. I'll wait until three. At three o'clock he still had not come back. I'm going home, I said to myself. But tomorrow I'll talk to him.

I left the key at the bacal and went home. On the way I was thinking: What a house to work in! Every day it's worse than the day before. I can't live this way! But there's no other work. I've got to stand it until Allah sends me something else. The day has to come soon.

The next morning when I knocked, Mseud opened the door for me. I went upstairs and found François lying on the mattress. All he wore was a pair of silk underpants. They were the kind girls wear.

Buenos días. Mseud lay down beside François and went to sleep.

Make the coffee, said François.

When the coffee was ready, I took it upstairs and left it on the floor beside the mattress. Then I sat down on a crate.

I waited for you yesterday, I told François. You told me you'd be back at one o'clock. I waited until three and you didn't come.

Another time, if you're not coming to pay me, tell me before you go out, so I won't have to sit waiting for you.

I owe you for yesterday and today, he said. But tomorrow I'm going to have some money, and I'll pay you.

Ouakha.

We're going out. When you finish, go home.

Yes, I said. And please, when you come home at night, don't piss on the walls and the floor. Go inside the latrine and do it. I clean it every day. It's not hard to open the door and go in. When I come here in the morning, the house smells very bad, and you're sleeping in the middle of the smell. It's bad for you, not for me. I don't sleep here.

All right, Ahmed. All right.

The next time I find filth in the room outside the latrine, I'm going to leave it. I'm not going to clean it up. I'm tired of mopping up everything. Even the hall.

That's enough, said François. We're going out. When you finish, go home.

I had to get four pails of water to clean the latrine and the room next to it. When I went home I was angry. And the next day I was angrier.

Those people owe me two days' wages. When I go to their house they run out and leave me alone. They think I have money hidden away to eat with. And all I eat is bread.

I banged on the door. François came to open it. Buenos días.

Then I said to him: Have you got the money? I haven't one franc. I can't even buy a piece of bread.

Wait a little. I'm going out in a little while. I'll bring you back some money. You wait for me until one o'clock.

Mseud got up and dressed, and they went out in the car. And at one o'clock they were not there. I went on waiting until two. I was very hungry. He's not coming. He's doing the same thing again. I don't know where to go to find him. But I'm going to look for him.

I shut the house and went out into the street. Then I began to go into all the bars as I walked along. He was not in any of them. I kept looking in bars and cafés. In front of the park at Sidi Boukhari I saw the car going past. Mseud was driving it. François was not with him. I shouted, and he stopped.

Where's François?

In the Sevillana eating.

Where are you going?

I have to buy something for him, he said.

I went to the Sevillana. François was sitting there. The food

216

was on the table. A minute later Mseud came in. He put seven thousand francs down by François's plate.

I stood by the table. Have you got my money? I said.

No. But I'll bring it later to your house.

They were eating beefsteak and eggs. François had a bottle of wine, and Mseud had a glass of beer. They began to talk and laugh together.

And that money there on the table? I said.

Oh, that's not mine.

Whose is it?

Mseud's.

Yes. Mseud has a lot of money, I said. But how much did he have when he came to your house?

We're not going to talk about it here, he told me.

It's shameful, I said. You've got money. For three days I've been waiting, and you won't pay me. You know I don't earn, enough with you to save anything from one day to the next.

Ahmed, I told you I didn't want to talk about it, he said.

If you can't pay me what you owe me, give me five hundred francs now, and we'll talk about it tomorrow at the house.

All right. Take this and go.

He handed me five hundred francs.

Thank you.

I went home and ate that night. See what the world is like. The Nazarene has money in his hand, and he tells me it isn't his. He says it's Mseud's. He's never done that before. But this is a bad time in the world. I've got to keep this work. I'll go every day and get whatever I can. When Omar had power in the Nazarene's house, I hated him. And now maybe Mseud is going to turn out even worse. But what difference does it make? Allah pays every man for what he does in the world.

The next day I knocked on the door, and François came and let me in. Buenos días, I said.

François said: Buenos días. But he did not say it the same as he always said it. There was something wrong with his good morning. As soon as he spoke, I knew that something was going to happen.

Ah! I thought. That Nazarene's not happy today!

I went upstairs and sat down.

There's no coffee in the house, I told François. Do you want me to go to the bacal and get some?

If you want coffee, buy it yourself, he told me.

What's the matter with you? I said. All this time I've been working for you. Nearly two years. And you've never said that

217

to me before. Tell me what's wrong.

Nothing's the matter with me, François said. You're not going to work for me any longer, that's all. Get out of my house! That's all I have to say to you.

Yes, I said. If you don't want me to work for you, pay me and I'll leave. But first I want to know why.

Yesterday you came to the restaurant and asked me for money. And you talked too loud.

I talked the way I always talk. I was trying to get what belonged to me. I said good afternoon and asked for my money. Nothing more. I said to you: Please pay me. And you said you had no money. There was a lot of money on the table. You gave me five hundred francs out of all that money that was lying there. And you said it wasn't yours. You said it was Mseud's. How can it be his? He came here without anything. He didn't even have a whole pair of pants. And now all the money's his? What sort of game are you playing with me?

Mseud jumped up from the bed.

Don't talk about me! he cried.

All you have to do is keep your mouth shut, I told him. I'm talking to the Nazarene. You've got nothing to do with it. I'll give you time to talk later. Lie down and keep still.

And if I don't?

I'll show you how!

No, no! said François. Please! That's enough! Mseud, keep still.

Mseud did not say any more.

Now you can talk, I told François. What were you saying? You want me to go?

Yes. Go.

Good. Pay me. I'll go.

He pulled out a thousand francs. Take it, he said.

You owed me this, I told him. I came today. Pay me for today, too.

He gave me another five hundred francs.

Good-bye, I said. The God who made me will give me better luck some day.

I went home and ate. For a few days I looked around the city for work. There was no work. No one was working, and no one was eating.

A few days later I was walking in front of the Spanish school. I saw the yellow car coming along, full of people. When it was beside me, François stopped it. I walked over and looked in. He had only Moslems inside. Omar was there with his wife and his two brothers who had just come from the war in Algeria. And there were two women in djellabas with them. They were going to Hajra den Nhal.

Look, Ahmed, said François. Please come tomorrow to the house.

If you want me there, I'll come.

Yes. Come, he said. Adiós.

And I walked along thinking: Omar's still working on him. He's probably going to feed him more tseuheur.

The next day I went back and started to work again for François. He did not say why he had asked me to come back, but I knew it was because the house was dirty. It was so filthy that he could not live in it any more unless it was cleaned out.

Now there was not even coffee in the kitchen. Each day when Mseud and François got up, they drove away in the car to have their breakfast. And they did not come back before I left. I went home without any money.

I waited a few days. One morning I was scrubbing the floor upstairs. I thought: I've got to talk to him. I'll starve if I don't. I called down to François: When you come up, may I talk to you a minute?

A little later he came upstairs.

What is it?

Look, I said. Please. You asked me to come back and work. And I'm here working every day. And you haven't paid me at all. You always tell me to wait. If you don't want me to work for you, just say to me: I have no work for you here, Ahmed. And I won't come any more. I walk all the way from Mstakhoche to Mtafi, and many times it's raining, and I'm not earning any money at all. What's the use of coming here every day, unless you're going to pay me?

But we're going to have a lot of money soon, he told me. I'll pay you then.

I've waited and waited. A man can be hungry only for so long. He can't go on for ever. Can't you understand that? Haven't you any respect for the people who work for you?

Yes, yes, yes, he said. And there's going to be money. Just be patient.

I know. But I have no food and no money to buy any with. I can't even buy one cigarette if I want to smoke. And I'm hungry. How can I be patient?

François put his hand into his pocket and pulled out some coins. There were about seven hundred francs there. Look! This is all I have.

It's impossible! I said. You get money in the mail. Where does it go?

You know I'm always going to bars with Mseud at night. I get drunk every night. That takes all my money.

Buy why? I said. Why do you do that? Nobody makes you go out and get drunk. Can't you remember that you need money in your house? Once you've paid all your bills and don't owe anybody anything, then you can go and get drunk.

Whenever I said anything like that to François, he got angry.

I saw that there was nothing I could do. I won't get any more bread from him, I thought. It's really finished.

He gave me three hundred francs for three days' work. That's all, he said. Come back tomorrow. There's an American lady coming. Maybe we'll have some money afterwards.

I took the three hundred francs. The next day I went back. I was cleaning out the latrine when the American lady knocked on the door. Mseud was downstairs washing his face, and he let her in. They were speaking English. Hello! Hello!

She came upstairs. She had blonde hair. She wore trousers and a man's shirt with the sleeves rolled up. Her face was painted in different colors. Green and blue around her eyes, and orange on her mouth. She had no eyebrows. Only two lines of black paint. Hello, she said.

Buenos días, I said. I was standing on the stairs that went up to the roof, looking at her.

François opened the door of the bedroom. A Spanish boy who was a friend of Mseud's had been sleeping there the night before, and he was still lying on the mattress. François was saying: Levántate. You've got to get up now. Then François came out and shut the door. He was putting on his shirt. They sat down and began to talk.

Mseud came upstairs. He was wearing nothing but some girls' undershorts, like the ones François wore. They were like a window to show everything inside. And he was not ashamed to walk around the room in front of the American lady. François liked to have him dress that way.

Make us a little tea, Ahmed, said François.

There's no sugar.

He gave me some money. I went to the bacal and brought back the sugar. While I was making the tea, Omar came to the house. Pepe, the Spanish boy, got up and dressed and went to sit with the others. I took five glasses of tea upstairs. I had to wash the steps to the roof. I was thinking: They'll be finished talking in a little while. Then I can clean the room where they're sitting.

Pepe began to play records on the phonograph. They went on talking, François, Mseud, Omar, Pepe and the American lady. They were having a good time. I went up to the roof and began to wash the steps from the top, until I got down to where they were.

Mseud looked at Pepe and winked at him. The two started to laugh. Then all of them were laughing. Ka! Ka! Kakaka!

They're laughing because I'm washing the stairs, I thought. And because I'm wearing these old trousers. And because I'm hungry. They think I'm something to laugh at.

My mouth filled with saliva. I walked toward Mseud and spat it all into his face. It ran down his cheek and across his mouth. They all stopped laughing. All but Omar. He laughed harder than before.

Why don't you laugh now? I said to Mseud. Go on. Laugh. François looked at me. His face had turned yellow. Then the American lady laughed again two or three times.

I put the rag into the pail of water. I wrung it out and went on washing the stairs. When I had finished, I went up onto the roof. There was a welding torch on the floor. It had a rubber tube that was connected to a big tank of gas. I lighted the torch and played with it for a few minutes. I was still thinking about the way they all had laughed.

Then Mseud came up the stairs. He had his jacket in his hand. His face was very angry.

Why did you spit on me? he cried.

Who are you? Why were you laughing?

He kept coming nearer. I opened the flame wider. It was making a loud noise.

Come nearer, I told him. I won't spit at you. I'll just make a hole in your face with this.

I turned the torch on him. He yelled and jumped back. I wanted to burn Mseud and the house and all of them. François ran onto the roof. He pushed Mseud back through the door. Mseud ran downstairs, and then François ran down. I stayed alone on the roof. After a while I put the welding torch down and turned off the gas.

I heard François go down to the street with the American lady. She got into her car and drove away. As soon as she was gone, François called me.

Ahmed!

What is it?

Come down.

I went downstairs.

He said to me: Now. Take your jacket and get out.

Why? I said.

You think it's good to spit at Mseud in front of my guests? And with a lady here who knows me?

And you think it's good to sit and laugh at me while I work? Why did you laugh? I'm not a person the same as you? Is it funny to see somebody wash the stairs?

You should have respect for the lady who was here, he said. She's a friend of mine.

And I'm not a friend of yours? I asked him. How long have I been working with you?

I've had enough! he shouted. He was swearing at me in French.

If you don't want me to work, pay me and I'll go. But look out! The curses you're giving me will make trouble for you. Because I'm right and you're wrong.

He went on cursing. Mseud stood up. When Pepe saw Mseud get up, he got up, too. They were both looking at me.

Why are you getting up, you two? I said. Stay in your corner. All this is your fault.

Sit down, Mseud, said François.

Omar sat watching by himself. He was still laughing.

Go on talking, I told François.

Get out!

Pay me. I'm going.

He took out a thousand francs.

Here. Get out of my house.

Good-bye, I told him. Some day you'll see where all this is going to take you. Instead of saying: I'm sorry, Ahmed, you're throwing me out with curses. Good!

I went out. It was still early. I walked down to Mustapha's café.

He was there. Ahmed! You've come early today.

A little, I said.

He asked the qahouaji for the kif pipe. Fill it up, he told me.

I had no kif. I borrowed a naboula and filled the bowl, and began to smoke.

It's good kif, said Mustapha.

Yes. It's not mine.

Are you still working?

How did you know? I just stopped. It's all finished.

It doesn't matter, he said. You've lived a lot of years. Sometimes you've worked. Sometimes you haven't.

If you want to come back here and sleep on the floor, you can come, he said.

No, Mustapha. Thank you. Not now.

I can't do more than that for you.

Thank you, Mustapha.

I was thinking: Look at all the work I did for that Nazarene! And when it ended, he cursed me and threw me out. But that's all right. The stork has to wait a long time for the locusts to come. Then he eats.

Selected Grove Press Paperbacks

GROVE PRESS, INC., 196 West Houston St., New York, N.Y. 10014